Also by Evan S. Connell

The Anatomy Lesson
Mrs. Bridge
The Patriot
Notes from a Bottle
    Found on the Beach at Carmel
At the Crossroads
Diary of a Rapist
Mr. Bridge
Points for a Compass Rose
The Connoisseur
Double Honeymoon
A Long Desire
The White Lantern

Saint Augustine's Pigeon

The Selected Stories of
Evan S. Connell

Edited by Gus Blaisdell

North Point Press
San Francisco
1982

Grateful acknowledgement is made to the following magazines where some of these stories first appeared: *Accent, Denver Quarterly, Escapade, Esquire, Greensleeves, The Paris Review, Saturday Evening Post, Southern Review, Transatlantic Review,* and *Western Review.*

Some of the stories in this volume were collected in two earlier books by Mr. Connell, THE ANATOMY LESSON AND OTHER STORIES (The Viking Press, 1957) and AT THE CROSSROADS (Simon and Schuster, 1965).

Cover photograph of the 9th century head of Christ from Kloster Lorsch by Sonia Halliday and Laura Lushington, printed with their permission and the permission of the Landesmuseum at Darmstadt, Germany.

to Calvin Kentfield

Contents

The Yellow Raft   3

The Marine   8

The Fisherman from Chihuahua   13

At the Crossroads   25

The Walls of Ávila   33

The Palace of the Moorish Kings   60

Arcturus   84

Otto and the Magi   128

Saint Augustine's Pigeon   179

The Short Happy Life of Henrietta   225

The Corset   228

Promotion   235

The Caribbean Provedor   245

The Scriptwriter   262

Mademoiselle from Kansas City   271

A Brief Essay on the Subject of Celebrity   280

Saint Augustine's Pigeon

The Yellow Raft

From the direction of the Solomon Islands came a damaged Navy fighter, high in the air, but gliding steadily down upon the ocean. The broad paddle blades of the propeller revolved uselessly with a dull whirring noise, turned only by the wind. Far below, quite small but growing larger, raced the shadow of the descending fighter. Presently they were very close together, the aircraft and its shadow, but each time they seemed about to merge they broke apart—the long fuselage tilting backward, lifting the engine for one more instant, while the shadow, like some distraught creature, leaped hastily through the whitecaps. Finally the engine plunged into a wave. The fuselage stood almost erect—a strange blue buoy stitched with gunfire—but then, tilting forward and bubbling, it disappeared into the greasy ocean. Moments later, as if propelled by a spring, a small yellow raft hurtled to the surface where it tossed back and forth, the walls lapped with oil. Suddenly, as though pursuing it from below, a bloody hand reached out of the water. Then for a while the raft floated over the deep rolling waves and the man held on. At last he drew himself into the raft where he sprawled on the bottom, coughing and weeping, turning his head occasionally to look at the blood on his arm. A few minutes later he sat up, cross-legged, balancing himself against the motion of the sea, and squinted toward the southern horizon because it was in that direction he had been flying and from that direction help would come. After watching the horizon for a long time he pulled off his helmet and appeared to be considering it while he idly twisted the radio cord. Then he lay down and tried to make himself comfortable. But in a little while he was up. He examined his wound, nodded, and with a cheerful expression he began to open a series of pouches attached to the inner walls of his raft: he found dehydrated rations, a few small luxuries, first-aid equipment, and signal flares. When the sun went down he had just finished eating a tablet of candy. He smacked his lips, lit a cigarette, and defiantly blew several smoke rings; but the wind was beginning to rise and before long he quit pretending. He zipped up his green canvas coveralls to the neck, tightened the straps and drawstrings of his life jacket, and braced his feet against the tubular yellow walls. He felt sick at his stomach and his wound was bleeding again. Several hours passed quietly except for the indolent rhythmic slosh of water and the squeak of rubber as the raft bent over the crest of a wave. Stars emerged, surrounding the raft, and spume broke lightly, persistently, against the man huddled with his back to the wind. All at once a rocket whistled up, illuminating the watery scene. No sooner had its light begun to fade than another rocket exploded high above; then a third, and a fourth. But darkness prevailed: overhead wheeled the Southern Cross, Hydra, Libra, and Corvus. Before dawn the pilot was on his hands and knees, whispering and stubbornly wagging his head while he waited to meet the second day. And as he peered at the horizon it seemed to him that he could see a marine reptile the size of a whale, with a long undulating swan-like neck, swimming toward him. He watched the creature sink into the depths and felt it glide swiftly under the raft. Then the world around him seemed to expand and the fiery tentacles of the sun touched his face as he waited, drenched with spray, to challenge the next wave. The raft trembled, dipped, and with a sickening, twisting slide, sank into a trough where the ocean and the ragged scud nearly closed over it. A flashlight rolled to one side, hesitated, and came rolling back while a pool of water gathered first at the pilot's feet, then at his head, sometimes submerging the flashlight. The walls of the raft were slippery, and the pouches from which he had taken the cigarettes and the food and the rockets were now filled with water. The drawstrings of his life jacket slapped wildly back and forth. He had put on his helmet and a pair of thin leather gloves to protect himself from the stinging spray. Steep foaming waves swept abruptly against the raft and the horizon dissolved into lowering clouds. By noon he was drifting through a steady rain with his eyes closed. Each time the raft sank into a trough the nebulous light vanished; then with a splash and a squeak of taut rubber it spun up the next slope, met the onrushing crest, whirled down again into darkness. Early that afternoon a murky chocolate streak separated the sea from the sky. Then the waves imperceptibly slickened, becoming enameled and black with a deep viridian hue like volcanic glass, their solid green phosphorescent surfaces curved and scratched as though scoured by a prehistoric wind; and the pilot waited, motionless, while each massive wave dove under the bounding yellow raft. When the storm ended it was night again. Slowly the constellations reappeared.

At dawn, from the south, came a Catalina flying boat, a plump and graceless creation known as the PBY—phlegmatic in the air, more at home resting its deep snowy breast in the water. It approached, high and slow, and almost flew beyond the raft. But then one tremendous pale blue wing of the PBY inclined toward a yellow dot on the ocean and in a dignified spiral the flying boat descended, keeping the raft precisely within its orbit until, just above the water, it skimmed by the raft. Except for the flashlight rolling back and forth and glittering in the sunshine the yellow raft was empty. The PBY climbed several hundred feet, turned, and crossed over the raft. Then it climbed somewhat higher and began circling. All morning the Catalina circled, holding its breast high like a great blue heron in flight, the gun barrels, propellers, and plexiglass blisters reflecting the tropical sun. For a while at the beginning of the search it flew tightly around the raft, low enough to touch the water almost at once, but later it climbed to an altitude from which the raft looked like a toy on a pond. There was nothing else in sight. The only shadow on the sea was that of the Navy flying boat moving in slow, monotonous circles around and around the deserted raft. At one time the PBY angled upward nearly a mile, its twin engines buzzing like flies in a vacant room, but after about fifteen minutes it came spiraling down, without haste, the inner wing always pointing at the raft. On the tranquil sunny ocean no debris was floating, nothing to mark the place where the fighter sank—only the raft, smeared with oil and flecked with salt foam. Early in the afternoon a blister near the tail of the Catalina slid open and a cluster of beer cans dropped in a leisurely arc toward the sea where they splashed like miniature bombs and began filling with water. Beyond them a few sandwich wrappers came fluttering down. Otherwise nothing disturbed the surface of the ocean; nothing changed all afternoon except that a veil gathered softly across the sky, filtering the light of the sun, darkening the metallic gleam of the Coral Sea. At five o'clock the PBY banked steeply toward the raft. Then it straightened up and for the first time in several hours the insignia on its prow—a belligerent little duck with a bomb and a pair of binoculars—rode vertically over the waves. The prow of the Catalina dipped when it approached the raft and the pitch of the engines began to rise. The flying boat descended with ponderous dignity, like a dowager stooping to retrieve a lost glove. With a hoarse scream it passed just above the raft. A moment later, inside the blue-black hull, a machine gun rattled and the raft started bouncing on the water. When the gunfire stopped the strange dance ended; the yellow raft fell back, torn into fragments of cork and deflated rubber that stained the ocean with an iridescent dye as green as a rainbow. Then the Catalina began to climb. Higher and higher, never again changing course, it flew toward the infinite horizon.

The Marine

In the officers' quarters of the naval hospital at Bremerton, Washington, two men lay on adjoining beds. One was a Marine captain who had been wounded in the fighting at Guadalcanal and the other was a Navy pilot with catarrhal fever who had not yet left the United States. The pilot had expected to start for his assignment in the South Pacific on the following day, but now he was delayed by the fever and was asking the marine what it was like on the front lines.

The captain, whose legs had been amputated, did not feel like talking but had answered a number of questions out of courtesy, and now was resting with his eyes shut. He had said to the pilot that many of the men under his command were very young and that many of them were volunteers, and that for the most part they were excellent shots. Some of them, the captain said, were the finest marksmen he had ever seen, although he had put in almost twenty years as a marine and had seen more good shooting than he could begin to remember. Many of these boys had come from small towns or from farm country and had grown up with a rifle in their hand, which was the reason they were so deadly. They had been picking Jap snipers out of trees as though they were squirrels. Often the Japs tied themselves to the trunk of a palm or into the crotch where the coconuts grew, so that if they were hit they would not fall, and when they were hit sometimes it seemed as if there was an explosion among the palm fronds as the man thrashed about. Other times an arm might be seen suddenly dangling alongside the trunk while the man's weapon dropped forty feet to the ground. Or nothing at all would happen, except that no more shots came from the tree. The captain had narrated these things with no particular interest, in a courteous and tired voice.

The pilot understood that he had been too inquisitive and he had decided not to ask any more questions. He lay with his arms folded on his chest and stared out the window at the pine trees on the hill. It had been raining since dawn but occasional great columns of light thousands of feet in height burst diagonally through the clouds and illuminated the pines or some of the battleships anchored in Puget Sound. The pilot was watching this and thinking about Guadalcanal, which he might see very soon. He felt embarrassed because the captain had talked so much and he felt to blame for this. He was embarrassed, too, about the fact that he himself would recover while the captain was permanently maimed, but there was nothing he could say about that without making it worse.

Presently the captain went on in the same tired and polite voice.

Lieutenant, he said without opening his eyes, I can tell you everything you need to know about what the war is like on Guadalcanal, although I don't know about the other islands because I was only on Guadalcanal. Listen. In my company there was a boy from southern Indiana who was the best shot I believe I ever saw. I couldn't say how many Japs he killed, but he thought he knew because he would watch where they fell and keep track of them. My guess is that he accounted for at least twenty. There were times when he would get into arguments over a body we could see lying not very far away from us in the jungle. He was jealous about them. One night I observed him crawl beyond his post, which was the perimeter of our defense, and go some distance into the jungle. The night was not very dark and I observed him crawling from one body to another. I thought he was going through their wallets and pulling the rings off their fingers. The men often did that although they were not supposed to. However I was puzzled by what this boy was doing because he made a strange motion over several of the Jap bodies. He appeared to be doing some sort of difficult work, and when he crawled back into the camp I went over to him and lay down next to him and asked what he had been doing. He told me he had been collecting gold teeth. He carried a tobacco pouch in his pocket, which he showed me. It was half-filled with gold and he told me how much gold was selling for by the ounce in the United States. He said that if he lived long enough and got onto enough islands he expected that he would be a rich man by the time the war ended. It was not uncommon to collect teeth and I had suspected he might be doing that also, but I told him I had been watching and was puzzled by the strange movements he had made over several of the bodies. He explained that he had been cutting off their heads and what I had observed was him cutting the spinal cord and the neck muscles with his knife. I asked why he had done this, if it was just for the sake of cruelty, although the men were dead, and he seemed very much surprised by this and looked at me carefully to see why I wanted to know. 'They're mine, sir,' he said to me. He thought that the bodies of the men he killed belonged to him. Then he said that he did not sever a head unless the man had died face down. I didn't understand what this meant. I thought perhaps it served some purpose that I knew nothing about, relating possibly to the way animals were butchered, but his explanation was so simple and so sensible that I felt foolish not to have thought of it. He reminded me that the jungle was full of snipers and that he did not want to expose himself more than necessary. In order to get at the mouths of the men who had died face down it would have been necessary to turn them over, and he did not want to risk this. A dead man is heavy and it takes a lot of work to turn him over if you yourself are lying flat, so he had severed these heads which, by themselves, could be turned over easily. You wished to know what the war is like on Guadalcanal, Lieutenant, although as I say, it may be different on other islands.

The captain had not opened his eyes while he was talking, and having said this much he cleared his throat, moved around slightly on his bed and then lay still. The pilot decided that the captain wanted to sleep, so he too lay still on his painted iron bed and listened to the rain and gazed at the fleet anchored in the sound.

There's one other thing, the captain continued. I had not known how old the boy was, except that he was very young. I thought he might be eighteen or nineteen, or twenty at the most. It's hard to tell with some of them. They look older or younger than they are. I've seen a man of twenty-six who looked no more than eighteen. At any rate this boy soon afterward was discharged from the service because he had run away from home in order to enlist and managed to get all the way to Guadalcanal before his mother, who had been trying to locate him, discovered what had happened. He was fourteen when he was sworn in and apparently he celebrated his fifteenth birthday on the island with us, telling his buddies it was his nineteenth. But finally, as I say, it caught up with him and he was sent home. His mother, I was told, was very anxious for her son to finish high school. Perhaps he's there now.

I believe what I'm going to remember longest, the captain added in a mild voice, is the moment he stared at me while we were lying side by side. We were closer than you and I. He was young enough to be my own boy, which is a thought that occurred to me at the time, although it seems irrelevant now. Be that as it may, when I looked into his eyes I couldn't see a spark of humanity. I've often thought about this without deciding what it means or where it could lead us, but you'll be shipping out presently, as soon as your fever subsides, and will experience the war yourself. Maybe you'll come to some conclusion that has escaped me.

The captain said nothing more and when the nurse came around a few minutes later, after looking at him, she held one finger to her lips because he had gone to sleep.

The Fisherman
from Chihuahua

Santa Cruz is at the top of Monterey Bay, which is about a hundred miles below San Francisco, and in the winter there are not many people in Santa Cruz. The boardwalk concessions are shuttered except for one counter-and-booth restaurant, the Ferris-wheel seats are hooded with olive green canvas and the powerhouse padlocked, and the rococo doors of the carousel are boarded over and if one peers through a knothole into its gloom the horses which buck and plunge through summer prosperity seem like animals touched by a magic wand that they may never move again. Dust dims the gilt of their saddles and sifts through cracks into their bold nostrils. About the only sounds to be heard around the waterfront in Santa Cruz during winter are the voices of Italian fishermen hidden by mist as they work against the long pier, and the slap of waves against the pilings of the cement dance pavilion when tide runs high, or the squeak of a gull, or once in a long time bootsteps on the slippery boards as some person comes quite alone and usually slowly to the edge of the gray and fogbound ocean.

The restaurant is Pendleton's and white brush strokes on the glass announce *tacos, frijoles,* and *enchiladas* as house specialties, these being mostly greens and beans and fried

meat made arrogant with pepper. Smaller letters in pseudo-
Gothic script say *Se Habla Español* but this is not true; it was
the man who owned the place before Pendleton who could
speak Spanish. From him, though, Pendleton did learn how
to make the food and this is the reason a short fat Mexican
who worked as a mechanic at Ace Dillon's Texaco station
continued eating his suppers there. He came in every night
just after eight o'clock and sat at the counter, ate an astound-
ing amount of this food, which he first splattered with
tabasco sauce as casually as though it were ketchup, and
then washed it farther down with beer. After that he would
feel a little drunk and would spend two or three dollars
playing the pinball machine and the great nickelodeon and
dancing by himself, but inoffensively, contentedly, just
snapping his fingers and shuffling across the warped boards
often until Pendleton began pulling in the shutters. Then,
having had a suitable evening, he would half-dance his way
home, or at least back in the direction of town. He was a
squat little man who waddled like a duck full of eggs and he
had a face like a blunt arrowhead or a Toltec idol, and he was
about the color of hot sand. His fingers were much too thick
for their length, seemingly without joints, only creases where
it was necessary for them to bend. He smelled principally of
cold grease and of urine as though his pants needed some
air, but Pendleton who did not smell very good himself did
not mind and besides there were not many customers during
these winter months.

So every evening shortly after dark he entered for his food
and some amusement, and as he appeared to contain all
God's world within his own self Pendleton was not disinter-
ested when another Mexican came in directly behind him
like a long shadow. This new man was tall, very tall, six feet
or more, and much darker, almost black in the manner of a
sweat-stained saddle. He was handsome, silent, and perhaps

forty years of age. Also he was something of a dandy; his trousers, which were long and quite tight, revealed the fact that he was bowlegged, as befits certain types of men, and made one think of him easily riding a large fast horse, not necessarily toward a woman but in the direction of something more remote and mysterious—bearing a significant message or something like that. Exceedingly short black boots of finest leather took in the cuffs of his narrow trousers. For a shirt he wore long-sleeved white silk unbuttoned to below the level of his nipples which themselves were vaguely visible. The hair of his chest was so luxuriant that an enameled crucifix there did not even rest on the skin.

These two men sat at the counter side by side. The tall one lifted off his sombrero as if afraid of mussing his hair and he placed it on the third stool. His hair was deeply oiled, and comb tracks went all the way from his temples to the back of his thin black neck, and he reeked of green perfume. He had a mustache that consisted of nothing but two black strings hanging across the corners of his unforgiving mouth, ending in soft points about an inch below his chin. He seemed to think himself alone in the restaurant because, after slowly licking his lips and interlacing his fingers, he just sat looking somberly ahead. The small man ordered for them both.

After they had eaten supper the little one played the pinball machine while this strange man took from his shirt pocket a cigarillo only a little bigger than his mustache and smoked it with care; that is, he would take it from his mouth between his thumb and one finger as if he were afraid of crushing it, and after releasing the smoke he would replace it with the same care in the exact center of his mouth. It never dangled or rolled; he respected it. Nor was it a cheap piece of tobacco; the smoke ascended heavily, moist and sweet.

Suddenly the fat Mexican kicked the pinball game and with a surly expression walked over to drop a coin into the nickelodeon. The tall man had remained all this time at the counter with his long savage eyes half-shut, smoking and smoking the fragrant cigarillo. Now he did not turn around — in fact all he did was remove the stump from his lips — but clearly he was disturbed. When the music ended he sat motionless for several minutes. Then he lifted his head and his throat began to swell like that of a mating pigeon.

Pendleton, sponging an ash tray, staggered as if a knife had plunged through his ribs.

The Mexican's eyes were squeezed shut. His lips had peeled away from his teeth like those of a jaguar tearing meat, and the veins of his neck looked ready to pop. In the shrill screams bursting from his throat was a memory of Moors, the ching of Arab cymbals, of rags and of running feet through all the market places of the East.

His song had no beginning; it had no end. All at once he was simply sitting on the stool looking miserably ahead.

After a while the small fat Mexican said to Pendleton "Be seeing you, man," and waddled out the door. A few seconds later the tall one's stool creaked. He put on the high steepled sombrero as though it were a crown and followed his friend through the door.

The next night there happened to be a pair of tourists eating in the back booth when the Mexicans entered. They were dressed as before except that the big one's shirt was lime green, and Pendleton noticed his wrist watch — fastened not to his wrist but on the green shirtsleeve where it bulged like an oily bubble. They took the same stools and ate fried beans, tacos, and enchiladas for half an hour, after which the short one who looked like his Toltec ancestors gently belched, smiled in a benign way, and moved over to his machine. Failing to win anything he cursed it and kicked it before selecting some records.

This time Pendleton was alert; as the music ended he got

ready for the first shriek. The tourists, caught unaware, thought their time had come. When they recovered from the shock they looked over the top of the booth and then the woman stood up in order to see better. After the black Mexican's song was finished they all could hear the incoming tide, washing softly around the pillars of the pavilion.

Presently the two men paid their bill and went out, the short one leading, into the dirty yellow fog and the diving, squeaking gulls.

"Why, that's terrible," the woman laughed. "It wasn't musical." Anyone who looked at her would know she was still shuddering from the force of the ominous man.

Her husband too was frightened and laughed. "Somebody should play a little drum behind that fellow." Unaware of what a peculiar statement he had made he formed a circle of his thumb and forefinger to show how big the drum should be.

She was watching the door, trying to frown compassionately. "I wonder what's the matter with that poor man. Some woman must have hurt him dreadfully."

Pendleton began to wipe beer bracelets and splats of tabasco sauce from the lacquered plywood counter where the men had been eating.

"We're from Iowa City," the woman said with a smile.

Pendleton had never been to Iowa City or anywhere near it even on a train, so he asked if they would like more coffee.

"Those two fellows," her husband said, "do they come here every night?"

Pendleton was seized with contempt for this domestic little man, though he did not know why. He walked stiffly away from their booth and stood with both hairy hands on his hips while he listened to the sea thrashing and rolling in the night.

"Who?" he demanded. "Them two?"

The couple, overpowered by his manner, looked at each other uneasily.

On the third night when the Mexicans sat down at the counter Pendleton said to the one who spoke English, "Tell your buddy no more yowling."

"Tell him yourself," the Toltec replied. "Eight tacos, four beers, and a lot of beans, man."

"What do you think this is, buster, some damn concert hall?"

For a moment the little Mexican became eloquent with his eyebrows; then both he and Pendleton turned their attention to the silent one who was staring somberly at the case of pies.

Pendleton leaned on his hands so that his shoulders bulged. "Now looky, Pablo, give him the word and do it quick. Tell him to cut out that noise."

This enraged the small man whose voice rose to a snarl. "Pablo yourself. Don't give me that stuff."

Pendleton was not angry but set about cleaving greens for their tacos as though he was furious. While the blade chunked into the wood beside his thumb he thought about the situation. He did not have anything particular in mind when all at once he slammed down the cleaver and with his teeth clenched he began bending his eyes toward the two.

"*No debe cantar,*" said the little one hurriedly, waggling a negative finger at his companion. "*No más.*"

"All right, by God," Pendleton muttered as though he understood. He wished to say something in Spanish but he knew only *mañana, adiós,* and *señorita,* and none of these seemed to fit. He resumed work, but doubtfully, not certain if the silent one had heard either of them. Without turning around he explained his attitude: "People come here to eat supper."

Abel W. Sharpe, who had once been county sheriff and

who now lived in a retirement home, came through the door alone but arguing harshly. He took a stool beside the tall Mexican, looked up at him twice, and then ordered hot milk and a waffle. While he was pouring syrup into the milk the nickelodeon music stopped and the black Mexican did it again.

At the first note the old man jumped off his stool and crouched several feet away, a spoon in one hand and his cup of sweet milk in the other. "Can't hear nothing," he said angrily to Pendleton. "The bastard deefened me."

The Toltec, who was playing pinball, paid not the least attention because he had lighted four pretty girls which meant he probably would win several games. His friend, now motionless, sat on the stool and gazed ahead as though he could see clear into some grief-stricken time.

Not until the eighth or ninth night did Pendleton realize that the restaurant was drawing more customers; there would be half-a-dozen or so extra for dinner, maybe more.

Then there came a night when the Toltec waddled in as usual but no one followed. That night the restaurant was uneasy. Things spilled, and while cleaning up a table Pendleton discovered a menu burned through and through with cigarette holes. By ten-thirty the place was deserted.

Pendleton said, "Hey, Pablo."

The Toltec gave him a furious look.

"All right," Pendleton apologized, "what's your name?"

"What's yours?" he replied. He was insulted.

"Where's your buddy?"

"He's no friend of mine."

Pendleton walked down the counter behind a damp rag, wrung it over the sink, and then very casually did something he never even thought of doing: he opened a bottle of beer and indicated to the Mexican that it was free.

Toltec, though still aggrieved, quickly accepted this gift,

saying, "I just met the guy. He asked me where to get some decent food."

Pendleton wiped a table and for a while appeared to be idly picking his teeth. When he judged enough time had gone by he said, "Got tired of my grub, I guess."

"No, tonight he's drunk. Man, he's out of his skull."

Pendleton waited a couple of minutes before saying, "He looks like a bullfighter I saw once in Tijuana called Victoriano Posada."

This proved to be a shrewd inquiry because after drinking some more of the free beer the fat Mexican remarked, "He calls himself Damaso."

Pendleton, wondering if some other information would follow, pretended to stretch and to yawn and smacked his chops mightily. He thought that tomorrow, when the tall man arrived, he would call him by name.

"Know what? He goes and stands by himself on the sea wall a lot of times. Maybe he's getting ready to knock himself off."

"Tell him not to do it in front of my place," Pendleton answered.

Through the screen door could be seen a roll of silvery yellow fog with the moon just above it, but the sea was hidden.

"These Santa Cruz winters," Pendleton said. Opening the icebox he chose a beer for himself and leaned against the counter, far enough away that his guest might not feel the friendship was being forced. Peeling off the wet label he rolled it into a soggy gray ball which he dropped into a bucket. "Singers make plenty money, I guess."

The Mexican looked at him slyly. "What are you talking about?"

Pendleton, after scratching his head, yawned again.

"Huh? Oh. I was just thinking about what's-his-name. That fellow you come in here with."

"I know it," the Mexican said, laughing.

For a while Pendleton studied his beer and listened to the combers, each of which sounded as if it would smash the door. "Feels like something standing up in the ocean tonight," he said. "I could use a little summer."

"You want the town full of tourists? Those sausages? You're crazy. You're off the rocks."

Pendleton judged that the Mexican was about to insult the summer people still more, so he manipulated the conversation once again. "Somebody told me your friend got himself a singing job at that night spot near Capitola."

"Look," said the Toltec, patient, but irritated, "I just met the guy a couple of weeks ago."

"He never said where he's from, I guess."

"Chihuahua, he says. That's one rough town. And full of sand. That Chihuahua — it's noplace."

Breakers continued sounding just beyond the door and the fog now stood against the screen like a person.

"What does he do?"

The Mexican lifted both fat little shoulders.

"Just traveling through?"

The Mexican lifted both hands.

"Where is he going?"

"All I know is he's got a pretty good voice."

"He howls like a god-damn crazy wolf," Pendleton said, "howling for the moon."

"Yah, he's pretty good. Long time ago I saw a-murder down south in the mountains and a woman screamed just like that."

Pendleton opened the icebox for two more beers. The Mexican accepted one as though in payment for service. For some seconds they had been able to hear footsteps approaching, audible after every tunnel of water caved in. The footsteps went past the door but no one could be seen.

"Know what? There was an old man washed up on the beach the other day."

"That so?" said Pendleton. "Everything gets to the beach sooner or later."

The Mexican nodded. Somewhere far out on the bay a little boat sounded again and again. "What a night," he said.

Pendleton murmured and scratched.

"Know something, mister? That Damaso, he ain't no Mexicano."

"I didn't think so," Pendleton lied.

"No, because he's got old blood. You know what I mean? I think he's a gypsy from Spain, or wherever those guys come from. He's dark in the wrong way. He just don't *feel* Mexicano to me. There's something about him, and besides he speaks a little Castellano."

Both of them considered this.

"What's he howling about?" Pendleton asked. "Some girl?"

"No, nothing like that."

"Then why the hell does he do it?"

But here the little Mexican lost interest; he revolved on the stool, from which only his toes could reach to the floor, hopped off, and hurried across to the nickelodeon. Having pushed a nickel through the slit he studied the wonderful colors and followed the bubbles which fluttered up the tubes to vanish; next, he dialed *"Tuxedo Junction"* and began shuffling around the floor, snapping his fingers and undulating so that in certain positions he looked about five months pregnant.

"Who knows?" he asked of no one in particular while he danced.

The next night he again came in alone. When Pendleton mentioned this he replied that the dark one was still drunk.

And the next night when asked if the drunk was going into its third day he replied that Damaso was no longer drunk, just sick from being so, that he was at present lying on the wet cement having vomited on his boots, that probably by sunrise he would be all right. This turned out to be correct because both of them came in for supper the following night. Toltec, smiling and tugging at his crotch, was rumpled as usual and smelled human while his tall companion was oiled and groomed and wearing the white silk again. A good many people were loitering about the restaurant—every booth was full—because this thing had come to be expected, and though all of them were eating or drinking or spending money in some way to justify themselves, and although not everybody looked up at the entrance of the two Mexicans, there could be no doubt about the situation. Only these two men seemed not to notice anything; they ate voraciously and drank quite a few beers after which the Toltec began playing pinball and Damaso remained on the stool with his long arms crossed on the counter.

Later the nickelodeon lighted up. When at last its music died away there was not a sound in the restaurant. People watched the head of the dark man bow down until it was hidden in his arms. The crucifix disentangled itself and dropped out the top of his gaucho shirt where it began to swing to and fro, glittering as it twisted on the end of its golden chain. He remained like that for quite some time, finally raised his head to look at the ticket, counted out enough money, and with the sombrero loosely in one hand he stumbled through the door.

The other Mexican paid no attention; he called for more beer, which he drank all at once in an attempt to interest a young girl with silver slippers and breasts like pears who was eating supper with her parents, but, failing to win anything at this or again at the machine, he suddenly grew bored with the evening and walked out.

The next night he entered alone. When asked if his companion had started another drunk he said Damaso was gone.

Pendleton asked late in the evening, "How do you know?"

"I feel it," he said.

Then for awhile Pendleton stood listening to the advancing tide which had begun to pat the pillars like someone gently slapping a dead drum. After taking off his apron he rolled it up, as he always did, and put it beneath the counter. He untied the sweaty handkerchief from around his neck and folded it over the apron, but there his routine altered; before pulling in the shutters he stopped at the screen door and looked out and listened, but of course did not see or hear any more than he expected.

Sharply the Toltec said, "I like to dance." And he began to do so. "Next summer I'm really going to cut it up. Nothing's going to catch me." He read Pendleton's face while dancing by himself to the odd and clumsy little step he was inventing, and counseled, "Jesus Christ, he's gone. Forget about it, man."

At the Crossroads

A red-bearded tramp with quick blue eyes and an old woman who calls herself Letty are standing at the intersection of two highways in the desert. The old woman feels death not far away so she is returning to West Virginia where she was born, but the tramp sees a different future — he is headed for California where he believes his luck will change.

It is almost noon. Old Letty, with head bowed, does not move, but the tramp is growing restless and begins to kick at the gravel. Now and again he shakes his head in despair. All at once Letty turns to him with a beseeching expression; she has just found out she cannot make it back to the town in the Cumberland Mountains where she was born. She has waited too long. Death is following her and will not wait. It does not seem possible. She is both weakened and thrilled by the idea, yet there can be no mistake — her time has come. Presently she is obsessed by a singular desire: she must explain to someone what life actually is. Now that she has been overtaken it is dreadfully important that someone remember her, remember and never forget that she too was once here on earth. A lazy vagabond is not the audience she would have selected but such is the will of God and to this man, therefore, whoever he may be, she intends to confide the meaning of her life.

Without preamble she walks over to him and begins in a quavering voice, "There was a time in Ely, Nevada, when the Lord appeared in the bright sunlight and said I was doing about as well as could be expected."

The tramp gazes at her incuriously; he wonders if she can be mad. He does not know where this old woman is going or where she came from or why, and cares not the slightest. His own plans are much too absorbing. It is very strange how any man should have all the bad luck he has had, very strange indeed, but if only he can reach the coast things will be different. He thinks about the many stingy people there are in the world; while he broods on how they conspire against him his lips puff out through his beard. Shading his eyes, he squints along the broad federal highway that comes sweeping out of the waterless eastern hills, but all he can see is cactus standing on the slope with arms uplifted like railroad signals. He looks north along the graveled state highway to an abandoned borax flat and beyond that to a low blunt range of old brown mountains upon which no snow ever falls and where nothing lives. There is not a sign of movement on either road, and when he squints to the south he cannot see much because the horizon is swimming in waves of heat. He feels a tug at his belt and looks down at the old woman with some irritation, noticing once again that she has en envelope fastened to her dress with a safety pin. Women are apt to do things like that; his mother used to leave messages pinned to a lace curtain in the parlor. So he is not particularly surprised or amused; however, he is a cautious man and after studying her anxious face he thinks he will keep her in sight. It might not be wise to turn his back on her any more.

Letty has forgotten what she meant to say to him and so draws herself up with a severe expression; but when at last it comes back to her she cannot repress a smile. All memories cause her to smile no matter what they might be. Her chin begins to tremble and then without warning her eyelids close. Now she is prepared to tell her companion all about it, but upon looking up she is distressed to find he has crossed the highway and she realizes that she has just had a little nap. She picks up her satchel and begins walking after him. It seems that the intersection is completely under water but she knows this is only an illusion caused by the desert heat, and so with her satchel firmly in one hand and her bamboo stick in the other she marches against the waves which obligingly recede very much as they did for the oppressed Jews.

The tramp, squatting in the gravel, is considerably interested in something he has just discovered. At first he thought it was the metal casing of a machine gun bullet but it turned out to be a lipstick cylinder. He pulls at the cap which comes off with a plop, he twists the base to see how much is left and then smears his thumb with it, and with a sly expression he lifts his pink thumb to his nose: the odor takes him by surprise even though he expected it. Assaulted by memories, he jumps to his feet and throws the lipstick as high and as far as he can. It comes down in a mirage out among the cactus — a dry lake bed has filled with rippling water and a black-tailed jackrabbit is leaping through it. He watches the rabbit jump out of the water and go leaping away over the brush. Now the lake is dry again, exposing its cracked, sodium-crusted bed. Everything is illusion. The tramp sits on his knapsack, bitterly discouraged, and holds his hands above his head to combat the sun.

Letty thinks he is listening to the story of her life. She goes on talking to him and he does not move. She tells the tramp about her brothers, Noah, Jonathan, Ephraim, Willard, and Thomas, and at the mention of their names her shameless eyes begin to weep. She fumbles for the letter at her breast. It is securely pinned and her old fingers do not very much care what she orders them to do—they go dancing away to the side—but after a while she gets the pin undone. Now the frayed, yellowed envelope is in her hand. She turns it about until she has located the flap, and a moment later she has the message itself, folded and unfolded so many times that it is in two pieces. She holds it out to the tramp, but he only looks at her in astonishment. Lifting one half of the brown spidery script close to her eyes, she commences to read aloud as though she were giving him a lecture:

> *Jonathan's going was a blessed release for there was, of course, no hope that he could ever get better. We held the funeral right at two* P.M. *this afternoon and then Melinda, Jackie Lu, and I drove to Blue Springs to bury him. As you know, Aunt Letty, your own father, grandfather, and great-grandfather are buried there, and young David was most curious about all those graves. He's come to resemble a picture in the album of Grandfather Shelby except for the beard, and has the meanness of menfolk. We think that he will be a big one like his great-uncles. It was but last night whilst we were gathered on the porch the child stood by my knee and gravely asked when you are coming home, so I kissed him and pushed back his hair and said to him it will be soon. . . .*

She cannot read any more; the sunlight is shattering. The letter wanders about in front of her eyes. She decides to tuck it away but the envelope has disappeared. Now she locates the envelope lying in the gravel near her feet. She is afraid to bend down and she does not know what to do. Alkali dust has gotten all over her shoes. The highways weave and shimmer. For a moment she is a little girl and her twin brother Ephraim has just waked her by saying, "Letty, Mamma is dead, and I think he is too." So she got out of her bed and went with Ephraim, and what he had said was true—they lay there in each other's arms, neither of them smiling, and nobody ever could understand what had caused them to die at the same time. Noah and Ephraim had pulled down the shades in the bedroom but the windows were open and as the wind blew in gustily the shades billowed and flapped as if waving goodbye to the dead. She could hear Noah out of doors crying and working the pump, but Ephraim stood dumbly beside the deathbed with his mouth open and his hands thrust into his pockets. She heard the dogs howling in the cellar and presently noticed how the hair on Ephraim's neck was standing straight out. She lifted the shade from the back window and found the sun had just started through the notch in the mountains. Overnight the snow had been melting; the barn roof was almost clear. The young sow lay motionless in her pen and her head was half-buried in a mound of snow and straw. Some chickens were picking their way across a patch of red mud beside the cistern where Noah in his overalls was still pumping water, though the bucket had long since filled and now each time he leaned on the pump handle the bucket overflowed.

Next she dreams of visiting Willard who is in the state penitentiary for life. He has grown into the biggest man of the family, taller than Noah, yet as strong as Thomas. She has brought him a sack of black walnuts which he likes and which he will crack in the palm of his hand, but all the time she is visiting he complains of the warden's yellow hound which bays at night just outside the wall. Willard believes the hound is challenging him to escape.

Now she is with a strange young man who limps, whose name she has forgotten. They have been walking somewhere for some important reason and he is tremendously excited by the election of President Hayes; they stop to rest on a fallen log but he is unable to sit still; he goes limping around the clearing while he tells her of the election and what it is going to mean, and often he looks over his shoulder at her with radiant eyes to see if she comprehends.

The air is piquant with the odor of turpentine from slashed pines nearby and while she is reaching for a sprig of wild mint beside the log he cries, "Oh, Letty! Aren't you listening?" But for the election she cares nothing; she wants to get married. A look of shock appears on his face when she suggests he marry her. They gaze at each other in dismay.

The tramp does not hear a single word of it. This old woman has been talking for an hour but it would take some kind of a professor to understand her. He has listened enough to know that she preaches for a living, not in a church but along the wayside, and in the satchel she carries along with her other belongings a tambourine for taking up the collection. Well, he thinks, there is nothing more satisfactory than the gospel—he has shouted himself drunk and jumped in the water at more than one meeting. Preachers lead a good life. There are times when he thinks about stealing a Bible and going into the business.

Briefly he listens to her reedy little voice, quavering and righteous and alone in the desert. She is talking about one of the grandsons she has never seen. He cannot imagine why she talks so much, but women are like that and he has long since realized that the less they say the more sense they make. He decides to eat an apple which is in his knapsack.

Letty feels some time has slipped away. The letter, dated nineteen years ago, is back in its envelope and again is pinned to her dress although she cannot remember doing it. She looks around for her companion and finds him across the road eating something—she watches steadily but cannot make out what it is. Soon she forgets this terrible afternoon and stands content at the crossroads, swaying a little, her eyes closed. Minutes drift by without a sound. On the desert nothing moves. Old Letty dreams, and occasionally speaks out in a sharp, critical tone, but if the tramp hears whatever she says he makes no attempt to answer. He dreams very seldom but when he does there is certainly no doubt about the meaning: principally he dreams of finding money while running through a forest. Joyously he flings himself high up among the cool dark boughs and then with moist leaves brushing his cheeks he comes floating down very casually, though somewhat reluctantly, clutching in both hands an impossibly thick clump of dollars. For some reason a few of these notes always float out of his grasp and with a sudden movement flatten themselves against the bark of passing tree trunks. A few more of the bills wad themselves up and are sucked into the forks of branches where they disappear like leaves spinning into a whirlpool. He realizes it is idle to do nothing but stare at this money while it gets away, and proof lies in the fact that his hands are empty every time he touches the ground, still he cannot stop himself in the air or turn around, or even reach for it, because once again he finds himself graciously descending, wrenching loose from the boughs these turgid clumps which break off like heads of lettuce in rich black loam. Whenever the tramp thinks about this particular dream his beard begins to quiver and he is apt to choke or cough, and often he looks narrowly over his shoulder to see if anyone has read his thoughts.

Letty is awake again, looking sternly at her companion because she imagines he has just insulted her. Her fear is confirmed when she notes that his beard is moving gently, as though he were laughing deep in his throat. She knows what he thinks of her—that nobody has ever loved her. Why should anyone laugh at that? Besides, it is not true. Almost immediately she has the facts to make him change his opinion. She intends to tell him about just a few of the bold young gentlemen and she will conclude her triumph by letting him know that she spurned every suitor and of her own free will chose God, yet even as she begins to speak the truth comes flying home, and trembling a little, she must stop. She staggers into the middle of the highway to gaze at him. Cautiously the tramp returns her look as if he reads her desperation at last and wonders what can be wrong.

Letty nods and smiles at him. She beckons to him.

The tramp becomes embarrassed. He kicks at the gravel and looks away, scanning the empty highways, and when after some moments he looks around at her again she has bowed her head. He plucks thoughtfully at his beard.

It is late afternoon now. The heat is stupefying, and for a long time the tramp has been squatting on his heels sifting hot pebbles and sand through his fingers while he thinks how much better life will be in California. Impatiently he waits; surely someone besides himself is going that way. It occurs to him that the old woman has stopped talking — he squints over his shoulder. She is on her feet but asleep, and while he is watching her she wakes up, stares at him blindly, and closes her eyes again.

Death is very close now. Very near to her, only a few minutes away. She is thinking of a morning eighty years ago. Someone had propped her up against a rail fence and there she was waiting for something, or someone, and presently two little boys came clambering over the fence. She knew they were her brothers Noah and Willard. They were climbing out of the field where they had made cornstalk fiddles. They walked up to her and Noah said, "Here, Letty, we have brought you one too," and placing a fiddle and bow in her hands he showed her what to do. She saw they were smiling down at her, so she began to laugh and they joined in, and she was sure the frogs and crickets and birds joined in while they performed upon their father's land.

The Walls of Ávila

Thou shalt make castels in Spayne,
And dreme of joye, al but in vayne.
— ROMAUNT OF THE ROSE

Ávila lies only a few kilometers west and a little north of Madrid, and is surrounded by a grim stone wall that was old when Isabella was born. Life in this town has not changed very much from the days when the earth was flat; somehow it is as though news of the passing centuries has never arrived in Ávila. Up the cobbled street saunters a donkey with a wicker basket slung on each flank, and on the donkey's bony rump sits a boy nodding drowsily in the early morning sun. The boy's dark face looks medieval. He is delivering bread. At night the stars are metallic, with a bluish tint, and the Spaniards stroll gravely back and forth beside the high stone wall. There are not so many gypsies, or *gitanos,* in this town as there are in, say, Valencia or Seville. Ávila is northerly and was not impressed by these passionate Asiatic people, at least not the way Córdoba was, or Granada.

These were things we learned about Ávila when J.D. returned. He came home after living abroad for almost ten years. He was thinner and taller than any of us remembered, and his crew-cut hair had turned completely gray although he was just thirty-eight. It made him look very distinguished, even a little dramatic. His skin was now as brown as coffee, and there were wind wrinkles about his restless

33

cerulean blue eyes, as though the light of strange beaches and exotic plazas had stamped him like a visa to prove he had been there. He smiled a good deal, perhaps because he did not feel at ease with his old friends any more. Ten years did not seem long to us, not really long, and we were disconcerted by the great change in him. Only his voice was familiar. At the bus station where three of us had gone to meet him only Dave Zobrowski recognized him.

Apparently this town of Ávila meant a great deal to J.D., although he could not get across to us its significance. He said that one night he was surprised to hear music and laughter coming from outside the walls, so he hurried through the nearest gate, which was set between two gigantic watch towers, and followed the wall around until he came to a carnival. There were concessions where you could fire corks at cardboard boxes, each containing a chocolate bar, or dip for celluloid fishes with numbered bellies, and naturally there was a carousel, the same as in America. It rotated quite slowly, he said, with mirrors flashing from its peak while enameled stallions gracefully rose and descended on their gilded poles. But nothing was so well attended as a curious swing in which two people stood, facing each other, grasping a handle, and propelled themselves so high that at the summit they were nearly upside down. The shadow of this swing raced up the wall and down again. "Like this!" J.D. exclaimed, gesturing, and he stared at each of us in turn to see if we understood. He said it was like the shadow of some grotesque instrument from the days of the Inquisition, and he insisted that if you gazed up into the darkness long enough you could make out, among the serrated ramparts of the ancient wall, the forms of helmeted men leaning on pikes and gazing somberly down while their black beards moved in the night wind.

He had tales of the Casbah in Tangiers and he had souvenirs from the ruins of Carthage. On his key chain was a fragment of polished stone, drilled through the center, that he had picked up from the hillside just beyond Tunis. And he spoke familiarly of the beauty of Istanbul, and of Giotto's tower, and the Seine, and the golden doors of Ghiberti. He explained how the Portuguese are fuller through the cheeks than are the Spaniards, their eyes more indolent and mischievous, and how their songs—*fados,* he called them—were no more than lazy cousins of the fierce flamenco one heard throughout Andalusia.

When Zobrowski asked in what year the walls of Ávila were built, J.D. thought for quite a while, his lean face sober while he gently rocked a tumbler of iced rum, but at last he said the fortifications were probably begun seven or eight hundred years ago. They had been repaired occasionally and were still impregnable to primitive force. It was queer, he added, to come upon such a place, indestructible when assaulted on its own terms, yet obsolete.

He had postal cards of things that had interested him. He had not carried a camera because he thought it bad manners. We did not completely understand what he meant by this but we had no time to discuss it because he was running on, wanting to know if we were familiar with Giambologna, saying, as he displayed a card, "In a grotto of the Boboli Gardens not far from the Uffizi—" He stopped abruptly. It had occurred to him that we might be embarrassed. No one said anything. None of us had ever heard of the Boboli Gardens, or of the sculptor Giambologna, or of the Venus that J.D. had wanted to describe.

"Here's the Sistine Chapel, of course," he said, taking another card from his envelope. "That's the Libyan sybil."

"Yes," said Zobrowski. "I remember this. There was a print of it in one of our high-school textbooks. Good God, how time does pass."

"Those damn textbooks," J.D. answered. "They ruin everything. They've ruined Shakespeare and the Acropolis and half the things on earth that are really worth seeing. Just like the Lord's Prayer — I can't hear it. I don't know what it says. Why wasn't I left to discover it for myself? Or the Venus de Milo. I sat in front of it for an hour but I couldn't see it."

He brought out a postal card of a church tower. At the apex was a snail-like structure covered with what appeared to be huge tile baseballs.

"That's the *Sagrada Familia*," he explained. "It's not far from the bull ring in Barcelona."

The *Sagrada Familia* was unfinished; in fact it consisted of nothing but a façade with four tremendous towers rising far above the apartment buildings surrounding it. He said it was a landmark of Barcelona, that if you should get lost in the city you had only to get to a clearing and look around for this weird church. On the front of it was a cement Christmas tree, painted green and hung with cement ornaments, while the tiled spires were purple and yellow. And down each spire ran vertical lettering that could be read a kilometer away. Zobrowski asked what was written on the towers.

"There's one word on each tower," said J.D. "The only one I recall is 'Ecstasy'."

Dave Zobrowski listened with a patient, critical air, as though wondering how a man could spend ten years in such idle traveling. Russ Lyman, who had once been J.D.'s closest friend, listened in silence with his head bowed. When we were children together it had been Russ who intended to go around the world some day, but he had not, for a number of reasons. He seemed to hold a monopoly on bad luck. The girl he loved married somebody else, then his business failed, and so on and on through the years. Now he worked as a drugstore clerk and invested his pitiful savings in gold mines or wildcat oil wells. He had been thirty-two when the girl he loved told him goodby, tapping the ash from her cigarette onto his wrist to emphasize that she meant it; he promptly got drunk, because he could not imagine anything else to do, and a few days later he began going around with a stout, amiable girl named Eunice who had grown up on a nearby farm. One October day when the two of them were walking through an abandoned orchard they paused to rest in the shade of an old stone wall in which some ivy and small flowers were growing. Eunice was full of the delicate awkwardness of certain large girls, and while Russell was looking at her a leaf came fluttering down to rest on her shoulder. He became aware of the sound of honey-bees flickering through the noonday sun, and of the uncommonly sweet odor of apples moldering among the clover, and he was seized with such passion that he immediately took the willing girl. She became pregnant, so they got married, although he did not want to, and before much longer he stopped talking about going around the world.

J.D., handing Russell a card of a little street in some North African town, remarked that on this particular street he had bought a tasseled red fez. And Russell nodded a bit sadly.

"Now, this is Lisbon," J.D. said. "Right over here on the far side of this rectangular plaza is where I lived. I used to walk down to the river that you see at the edge of the card, and on the way back I'd wander through some little shops where you can buy miniature galleons of filigreed gold."

"I suppose you bought one," said Zobrowski.

"I couldn't resist," said J.D. with a smile. "Here's a view of Barcelona at night, and right here by this statue of Columbus I liked to sit and watch the tide come sweeping in. An exact copy of the *Santa María* is tied up at the dock near the statue. And whenever the wind blew down from the hills I could hear the butter-pat clap of the gypsies dancing on the Ramblas." He looked at us anxiously to see if we were interested. It was clear that he loved Spain. He wanted us to love it, too.

"One time in Galicia," he said, "at some little town where the train stopped I bought a drink of water from a wrinkled old woman who was holding up an earthen jug and calling, *'Agua! Agua fría!'* " He drew a picture of the jug — it was called a *porrón* — and he demonstrated how it was to be held above your head while you drank. Your lips were never supposed to touch the spout. The Spaniards could drink without swallowing, simply letting the stream of water pour down their throats, and after much dribbling and choking J.D. had learned the trick. But what he most wanted to describe was the old woman who sold him the water. She could have been sixty or ninety. She was toothless, barefoot, and with a rank odor, but somehow, in some way he could not get across to us, they had meant a great deal to each other. He tried to depict a quality of arrogance or ferocity about her, which, in the days when she was young, must have caused old men to murmur and young men to fall silent whenever she passed by. He could not forget an instant when he reached out the train window to give her back the clay jug and met her deep, unwavering eyes.

"The train was leaving," he said, leaning forward. "It was leaving forever. And I heard her scream at me. I didn't know what she said, but there was a Spaniard in the same compartment who told me that this old Galician woman had screamed at me, 'Get off the train! Stay in my land!' " He paused, apparently remembering, and slowly shook his head.

It was in Spain, too, in a cheap water-front night club called *El Hidalgo* — and he answered Russell's question by saying that Don Quixote, for example, was an *hidalgo* — it was here that he fell in love for the only time in his life. The cabaret was in an alley of the Gothic quarter where tourists seldom ventured. J.D. often spent his evenings there, buying lottery tickets and brown paper cigarettes and drinking a yellowish wine called *manzanilla*. One night the flamenco dancers were in a furious mood — he said he could feel the tension gathering the way electricity will sometimes gather on a midwestern afternoon until it splits the air. An enormously fat gypsy woman was dancing by herself, dancing the symbols of fertility that have survived a thousand generations. She was dressed in what he likened to a bedspread covered with orange polka dots. Raising and lowering her vast arms she snapped her fingers and angrily danced alone; then all at once a savage little man in high-heeled boots sprang out of the crowd and began leaping around her. The staccato of his boots made the floor tremble and caused the *manzanilla* to sway inside the bottles.

"Everybody was howling and clapping," said J.D., and he clapped once as the gypsies clap, not with the entire hand but with three fingers flat against the palm. It sounded like a pistol shot. "Somebody was looking at me," he went on. "I could feel someone's eyes on me. I looked into the shadows and saw her. She was about nineteen, very tall and imperial, with her hair in braids. She began walking toward me, and she was singing. She sang to me that her name was Paquita—"

"She was improvising a song," said Zobrowski.

J.D. nodded. "It had the sound of a lament. Those old tragedies you hear in Spain, they're paralyzing."

"Just what do you mean?" Zobrowski asked.

"I don't know," said J.D. "It's as if a dagger was still plunged to the hilt in her breast."

Zobrowski smiled. "Go on. No doubt this young woman was beautiful."

"Yes. And she never stopped looking at me. I don't remember, but she must have walked across the room because

I realized I was standing up and she was standing directly in front of me, touching my lips with one finger."

"I have had similar dreams," said Zobrowski.

Russell was listening avidly. "I didn't think Spanish women could ever get away from their chaperons."

"*Dueña,* I believe, is the word," Zobrowski said.

"There was no *dueña* for that girl," answered J.D. He was silent for a little while and then concluded his story. "Later that night I saw her walking the streets."

"Well, that explains everything," Zobrowski smiled. "You simply mistook her professional interest in you for some sort of transcendental love."

J.D. looked at Dave Zobrowski for a long time, and finally said, "I didn't think I could make you understand." To Russell he said, "I find myself repeating her name. In the night I see her everywhere. In Paris, or in Rome, or even in this town, I see a girl turning away and my heart jumps the way it did that night in Barcelona."

"You should have married her," said Russell.

"I think he has done enough foolish things as it is," Zobrowski replied, and that seemed to end the matter. At least J.D. never referred to Paquita again. He spoke of the Andalusian gypsies, saying that they are a mixture of Arab and Indian, while the Catalonians are almost pure Sudra Indian. He gave this information as though it were important; he seemed to value knowledge for itself alone. But, looking into our faces, he saw that we could not greatly care about Spanish gypsies one way or another.

He had a pale gray cardboard folder with a drawing of St. George on the cover. Inside was a map of the geographical limits of the Catalan language, and this inscription : "With the best wishes for all the friends of the Catalan speaking countries once free in the past they will be free and whole again thanks to the will and strength of the Catalan people."

This was a folder of the resistance movement; it had been given to him, at the risk of imprisonment and perhaps at the risk of life itself, by a charwoman of Valencia. Zobrowski inquired if these were the people who opposed Franco. J.D. said that was correct. In Algiers he had met a waiter who had fought against Franco and barely escaped the country; this waiter had been in Algiers since 1938 and had no hope of seeing his family again, though he believed, as the charwoman believed, that one day Spain would be free.

After inspecting the pathetic little folder Zobrowski suggested, "I can easily appreciate your concern for these people. However you might also spend some time considering your own situation. Frankly, time is getting on, while you elect to dawdle about the waterfronts of the world."

J.D. shrugged.

"I've been meaning to ask," said Zobrowski. "Did you ever receive the letter I addressed to you in Vienna?"

"I don't remember it," said J.D.

"It concerned an executive position with the Pratt Hanover Company. They manufacture farm implements. I spoke to Donald Pratt about you and he was very much interested."

"No, I never got the letter," said J.D. and he grinned. "I was traveling quite a bit and I guess a lot of letters never caught up with me."

"Would you have come back if you had received the offer from Pratt?"

"No, I guess not," said J.D.

"We've known each other a long time, haven't we?"

J.D nodded. "Since we were kids, Dave."

"Exactly. I would like to know how you manage to live."

"Oh, I work here and there. I had a job at the American embassy in Switzerland for a while, and to be honest about it, I've done some black marketing. I've learned how to get along, how to pull the levers that operate the world."

Then he began to describe Lucerne. It seemed far distant, in every dimension, from the days when we were children and used to bicycle down the river road to the hickory woods and hunt for squirrels. Each of us had a .22 rifle, except J.D., who went hunting with a lemonwood bow. He had made it himself, and he had braided and waxed the string, and sewn a quiver, and planed his arrows. He did not hit many squirrels with his equipment, and we would often taunt him about losing the arrows among the high weeds and underbrush, but he never seemed to mind; he would go home to his father's tool chest in the basement and calmly set about planing another batch of sticks. We would watch him clip turkey feathers into crisp rhomboids and carefully glue them into place, bracing each feather with matchsticks until the glue hardened. We would sit on the wash tub, or on his father's work bench, and smoke pieces of grapevine while we studied the new arrows. When he fitted on the bronze tip and banded each arrow with hunter's green and white Russell would watch with an almost hypnotized expression. But Dave Zobrowski, even in those days, was puzzled and a trifle impatient with J.D.

Remembering such things as J.D.'s bow and arrow we could see that it was he, and not Russell, who was destined to go away. We thought he had left a good deal of value here in the midwest of America. Our town is not exotic, but it is comprehensible and it is clean. This is partly due to Dave Zobrowski, who has always been vehement about cleanliness. That he grew up to become a physician and a member of the sanitary commission surprised no one. He likes to tell of disgusting conditions he has seen in other cities. While he was in Chicago at a medical convention he investigated a hotel charging the same price as the Pioneer House here in town, and he reported, all too graphically, how the ceiling was stained from leakage, how there was pencil writing on the walls, together with the husks of smashed roaches, and how he found a red hair embedded in the soap. Even the towel was rancid. Looking out the smoky window he saw wine bottles and decaying fruit in the gutter.

Visitors to this town often wonder how it is possible to exist without ballet, opera, and so forth, but it usually turns out that they themselves attend only once or twice each season, if at all. Then, too, if you are not accustomed to a certain entertainment you do not miss it. Russell, for example, grew up in a home devoid of music but cheerful and harmonious all the same. To his parents music was pointless, unless at Christmas time, when the phonograph would be wound up, the needle replaced, and the carols dusted off; consequently Mozart means nothing to him.

A Brooklyn police captain named Lehmbruck drove out here to spend his vacation but went back east after a week, saying it was too quiet to sleep. However he seemed to be interested in the sunset, remarking that he had never seen the sun go down anywhere except behind some buildings. And he had never eaten old ham—he studied the white specks very dubiously, and with some embarrassment asked if the ham was spoiled. The Chamber of Commerce later received a wistful little note from Captain Lehmbruck, hinting that he might have another try at the prairie next summer.

Christmas here is still made instead of bought, even if we think no more of Christ than anyone else. And during the summer months the sidewalks are overhung with white or lavender spirea, and we can watch the rain approaching, darkening the farmland. Life here is reasonable and tradition not discounted, as evidenced by the new public library which is a modified Parthenon of Tennessee marble. There was a long and bitter argument about the inscription for its façade. One group wanted the so-called living letter, while the majority sought reassurance in the Doric past. At last we chiseled it with "Pvblic," "Covnty," "Strvctvre," and so forth.

J.D. knew about all these things, but he must have wanted more, and as he talked to us about his travels we could read in his restless blue eyes that he was not through searching. We thought he would come home when his father died, at least for a little while. Of course he was six thousand miles away, but most men would have returned from any distance. We did not know what he thought of us, the friends who had been closest to him, and this was altogether strange because our opinions about him were no secret — the fact that Russell envied him and that Zobrow-ski thought his life was going to rot.

Russell, to be sure, envied everybody. For a time after the marriage we believed Russell would collect himself, what-ever it was needed collecting, because he went around look-ing very pleased with himself, although Eunice seemed a bit confused. He began to go shooting in the hickory woods again, firing his old .22 more to exult in its noise than to kill a squirrel. Yet something within him had been destroyed. Whether it could have been an insufferable jealousy of J.D. — who was then in Finland — or love that was lost, or the hard core of another sickness unknown to anyone on earth, no one could say, but it was to be only a few years after J.D.'s visit that we would find Russell lying in the garage with his head almost torn off and a black .45 service auto-matic in his hand.

"Here is where Dante first met Beatrice," said J.D., add-ing with a smile that several locations in Florence claimed this distinction, even as half the apartments in Toledo insist El Greco painted there. And he had a picture of Cala Rat-jada where he had lived with a Danish girl named Vivian. We had forgotten, if indeed we had ever realized it, that in other countries people are not required to be so furtive about their affairs. We learned that Cala Ratjada was a fishing village on the eastern end of Majorca. Majorca we had heard of because the vacation magazines were publicizing it.

"I understand there's a splendid cathedral in the capital," Zobrowski said. "Palma, isn't it?"

J.D. agreed rather vaguely. It was plain he did not care much for cathedrals, unless there was something queer about them as there was about the *Sagrada Familia*. He preferred to tell about the windmills on Majorca, and about his bus ride across the island with a crate of chickens on the seat behind him. We had not known there was a bus across the island; the travel magazines always advised tourists to hire a car with an English-speaking driver. So we listened, because there is a subtle yet basic difference between one who travels and one who does not.

He had lived with this Danish girl all of one summer in a boarding house—a *pensión* he called it—and every afternoon they walked through some scrubby little trees to a white sandy beach and went swimming nude. They took along a leather bag full of heavy amber wine and drank this and did some fancy diving off the rocks. He said the Mediterranean there at Cala Ratjada was more translucent even than the harbor of Monte Carlo. When their wine was finished and the sand had become cool and the shadows of the trees were touching the water they walked back to the village. For a while they stopped on the embarcadero to watch the Balearic fishermen spreading their nets to dry. Then J.D. and the Danish girl returned to the *pensión* for dinner. They ate such things as fried octopus, or baby squid, or a huge seafood casserole called a *paella*.

"Where is she now?" Russell asked.

"Vivian?" said J.D. "Oh, I don't know. She sent me a card

from Frederikshavn a year or so ago. She'd been wanting to
go to India, so maybe that's where she is now."

"Didn't she expect you to marry her?"

J.D. looked at Russell and then laughed out loud; it was
the first time he had laughed all evening.

"Neither of us wanted to get married," he·said. "We had a
good summer. Why should we ruin it?"

This was a kind of reasoning we were aware of, via novels
more impressive for poundage than content; otherwise it
bore no relation to us. What bound them together was as
elementary as a hyphen, and we suspected they could meet
each other years later without embarrassment. They had
loved without aim or sense, as young poets do. We could
imagine this, to be sure, but we could not imagine it actually
happening. There were women in our town, matrons now,
with whom we had been intimate to some degree a decade
or so ago, but now when we met them, or were entertained
in their homes, we were restrained by the memory of the
delicate past. Each of us must carry, as it were, a balloon
inked with names and dates.

So far as we knew, J.D. looked up only one of the women
he used to know here in town. He called on Helen Louise
Sawyer who used to win the local beauty contests. When we
were young most of us were afraid of her, because there is
something annihilating about too much beauty; only J.D.
was not intimidated. Perhaps he could see then what we
learned to see years later — that she was lonely, and that she
did not want to be coveted for the perfection of her skin or
for the truly magnificent explosion of her bosom. When
Helen Louise and J.D. began going around together we
were astonished and insulted because Russell, in those days,
was much more handsome than J.D., and Dave Zobrowski
was twice as smart. All the same she looked at no one else.
Then he began leaving town on longer and longer expedi-
tions. He would return wearing a southern California sport

shirt, or with a stuffed grouper he had caught off Key West. Helen Louise eventually went into the real-estate business.

He telephoned her at the office and they went to dinner at the Wigwam, which is now the swank place to eat. It is decorated with buffalo skins and tomahawks and there are displays of flint arrowheads that have been picked up by farmers in neighboring counties. The only incongruities are the pink jade ashtrays that, by midnight, seem to have been planted with white, magenta-tipped stalks to remind the diners that a frontier has vanished. And well it has. The scouts are buried, the warriors mummified. Nothing but trophies remain: a coup stick hung by the Wigwam's flagstone hearth, a pipe smoked by Satanta, a cavalry saber and a set of moldering blue gloves crossed on the mantel, a tan robe laced to the western wall, a dry Pawnee scalp behind the bar. The wind still sweeps east from the lofty Colorado plains, but carries with it now only the clank of machinery in the wheat fields. The Mandans have gone, like the minor chords of an Iowa death song, with Dull Knife and Little Wolf whose three hundred wretched squaws and starving men set out to fight their way a thousand miles to the fecund Powder River that had been their home.

There is a gratification to the feel of history behind the places one has known, and the Wigwam's historical display is extensive. In addition, the food is good. There is hot biscuit with clover honey, and the old ham so mistrusted by Captain Lehmbruck of Brooklyn. There is Missouri fried chicken, spare ribs, venison with mushrooms, catfish, beef you can cut with a fork, wild rice and duck buried under pineapple sauce, as well as various European dishes. That evening J.D. asked for a certain Madeira wine and apparently was a little taken aback to find that the Wigwam had it. Travelers, real travelers, come to think of their homes as provincial and are often surprised.

Helen Louise had metamorphosed, as even we could see,

and we knew J.D. was in for a shock. Through the years she had acquired that faintly resentful expression that comes from being stared at, and she seemed to be trying to compensate for her beauty. Although there was nothing wrong with her eyes she wore glasses; she had cropped her beautiful golden hair in a Lesbian style; and somehow she did not even walk the way she used to. The pleasing undulations had mysteriously given way to a militant stride. Her concern in life was over such items as acreage and location. At the business she was quite good; every real-estate man in town hated her, no doubt thinking she should have become a housewife instead of the demon that she was. But apparently she had lost her desire to marry, or sublimated it. At the lunch hour she could be seen in an expensive suit, speaking in low tones to another businesswoman, and her conversation when overheard would be, " . . . referred the order to me . . . Mrs. Pabst's opinion . . . second mortgage . . . bought six apartments . . ."

We guessed that J.D.'s evening with Helen Louise might be an indication that he had grown tired of wandering around the earth, and that he wanted to come home for good. Helen Louise, if no longer as voluptuous as she had been at twenty or twenty-five, was still provocative, and if she married was it not possible she might come to look very much as she had looked ten years before? But J.D. had very little to say about his evening with her; and after he was gone Helen Louise never mentioned him.

"Did you know that in Cádiz," he said — because it was to him a fact worth noting, like the fact that in Lisbon he had lived on a certain plaza — "Did you know that in Cádiz you can buy a woman for three *pesetas*?" Whether or not he might have been referring to Helen Louise we did not know, nor did anyone ask.

"Once I talked with Manolete," he said, as though it was the first line of a poem.

"I've heard that name," Zobrowski answered. "He's a toreador, is he not?"

"I think 'toreador' was invented by Bizet," J.D. replied. "Manolete was a matador. But he's dead. It was in Linares that he was *cogido*. On the twenty-seventh of August in nineteen-forty-seven. At five in the afternoon, as the saying goes." And he continued, telling us that the real name of this bullfighter had been Manuel Rodriguez, and that after he was gored in Linares the ambulance which was taking him to a hospital started off in the wrong direction, and there was a feeling of bitterness in Spain when the news was broadcast that he was dead of his wounds.

"What you are trying to express," Zobrowski suggested, "is that this fellow was a national hero."

"Yes," said J.D.

"Like Babe Ruth."

"No," said J.D. instantly and with a vexed expression. He gestured helplessly and then shrugged. He went on to say that he happened to be in Heidelberg when death came to Manolete in the town of Linares. He looked around at us as if this circumstance were very strange. As he spoke he gestured excitedly and often skipped from one topic to another because there was so little time and he had so much to tell us. In a way he created a landscape of chiaroscuro, illuminating first one of his adventures and now another, but leaving his canvas mostly in shadow.

"One morning in Basel," he said, "it began to snow while I was having breakfast. Snow was falling on the Rhine." He was sitting by a window in a tea shop overlooking the river. He described the sunless, blue-gray atmosphere with large white flakes of snow piling up on the window ledge, and the dark swath of the river. Several waitresses in immaculate uniforms served his breakfast from a heavy silver tray. There was coffee in a silver pitcher, warm breads wrapped in thick linen napkins, and several kinds of jam and preserves; all the while the snow kept mounting on the ledge just outside the window, and the waitresses murmured in German. He returned to Basel on the same morning of the following year — all the way from Palermo — just to have his breakfast there.

Most of his ten years abroad had been spent on the borders of the Mediterranean, and he agreed with Zobrowski's comment that the countries in that area must be the dirtiest in Europe. He told about a servant girl in one of his *pensiones* who always seemed to be on her knees scrubbing the floor, but who never bathed herself. She had such a pervasive odor that he could tell whenever she had recently been in a room.

He said that Pompeii was his biggest disappointment. He had expected to find the city practically buried under a cliff of lava. But there was no lava. Pompeii was like any city abandoned and overgrown with weeds. He had visited the Roman ruins of North Africa, but the names he mentioned did not mean anything to us. Carthage did, but if we had ever read about the others in school we had long since stored their names and dates back in the dusty bins alongside algebra and Beowulf. Capri was the only celebrated spot he visited that surpassed all pictures of it, and he liked Sorrento too, saying that he had returned to the mainland about sundown when the cliffs of Sorrento become red and porous like the cliffs of the Grand Canyon. And in a town called Amalfi he had been poisoned — he thought it was the eggs.

All this was delivered by a person we had known since childhood, yet it might as well have come from a foreign lecturer. J.D. was not trying to flaunt his adventures; he described them because we were friends and he could not conceive of the fact that the ruins of Pompeii would mean less to us than gossip on the women's page. He wanted to tell us about the ballet in Cannes, where the audience was so quiet that he had heard the squeak of the dancers' slippers. But none of us had ever been to a ballet, or especially wanted to go. There was to us something faintly absurd about men and women in tights. When Zobrowski suggested as much, J.D. looked at him curiously and seemed to be struggling to remember what it was like to live in our town.

A number of things he said did not agree with our concept. According to him the Swedish girls are not in the least as they appear on calendars, which invariably depict them driving some cows down a pea-green mountainside. J.D. said the Swedes were long and gaunt with cadaverous features and gloomy dispositions, and their suicide rate was among the highest on earth.

Snails, he said, though no one had inquired, have very little taste. You eat them with a tiny two-pronged fork and some tongs that resemble a surgeon's forceps. The garlic-butter sauce is excellent, good enough to drink, but snail meat tasted to him rubbery like squid.

About the taxi drivers of Paris: they were incredibly avaricious. If you were not careful they would give you a gilded two-franc piece instead of a genuine fifty-franc piece for change, and if you caught them at it they became furious. But he did say that the French were the most urbane people to be found.

He had traveled as far east as Teheran and as far north as Trondheim. He had been to Lithuania and to Poland, and to Egypt and to the edge of the Sahara, and from the animation of his voice we could tell he was not through yet. While he was telling us about his plans as we sat comfortably in the cocktail lounge of the Pioneer House, a bellboy came in and respectfully said to Dave, "Dr. Zobrowski, the hospital is calling."

Without a word Zobrowski stood up and followed the

boy. A few minutes later he returned wearing his overcoat and carrying his gray Homburg. "I'm sorry, but it's an emergency," he said to us all, and then to J.D., "Since you are not to be in town much longer I suppose this is good-by."

J.D. uncrossed his long legs and casually stood up.

"No doubt you lead an entertaining life," Zobrowski observed, not bothering to conceal his disapproval. "But a man cannot wander the face of the earth forever."

"That's what everybody tells me," J.D. answered with a grin. "It doesn't bother me much any more."

Zobrowski pulled on his yellow pigskin gloves and with a severe expression he began to settle the fingers as carefully as though he had put on surgical gloves. "In my opinion," he said suddenly, and lifted his eyes, "you are a damn fool."

They stared at each other not with hostility, nor exactly with surprise, but as though they had never quite seen each other until that instant. Yet these were the two men who, about thirty years previously, had chipped in equal shares to buy a dog, a squat little beast with peculiar teeth that made it look like a beaver.

"From birth we carry the final straw," said Zobrowski at last.

J.D. only smiled.

Zobrowski's normally hard features contracted until he looked cruel, and he inclined his head, saying by this gesture, "As you wish." He had always known how to use silence with devastating force, yet J.D. was undismayed and did nothing but shrug like a Frenchman.

Zobrowski turned to Russell. "I had lunch with my broker the other day. He has some information on that Hudson's Bay mining stock of yours that makes me feel we should have a talk. Stop by my office tomorrow morning at eight-thirty. I have had my receptionist cancel an appointment because of this matter."

Russell's mouth slowly began to drop open as he gazed at Zobrowski. He never made reasonable investments and several times had been saved from worse ones only because he confided his financial plans, along with everything else, to anybody who would listen. Then, too, the making of money necessitates a callousness he had never possessed.

"That stock's all right," he said weakly. "I'm positive it's all right. Really it is, Dave. You should have bought some."

"Yes," Zobrowski said, looking down on him with disgust. And turning to J.D. he said, "Let us hear from you. Good-by." Then he went striding across the lounge.

"Oh, God!" mumbled Russell, taking another drink. He was ready to weep from humiliation and from anxiety over the investment. In the past few years he had become quite bald and flabby, and had taken to wearing suspenders because a belt disturbed his intestines. He rubbed his jowls and looked around with a vague, desperate air.

"Whatever happened to little Willie Grant?" J.D. asked, though Grant had never meant a thing to him.

"He's — he's in Denver," Russell said, gasping for breath.

"What about Martha Mathews?"

This was the girl who rejected Russell, but J.D. was abroad when it happened and may never have heard. He looked astonished when Russell groaned. Economically speaking, she was a great deal better off than if she had married Russell. She had accepted a housing contractor with more ambition than conscience, and now spent most of her time playing cards on the terrace of the country club.

J.D. had been in love, moderately, in the abstract, with a long-legged sloe-eyed girl named Minnette whose voice should have been poured into a glass and drunk. Her mother owned a bakery. We usually saw Minnette's mother when we came trotting home from school at the noon hour; she would be standing at the door with arms rolled in her apron while she talked to the delivery man, or, in winter time, we would often seen her as she bent over, pendulous, tranquil, somehow everlasting, to place chocolate éclairs in the bakery window while sleet bounced indignantly off the steaming glass. At such moments she looked the way we always wanted our own harried mothers to look. If the truth were known it might be that we found her more stimulating than her daughter, although this may have been because we were famished when we passed the bakery. In any event he inquired about Minnette, so we told him her eyes still had that look, and that she was married to the mortician, an extremely tall man named Knopf who liked to underline trenchant phrases in the little books on Success that you buy for a quarter.

Answering these somehow anachronistic questions stirred us the way an old snapshot will do when you come upon it while hunting for something else. Later on Russell was to say that when J.D. mentioned the yellow brick building where the four of us began our schooling he remembered for the first time in possibly a decade how we used to sit around a midget table and wield those short, blunt, red-handled scissors. We had a paste pot and sheets of colored paper, and when our labors were done the kindergarten windows displayed pumpkins, Christmas trees, owls, eggs, rabbits, or whatever was appropriate to the season. J.D. could always draw better than anyone else. When visiting night for parents came around it would be his work they admired. David Zobrowski, of course, was the scholar; we were proud to be Dave's best friends. Russell managed to remain undistinguished in any way until time for the singing class. Here no one could match him. Not that anyone wanted to. He sang worse than anyone who ever attended our school. It was as if his voice operated by a pulley, and its tenor was remotely canine. The class consisted of bluebirds and robins, with the exception of Russ who was placed at a separate desk and given no designation at all. Usually he gazed out the window at the interminable fields, but when it came to him that he, too, could sing, and his jaw began to work and his throat to contract, he would be warned into silence by the waving baton.

Going to and from the business district ordinarily meant passing this musty little building, which had long since been converted into headquarters for the Boy Scout troop, and which now related to us no more than the Wizard of Oz, but until J.D. spoke of it we had not realized that the swings and the slide were gone, and crab grass was growing between the bricks of the front walk.

When we were in high school J.D. occasionally returned to wander the corridors of the elementary school. The rest of us had been glad enough to move on and we considered his visits a bit queer, but otherwise never paused to think about them.

These were the streets where we had lived, these the houses, during a period of time when today could not influence tomorrow, and we possessed the confidence to argue about things we did not understand. Though, of course, we still did that. On winter nights we dropped away to sleep while watching the snow come drifting by the street light, and in summer we could see the moths outside the screens fluttering desperately, as though to tell us something. Our childhood came and went before we were ready to grasp it. Things were different now. The winged seeds that gyrate down from the trees now mean nothing else but that we must sweep them from the automobile hood because stains on the finish lower the trade-in value. Now, in short, it was impractical to live as we used to live with the abandon of a mule rolling in the dust.

In those days our incipient manhood had seemed a

unique power, and our single worry that some girl might become pregnant. We danced with our eyes closed and our noses thrust into the gardenias all the girls wore in their hair, meanwhile estimating our chances. And, upon discovering literature, thanks to the solemn pedantry of a sophomore English teacher, we affected bow ties and cigarette holders and were able to quote contemporary poets with a faintly cynical tone.

On a postcard of a Rotterdam chocolate factory, sent to Russell but addressed to us all, J.D. scribbled, "I see nothing but the noon dust a-blowing and the green grass a-growing." If not contemporary it was at least familiar, and caused Zobrowski to remark, with a certain unconscious measure, "As fond as I am of him I sometimes lose patience. In a furrow he has found a feather of Pegasus and what should have been a blessing has become a curse."

Now J.D. was inquiring after one or two we had forgotten, or who had moved away, leaving no more trace than a cloud, and about a piano teacher who had died one sultry August afternoon on the streetcar. Yet his interest was superficial. He was being polite. He could not really care or he would not have gone away for ten years. He wondered whatever became of the bearded old man who used to stand on a street corner with a stack of Bibles and a placard promising a free copy of the New Testament to any Jew who would renounce the faith. We did not know what happened to the old man; somehow he had just vanished. Quite a few things were vanishing.

J.D. cared very little for the men who had once been our fraternity brothers, which was odd because in our hearts we still believed that those days and those brothers had been so extraordinary that people were still talking about them. Yet we could recall that he took no pride in being associated with them. The militant friendship of fraternity life made him surly. He refused to shake hands as often as he was expected to. We had been warned that, as pledges, we would be thrown into the river some night. This was part of learning to become a finer man. When the brothers came for us about three o'clock one morning, snatching away our blankets and singing the good fellowship song, we put up the traditional fight—all of us except J.D. He refused to struggle. He slumped in the arms of his captors as limp as an empty sack. This puzzled and annoyed the brothers, who held him aloft by his ankles and who bounced his head on the floor. He would not even open his eyes. They jabbed him stiffly in the ribs, they twisted his arms behind his back, they kicked him in the seat, they called him names, and finally, very angry, they dragged him to the river and flung him in. But even when he went sailing over the bullrushes he was silent as a corpse. Strangely, he did not hit the water with a loud splash. Years later he told us that he twisted at the last moment and dove through the river scum, instead of landing flat on his back as Russell did. They vanished together, as roommates should, but Russell was again audible in a few seconds—thrashing back to shore, where the brothers helped him out and gave him a towel and a bathrobe and a drink of brandy.

J.D., however, did not reappear. Even before Russell had reached the shore we were beginning to worry about J.D. There was no moon that night and the river had an evil look. We stood in a row at the edge of the water. We heard the bullfrogs, and the dark bubbling and plopping of whatever calls the river home, but nothing more. And all at once the structure of the fraternity collapsed. The last vestige of unity disappeared. We were guilty individuals. Some people began lighting matches and peering into the river, while others called his name. But there was no answer, except in the form of rotten, half-submerged driftwood floating by, revolving in the sluggish current, and, beyond the confused whispering, the brief, crying shadows of night birds dipping in wild alarm over the slimy rushes.

When we saw him again we asked what happened, but several years passed before he told anyone. Then he said — and only then was his revenge complete — "Oh, I just swam under water as far as I could. After that I let the river carry me out of sight." He swam ashore a mile or two downstream, and by a back road he returned to the fraternity house. Nobody was there; everybody was at the river searching for his body. The fraternity was almost ruined because of J.D.

Now he had climbed the Matterhorn, and we were not surprised. He knew what it was like in Venice, or in Copenhagen, and as we reflected on his past we came to understand that his future was inevitable. We knew he would leave us again, perhaps forever.

Russell, tamping out a cheap cigar, said boldly, "Eunice and I have been thinking about a trip to the Bahamas next year, or year after." He considered the nicotine on his fingertips, and after a pause, because his boast was empty, and because he knew that we knew how empty it was, he added, "Though it depends." He began picking helplessly at his fingertips. He would never go anywhere.

"You'll like the Bahamas," J.D. said.

"We consider other places," Russell said unexpectedly, and there were tears in his eyes.

J.D. was watching him with a blank, pitiless gaze.

"I think I'll go to Byzantium," Russell said.

"That doesn't exist any more."

Russell took a deep breath to hush the panic that was on him, and at last he said, "Well, gentlemen, I guess I'd better get some shut-eye if I'm going to talk business with Dave in the morning."

"It's late," J.D. agreed.

Then we asked when he would be coming home for good, although it was a foolish question, and J.D. laughed at it. Later, in talking about him, we would recall his reason for not wanting to live here. He had explained that the difference between our town and these other places he had been was that when you go walking down a boulevard in some strange land and you see a tree burgeoning, you understand that this is beautiful, and there comes with the knowledge a moment of indescribable poignance in the realization that as this tree must die, so will you die. But when, in the home you have always known, you find a tree in bud you think only that spring has come again. Here he stopped. It did not make much sense to us, but for him it had meaning of some kind.

So we asked when he would be coming back for another visit. He said he didn't know. We asked what was next. He replied that as soon as he could scrape together a few more dollars he thought he might like to see the Orient.

"They say that in Malaya . . ." he began, with glowing eyes. But we did not listen closely. He was not speaking to us anyway, only to himself, to the matrix which had spawned him and to the private god who guided him. His voice reached us faintly, as if from beyond the walls of Ávila.

The Palace
of the Moorish Kings

Often we wondered why he chose to live as he did, floating here and there like a leaf on a pond. We had talked about this without ever deciding that we understood, although each of us had an opinion. All we could agree upon was that he never would marry. In some way he was cursed, we thought. One of those uncommon men who follow dim trails around the world hunting a fulfillment they couldn't find at home. Early in a man's life this may not be unnatural, but years go by and finally he ought to find a wife and raise children so that by the time his life ends he will have assured the continuation of life. To us that seemed the proper pattern because it was traditional, and we were holding to it as best we could. Only J.D. had not.

From the capitals and provinces of Europe he had wandered to places we had scarcely heard of—Ahmedabad, Penang, the Sulu archipelago. From the Timor coast he had watched the moon rise above the Arafura Sea. He had slept like a beggar beside the red fort in Old Delhi and had seen the Ajanta frescoes. Smoke from funeral pyres along the Ganges at Varanasi had drifted over him, and he'd been doused with brilliant powders during the festival of Bahag Bihn.

Three hundred miles south of Calcutta, he had told us, is a 13th century Hindu temple known as the Black Pagoda of Konorak which is decorated with thousands of sculptured sandstone figures—lions, bulls, elephants, deities, musicians, dancing girls and frankly explicit lovers. Its vegetable-shaped peak, the *sikhara,* collapsed a long time ago, but the *mandapa* is still there, rising in three stages. It represents the chariot of the sun. This fantastic vehicle is drawn by a team of elaborately carved horses and century after century it rolls toward the Bay of Bengal. Nothing equals it, he said. Nothing. The temple complex at Khajuraho is marvelous, but Konorak—and he gestured as he did whenever he could not articulate his feelings.

What he was after, none of us knew. Seasons turned like the pages of a familiar album while he traveled the byways of the world. He seemed to think his life was uncircumscribed, as though years were not passing, as though he might continue indefinitely doing whatever he pleased. Perhaps he thought he would outlive not only us but our children, and theirs beyond them.

We ourselves had no such illusions. We could see the clean sweep of youth sagging. Not that we had considered ourselves old, or even badly middle-aged, just that there was some evidence in the mirror. And there was other evidence. Zobrowski's son, for example, was in Asia fighting a war that had begun secretly, deceptively, like a disease, had gotten inside of us and was devouring us before we understood its course. We who had fought in the Second World War had gone along confidently supposing that if war broke out again we would be recalled for duty, but now the government ignored us. It was somewhat embarrassing, as if we were at fault. Young Dave Zobrowski did the fighting while all we did was drive to the office. A boy hardly old enough for long pants had been drafted.

The war offered a deep and bitter paradox. We had succeeded. Beyond all possible question we had succeeded: we had defeated the enemy, yet we had failed. Davy, too, attacked the riddle, unaware at his age that an insoluble problem existed, just as it had existed for us and as it existed for our fathers after the war they called The Great War. Maybe young Dave was more conscious of this than we had been, because we were more knowing than our fathers; still, not much had been changed by our evident sophistication. One conflict ended. Another began. Awareness was irrelevant.

So, against this, we were helpless. We could only hope that our bewilderment and dismay were misplaced. The acid we tasted while listening to newscasts and hearing the casualty figures — "body count" the Pentagon secretaries chose to call it — we could only hope that these falsified and shameful statistics would soon be forgotten. During the Second World War we would have thought it degenerate to gloat over corpses. Now this had become official practice. Apparently it was meant to reassure and persuade us that the government's cause was just.

The slow spectacle of ourselves aging, a dubious war, the decay of our presumably stable nation — these matters were much on our minds when J.D. wrote that he had decided to stop traveling. He was planning to come home. Furthermore, he intended to get married.

We were, of course, astonished. At an age when his friends might become grandfathers he had concluded that perhaps he should stop amusing himself like a college boy in the summertime.

Our wives were not surprised. They considered marriage inevitable and they were relieved that J.D. had at last come to his senses. They were merely irritated that he had waited so long. They regarded his solitary wandering as some kind of pretext for taking advantage of women all over the world. If we were in charge, they seemed to say, he'd have been suitably married years ago. The news affected them quite differently than it affected Zobrowski and Al Bunce and the others who used to play football and marbles with J.D. in those tranquil days when it was safe to walk the streets, and the air in the city was almost as sweet as it was on a farm.

Then we didn't think of our city the way we do now. Sometimes in winter or when the earth was soft after a rain we would find deer tracks across a vacant lot, and occasionally we caught a glimpse of what we thought must be a strange dog vanishing into the shrubbery — only to realize that it was a fox. Now we go about our business in a metropolis. The sizeable animals have disappeared, nobody knows quite where; but we don't see them, not even their prints. Gray squirrels once in a while, some years a good many, but little else. Robins, jays, bluebirds, cardinals, thrashers — we used to sprinkle breadcrumbs on the snowy back porch just to watch a parliament of birds arrive. Today our luncheon guests are the ubiquitous sparrows who can put up with anything.

Smoke fouls the sky and we find ourselves constantly interrupted by the telephone. Billboards, wires, garbage. We have difficulty accepting these everyday truths. How can we admit that the agreeable past, which we thought was permanent and inviolable, has slipped away like a Mississippi steamboat? We like to think that one morning we will see again those uncultivated fields thick with red clover, streams shaded by cottonwood and willow, and butterflies flickering through the sunlight as clearly as illustrations in the heroic books we read when we were eight.

We used to discuss what we would do when we grew up. We made splendid plans. First, of course, we would be rich. Next, we would marry beautiful exciting women with names like Rita, Hedy or Paulette. We would race speedboats and monoplanes, become as famous as Sir Malcolm Campbell and Colonel Roscoe Turner, or perhaps become wild animal trainers like Clyde Beatty, or hunters like Frank Buck, or great athletes like Glenn Cunningham and Don Budge. There were jungles to be explored, mountain peaks that had never been scaled, cities buried in the sand.

One after another these grandiose ideas acquired the patina of dreams. We could perceive as we grew older that we had not been realistic, so it was natural for Bunce to stop talking about an all-gold motorcycle. Art Stevenson would laugh when reminded of his vow to climb Mount Everest. But there were less ambitious adventures which still seemed reasonable. It's not so hard, for instance, to visit the ruins of Babylon; apparently you can go by jet to Baghdad and hire a taxi.

All of us intended to travel — we agreed on that — just as soon as matters could be arranged. As soon as we finished school. As soon as we could afford a long vacation. As soon as the payments were made on the house and the car. As soon as the children were old enough to be left alone. Next year, or the year after, everything would be in order.

Only J.D. had managed to leave. Surabaja. Brunei. Kuala Lumpur. The islands of Micronesia. He had sent us post-cards and occasionally a letter describing where he had been or where he thought he might go next, so in a sense we knew what the world was like.

Once he had returned for a visit. Just once. He stayed not quite three days. We felt obscurely insulted, without being able to explain our resentment. He was not obligated to us. We had played together, gone through school together and exchanged the usual juvenile confidences, but no pacts were signed. We couldn't tell him to come home at Christmas, or insist that he stop fooling around and get a job. Nevertheless, we wished he would; bitterness crept into our talk because we knew he meant more to us than we meant to him. We suspected he seldom thought about us. He could guess where we would be at almost any hour; he could have drawn the outline of our lives day after day and year after year. Why should he think about us? Who thinks about a familiar pair of shoes?

Nor could we explain why we so often discussed him. Perhaps we were annoyed by his indifference toward our values. The work we did was as meaningless to him as the fact that our children were growing up. To us nothing was more significant than our jobs and our families, but to J.D. these vital proceedings had less substance than breadcrumbs in the snow. When he wrote, usually to Zobrowski, he never asked what we were doing. He considered us to have a past — a childhood involved with his own — but a transitory nebulous present and a predictable future.

During his visit we questioned him as if we might not ever talk to him again. We asked about Africa — if he had seen Mount Kilimanjaro. He said yes, he had been there, but you seldom see much of Kilimanjaro for the clouds.

Millicent asked if he had shot anything. He said no, he was not a hunter. But he had met an Englishman who did some sort of office work in Bristol and every year came down to hunt, and they had sat up all night drinking gin and talking while the clouds opened and closed and opened again to reveal different aspects of Kilimanjaro in the moonlight, and it sounded as though the lions were only a few yards away. This was as close as he had gotten to hunting the big game of Africa he told her with mock seriousness. Unless you counted the flies, which were savage brutes.

Nairobi, he said, was a delightful town, surprisingly clean, and the weather was decent. We had assumed that it was filthy and humid.

The Masai live not far from Nairobi, he said, and you can visit their compounds if you care to. They eat cheese and drink the blood of cattle and have no use for 20th century marvels, except for ceramic beads with which they make rather attractive bracelets and necklaces. Their huts are plastered with animal dung, yet you can tell from watching a Masai warrior that once they were the lords of this territory just as you see in Spanish faces the memory of an age when Spaniards ruled Europe. But it's embarrassing to visit the Masai, he said, because they start to dance whenever a tourist shows up.

I should guess they look forward to the tips, Zobrowski remarked.

They get paid, J.D. said, but you don't tip a Masai. And nobody needs to tell you.

Barbara asked how he liked Ethiopia. He said he'd been there but hadn't stayed long because of the cholera and the mud. He mentioned this Ethiopian mud twice. We thought it strange that his principal memory of such an exotic country should be something as prosaic as mud.

Nor did we understand why he chose to cross and recross a world of dung-smeared huts, lepers, starvation and cholera. No doubt he had seen rare and wonderful sights, he must have met a good many unusual people, and he had tasted fruits we weren't apt to taste. Granted the entertainment value, what else is there? His pursuit of ephemeral moments through peeling back streets struck us as aimless. He is Don Quixote, Zobrowski observed later, without a lance, an opponent or an ideal.

Perhaps J.D. knew what he wanted, perhaps not. We wondered if the reason for his travels could be negative — ridiculing the purpose and substance of our lives. In any event, we had assumed that he would continue trudging from continent to continent as deluded as Quixote until death overtook him in a squalid cul de sac. We were wrong.

He was planning to settle down. Evidently he had decided to emulate us. When we recognized this we felt a bit more tolerant. After all, what sweeter compliment is there? Then, too, it should be interesting to learn what the Black Forest was like. Dubrovnik. Kabul. Goa. The South Seas. At our leisure we would be able to pick the richest pockets of his experience.

Leroy Hewitt was curious about Moslem Africa and meant to ask if there were minarets and cool gardens, and if it was indeed true that the great square at Marrakesh is filled with storytellers, dancers, acrobats and sorcerers just as it was hundreds of years ago. Once J.D. had traveled from Marrakesh to the walled city of Taroudent, rimmed by dark gold battlements, and he had gone over the Atlas mountains to Tiznit and to Goulimine to the lost Islamic world of women wearing long blue veils and of bearded warriors armed with jeweled daggers.

From there we had no idea where he went. Eventually, from Cairo, had come a torn postcard — a cheap colored photo of a Nile steamer. The penciled message told us that he had spent a week aboard this boat and the afternoon was hot and he was drinking lemonade. How far up the Nile he had traveled we didn't know, or whether he had come down from Uganda.

Next he went to some Greek island, from there to Crete, and later, as closely as we could reconstruct his path, to Cyprus. He wrote that the grapes on Cyprus were enormous and sweet and hard, like small apples, and he had bought an emerald which turned out to be fraudulent, and was recuperating from a blood infection which he'd picked up on the Turkish coast. Months passed before we heard any more. He wrote next from Damascus. The following summer he was in Iraq, thinking he might move along to Shiraz, wondering if he could join a camel train across the plateau. He wanted to visit Karachi. What little we knew of these places we had learned from melodramatic movies and the *National Geographic.*

But what brought J.D. unexpectedly into focus was the Indo-China war. We saw him the way you suddenly see crystals in a flask of treated water. Dave Zobrowski was killed.

When we heard that Davy was dead, that his life had been committed to the future of our nation, we perceived for the first time how J.D. had never quite met the obligations of citizenship. During the Second World War he had been deferred because his father was paralyzed by a stroke and his mother had always been in poor health, so he stayed home and worked in the basement of Wolferman's grocery. Nobody blamed him. Not one of us who went into the service blamed him, nor did any of us want to trade places with him. But that was a long time ago and one tends to forget reasons while remembering facts. The fact that now came to mind most readily concerning J.D. and the war was just that he had been deferred. We resented it. We resented it no more than mildly when we recalled the circumstances; nevertheless we had been drafted and he hadn't. We also knew that we had accomplished very little, if anything, while we were in uniform. We were bored and sometimes terrified, we shot at phantoms and made absurd promises to God. That was about the extent of our contribution toward a better world. It wasn't much, still there was the knowledge that we had walked across the sacrificial block.

After the war we began voting, obeying signs, watering the grass in summer, sowing ashes and rock salt in winter, listening to the six o'clock news and complaining about monthly bills. J.D. had not done this either. As soon as his sister graduated from secretarial school and got a job he packed two suitcases and left. He had a right to his own life; nobody denied that. Nobody expected him to give up everything for his parents' comfort. But he had left with such finality.

Problems sprang up around us like weeds, not just family difficulties but national and international dilemmas that seemed to need our attention, while J.D. loitered on one nutmeg-scented island after another. Did it matter to him, for instance, that America was changing with the malevolent speed of a slap in the face? Did it make any difference to him that American politicians now ride around smiling and waving from bullet-proof limousines? We wondered if he had an opinion about drugs, ghettos, riots, extremists and the rest of it. We suspected that these threatening things which were so immediate to us meant less to him than the flavor of a Toulouse strawberry. And now young Dave was among the thousands who had been killed in an effort to spread democracy—one more fact that meant nothing to J.D. He was out to lunch forever, as Bunce remarked.

While we waited for him to return we argued uncertainly over whether or not it was a man's privilege to live as he pleased. Wasn't J.D. obligated to share with us the responsibility of being human? We knew our responsibilities, which were clear and correct, and hadn't disclaimed them. Maybe our accomplishments were small, but we took pride in them. We might have no effect on these staggering days, no more than we had affected the course of the war, but at least we participated.

We waited through days charged with electric events which simultaneously shocked and inured us, shocking us until we could feel very few shocks, until even such prodigious achievements as flights to the moon appeared commonplace. At the same time our lives continued turning as slowly and methodically as a water wheel: taxes, business appointments, bills, promotions, now and then a domestic squabble. This was why we so often found ourselves talking about J.D. — the only one whose days dropped from a less tedious calendar. He had gone to sleep beside the Taj Mahal while we occupied ourselves with school bonds, mortgages, elections, auto repairs, stock dividends, cocktail parties, graduations and vacations and backyard barbecues.

Because we had recognized adolescent fantasies for what they are, and had put them away in the attic like childhood toys, we felt he should have done the same. What was he expecting? Did he hope somehow to seize the rim of life and force it to a stop? Implausibly, romantically, he had persisted — on his shoulders a rucksack stuffed with dreams.

He drifted along the Mediterranean littoral like a current, pausing a month or so in Yugoslavia or Greece, frequently spending Easter on the Costa del Sol; and it was after one of these sojourns in Spain that he came back to see us. His plans then concerned the Orient — abandoned temples in a Cambodian rain forest, Singapore, Macao, Burma, Sikkim, Bhutan. He talked enthusiastically, youthfully, as though you could wander about these places as easily as you locate them on a map.

He had met somebody just back from the foothills of the Himalayas who told him that at Gangtok you see colors more luminous than any you could imagine — more brilliant, more hallucinatory than the wings of tropical butterflies. The idea fascinated him. We asked what sense it made, quite apart from the danger and the trouble, to go such a long distance for a moment of surprise. He wasn't sure. He agreed that perhaps it didn't make sense.

He'd heard about prayer flags posted on bamboo sticks, the waterways of Kashmir, painted houseboats, mango trees on the road to Dharamasala. He thought he'd like to see these things. And there was a building carved from a cliff near Aurangabad. And there was a fortified city called Jai-salmer in the Rajasthan desert.

Then he was gone. Like a moth that flattens itself against a window and mysteriously vanishes, he was gone.

A friend of Art Stevenson's, a petroleum engineer who was sent to the Orient on business, told Art that he happened to see J.D. sitting under a tree on the outskirts of Djakarta. He did not appear to be doing anything, the engineer said; and as he, the engineer, was pressed for time he didn't stop to say hello. But there could be no doubt, he told Art, that it was indeed J.D. dressed in faded khaki and sandals, doing absolutely nothing there in the baking noon-day heat of Indonesia. He is mad, Zobrowski commented when we heard the story.

This, of course, was an overstatement. Yet by the usual standards his itinerant and shapeless life was, at the very least, eccentric; and the word 'madness' does become appropriate if one sits long enough beneath a tree.

However, some lunacy afflicts our own temperate and conservative neighborhood. We meet it on the front page every morning—a catalogue of outrageous crimes and totally preposterous incidents as incomprehensible as they are unremitting. What can be done? We look at each other and shrug and wag our heads as though to say well, suppose we just wait and maybe things will get back to normal. At the same time we know this isn't likely. So it could be argued that Zobrowski's judgment was a trifle narrow.

Anyway, regardless of who was mad, we waited impatiently for J.D. When he arrived we would do what we could to help him get settled, not without a trace of malicious satisfaction. But more important, we looked forward to examining him. We needed to know what uncommon kernel had made him different. This, ultimately, was why we had not been able to forget him.

Our wives looked forward to his return for another reason: if he was planning to get married they wanted to have a voice in the matter. They thought it would be foolish to leave the choice of a wife entirely up to him. They were quite in league about this. They had a few suitable divorcees picked out, and there were several younger women who might be acceptable.

We knew J.D. had spent one summer traveling around Ireland with a red-haired movie actress, and we had heard indirectly about an affair with a Greek girl who sang in nightclubs along the Riviera. How many others there had been was a subject for speculation. It seemed to us that he amused himself with women, as though the relationship between a man and a woman need be no more permanent than sea foam. Leroy Hewitt suggested, perhaps to irritate the ladies, that their intricate plans might be a waste of time because J.D. probably would show up with a Turkish belly dancer. But the ladies, like Queen Victoria, were not amused.

We tried to remember which girls interested him when we were in school. All of us agreed that he had been inconstant. It was one girl, then another. And as we thought back to those days it occurred to us that he had always been looking for somebody unusual—some girl with a reputation for brilliance, individuality or beauty. The most beautiful girl in school was Helen Louise Sawyer. J.D. would take her on long drives through the country or to see travel films, instead of to a dance where she herself could be seen. This may have been the reason they broke up. Or it might have been because she was conceited and therefore rather tiresome—a fact which took J.D. some time to admit.

For a while he dated the daughter of a Congregational minister who, according to the story, had been arrested for prostitution. Almost certainly there was no truth in it, but this rumor isolated her and made her a target. J.D. was the only one with enough nerve to date her publicly, and the only one who never boasted about what they had done.

His other girls, too, were somehow distinctive. Gwyneth, who got a dangerous reputation for burning her dates with a lighted cigarette at intimate moments. A cross-eyed girl named Grace who later became a successful fashion designer in New York. Mitzi McGill, whose father patented a vending machine that supposedly earned him a million dollars. The Lundquist twins, Norma and Laura. To nobody's surprise J.D. went out with both of them.

Rarities excited him. The enchanted glade. The sleeping princess. Avalon. We, too, had hoped for and in daydreams anticipated such things, but time taught us better. He was the only one who never gave up. As a result he was a middle-aged man without a trade, without money or security of any sort, learning in the August of life that he shouldn't have despised what might be called average happiness — 3% down the years, so to speak. It wasn't exhilarating, not even adventurous, but it was sufficient.

Now, at last, J.D. was ready to compromise.

I've expected this, Zobrowski said. He's our age. He's beginning to get tired.

He's lonely, said Millicent. He wants a home.

Are we echoing each other? Zobrowski asked.

On Thanksgiving Day he telephoned from Barcelona. He knew we would all be at Zobrowski's; we gathered there every Thanksgiving, just as it was customary to drop by the Hewitts' for eggnog on Christmas Eve, and to spend New Year's Day at the Stevensons'.

It was midnight in Barcelona when he called. Having gorged ourselves to the point of dyspepsia we were watching football on television, perfectly aware that we were defaulting on a classic autumn afternoon. Somebody in the next block was burning leaves, the air was crisp and through the picture window we could see a maple loaded like a treasure galleon with red gold. But we had prepared for the feast by drinking too much and by accompanying this with too many tidbits before sitting down to the principal business — split-pea soup, a green salad with plenty of Roquefort, dry heavy salty slices of sugar-cured Jackson County ham as well as turkey with sage and chestnut and onion dressing, mushroom and giblet gravy, wild rice, sweet potatoes, creamed asparagus, corn on the cob, hot biscuits with fresh country butter and honey that would hardly flow from the spoon. For dessert there were dense flat triangles of black mince pie topped with rum sauce. Nobody had strength enough to step outside.

As somnolent as glutted snakes we sprawled in Zobrowski's front room smoking cigars, sipping brandy and nibbling peppermints and mixed nuts while the women cleared the table. Embers snapped in the fireplace as group after group of helmeted young Trojans rushed across the miniature gridiron. It was toward such completed days that we had worked. For the moment we'd forgotten J.D.

His call startled us, though we were not surprised that he was in Spain again. He had gone back there repeatedly, as though what he was seeking he'd almost found in Spain. Possibly he knew the coast between Ayamonte and Port-Bou better than we knew the shore of Lake Lotawana. He had been to Gijón and Santander and famous cities like Seville. He'd followed baroque holy processions and wandered through orange groves in Murcia. During his visit he spoke fervently of this compelling, strict, anachronistic land — of the apple wine *manzanilla,* fringed silk shawls, bloody saints, serrated mountains, waterless valleys, burnt stony plateaus, thistles as tall as trees lining the road to Jaén.

We remembered his description of goat bells tinkling

among rocky Andalusian hills and we could all but feel the
sea breeze rise from Gibraltar. One afternoon he ate lunch in
a secluded courtyard beside a fountain—bread, a ball of
cheese and some sausage the color of an old boot. He
insisted he'd never eaten better.

He imitated the hoarse voices of singing gypsies — a strident unforgotten East beneath their anguished music—
and told us about a cataract of lavender blossoms pouring
across the ruined palace of the Moorish kings at Málaga. As
young as another Byron he had brought back these foreign
things.

There's a town called Ronda which is built along a precipice, and he told us that when he looked over the edge he
could feel his face growing damp. He was puzzled because
the sky was blue. Then he realized that spray was blowing up
the cliff from the river. It was so quiet, he said, that all he
heard was wind through the barranca and he was gazing
down at two soaring hawks.

He thought Granada might be Spain's most attractive
city. He had told us it was the last Arab bastion on the
peninsula and it fell because of rivalry between the Abence-
rrages and Zegris families—information anybody could
pick up in a library. But for him this was more than a musty
fact. He said that if you look through a certain grate beneath
the floor of the cathedral you can actually see the crude iron
coffins containing the bodies of Ferdinand and Isabella; or if
you go up a certain street near the Alhambra you pass a shop
where an old man with one eye sits at a bench day after day
meticulously fitting together decorative little boxes of inlaid
wood. And he liked to loiter in the Plaza España, particularly while the sun was going down, when swallows scour
the twilight for insects.

He had ridden the night train to San Sebastián along with
several members of the Guardia Civil in Napoleonic leather

hats who put their machine guns on an empty seat and played cards, with the dignity and sobriety peculiar to Spaniards, beneath the faltering light of a single yellow bulb. Outside a station in the mountains where the train paused to build up compression there was a gas lamp burning with vertical assurance, as though a new age had not begun. Wine bottles rolled in unison across the warped floor of the frayed Edwardian coach when the train creaked around a curve late at night, and the soldiers ignored a young Spaniard who began to speak of liberty. Liberty would come to Spain the young man believed — even though Franco's secret police were as common as rats in a sewer.

From everything J.D. said about Spain we thought it must be like one of those small dark green olives, solid as leather, with a lasting taste.

He returned to Barcelona more than to any other city, although it was industrial and enormous. He liked the Gothic *barrio,* the old quarter. He enjoyed eating outside a restaurant called *La Magdalena* which was located in an alley just off the Ramblas. Whenever a taxi drove through the alley the diners had to stand up and push their chairs against the wall so it could squeeze past. Whores patrolled the *barrio,* two by two, carrying glossy handbags. Children who should have been at home asleep went from cafe to cafe peddling cigarettes. Lean old men wearing flat-brimmed black hats and women in polka dot dresses snapped their fingers and clapped and danced furiously with glittering eyes on cobblestones that were worn smooth when the Armada sailed toward England.

Flowers, apple wine, moonlight on distant plazas, supper in some ancient alley, Arabs, implications, relics — that was how he had lived while we went to work.

Now he was calling to us from a boarding house in the cheap section of Barcelona. He was alone, presumably, in the middle of the night while we were as surfeited, prosperous and unrepentant as could be. It was painful to compare his situation with ours.

So, Zobrowski said to him on the telephone, you're there again.

J.D. said yes, he was in the same boarding house — *pensión,* he called it — just off Via Layetana. He usually stayed at this place when he was in Barcelona because it had a wonderful view. You could understand Picasso's cubism, he said with a laugh, if you looked across these rooftops.

I'm afraid my schedule won't permit it, Zobrowski remarked.

What a pity, said J.D.

Zobrowski took a fresh grip on the telephone. It would appear, he said, that Spain continues to stimulate your imagination.

Actually no, J.D. answered. That's why I'm coming back.

Then he explained. He wasn't altogether clear, but it had to do with progress. With jet planes and credit cards and the proliferation of luxury hotels and high rise apartments you could hardly tell whether you were in Barcelona or Chicago. Only the street signs were different. It wasn't just Barcelona, it was everyplace. Even the villages had begun to change. They were putting television sets in bars where you used to hear flamenco. You could buy *Newsweek* almost as soon as it was published. The girls had started wearing blue jeans. There was a Playboy club in Torremolinos.

Years ago he had mentioned a marble statue of a woman in one of the Barcelona plazas and he had said to us, with an excess of romantic enthusiasm, that she would always be there waiting for him.

Zobrowski asked about this statue. J.D. replied that she was growing a bit sooty because of the diesel trucks and cabs and motorbikes.

He said he had recently been up north. The mountain beyond Torrelavega was completely obscured by factory smoke and there was some sort of yellowish chemical or plastic scum emptying into the river with a few half-dead fish floating through it.

The first time he was in Spain he had walked from Santillana del Mar to Altamira to have a look at the prehistoric cave paintings. There wasn't a tourist in sight. He had passed farmers with long-handled scythes, larks were singing, the sky was like turquoise, and he waded through fields of flowers that reached to his knees. Now, he said, he was afraid to go back. He might get run over by a John Deere tractor, or find a motel across the road from the caves.

That bullfighting poster you had, Zobrowski said, the one with Manolete's name on it. Reproductions of that poster are for sale at a number of department stores.

You're flogging me, J.D. said after a pause.

I suppose I am, Zobrowski said.

However, I do get the point, J.D. said. Another decade and the world's going to be as homogenized as a bottle of milk.

Millicent is here, Zobrowski said. She would like a word with you.

J.D.! Millie exclaimed. How marvelous to hear you're coming home! You remember Kate Van Dusen, of course. Ray Van Dusen's sister?—tall and slim with absolutely gorgeous eyes.

J.D. admitted that he did.

She married Barnett Thomas of Thomas Bakery Products, but things just didn't work out and they've separated.

There was no response. Millie seemed about to offer a trans-Atlantic summary of the marriage. Separated was a euphemism, to say the least. Kate and Barnett were in the midst of a reckless fight over property and the custody of their children.

She's asked about you, Millie went on. She heard you might be coming back.

I'm engaged, J.D. said.

We didn't realize that, said Millie without revealing the horror that flooded the assembled women. We simply understood that you were considering marriage. Who is she?

Margaret Hobbs, he said.

Margaret Hobbs? Millie sounded uncertain. Is she British?

You know her, J.D. answered. She's been teaching kindergarten in Philadelphia.

Oh! Oh, my God! Millie said.

We had gone to grammar school with Margaret Hobbs. She was a pale dumpy child with a screeching voice. Otherwise she was totally undistinguished. Her parents had moved to Philadelphia while we were in the sixth grade and none of us had heard of her since. Her name probably hadn't been mentioned for twenty-five years.

We met by accident last summer, J.D. said. Margaret and some other schoolteachers were on a tour and we've been corresponding since then. I guess I've always had a special feeling for her and it turns out she's always felt that way about me. She told me she used to wonder what I was doing and if we'd ever meet again. It's as though in a mysterious way we'd been communicating all these years.

How interesting, Millie said.

It really is, isn't it! J.D. said. Anyhow, I'm anxious for all of you to make her acquaintance again. She's amazingly well informed and she remembers everybody.

I think it's just wonderful, Millie said. We're so pleased. I've always wished I could have known Margaret better. Now here's Leroy.

Is that you, young fellow? Leroy asked.

Hello, said J.D. You don't sound much different.

Leroy chuckled and asked if he'd been keeping himself busy. J.D. said he supposed so.

Great talking to you, Leroy said. We'll have a million

yarns to swap when you get home. Hang on, here's Aileen.

We look forward to hearing of your adventures, Aileen said. When do you arrive?

J.D. didn't know exactly. He was going to catch a freighter from Lisbon.

Aileen mentioned that last month's *Geographic* had an article on the white peacocks.

After a moment J.D. replied that the connection must be bad because it sounded as if she was talking about peacocks.

Have you been to Estoril? Aileen almost shouted.

Estoril? Yes, he'd been to Estoril. The casino was jammed with tourists. Germans and Americans, mostly. He liked southern Portugal better — the Algarve. Faro, down by the cape.

Faro, Aileen repeated, memorizing the name. Then she asked if he would stop in Philadelphia before coming home.

J.D. was vague. The freighter's first two ports of call were Venezuela and Curaçao. Next it went to Panama. He thought he might hop a bus from Panama, or maybe there would be a boat of some sort heading for British Honduras or Yucatán or maybe New Orleans.

Aileen began to look bewildered. She was sure that he and Margaret would be able to coordinate their plans and it had been a pleasure chatting. She gave the phone to Art Stevenson.

Art said a lot of water had flowed under the bridge and J.D. might not recognize him because he had put on a pound or two. J.D. answered that he himself had been losing some hair. Art proposed that they try to work out a deal.

Neither of them knew what to say next. Art gave the phone to Barbara.

Barbara asked if he and Margaret would be interested in joining the country club. If so, she and Al would be delighted to sponsor them.

Not at first, J.D. said. Maybe later. Let me talk to Dave again.

He was thinking of buying a car in Europe because he had heard he could save money that way, and he wanted Zobrowski's advice. He had never owned a car.

Zobrowski suggested that he wait until he got back. Bunce's brother-in-law was a Chevrolet dealer and should be able to arrange a price not far above wholesale. Zobrowski also pointed out that servicing foreign cars in the United States can be a problem. Then, too, you're better off buying from somebody you know.

J.D. inquired about jobs.

We had never learned how he supported himself abroad. As far as we could determine he lived from day to day. There have always been individuals who manage to do this, who discover how to operate the levers that enable them to survive while really doing nothing. It's a peculiar talent and it exasperates people who live conventionally.

A job could be found for him, that wasn't the issue. What disturbed us was that he had no bona fide skills. Zobrowski was a respected surgeon. Bunce was vice-president of the Community National Bank and a member of the Board of Education. Art Stevenson was director and part-owner of an advertising agency. Leroy Hewitt was a successful contractor, and so on. One or another of J.D.'s friends could find him a place, but there would be no way to place him on equal terms. He could speak French, Italian, Spanish, German and Portuguese well enough to make himself understood, besides a few necessary phrases of Arabic and Swedish and Hindi and several others, but language schools want instructors who are fluent. He knew about inexpensive restaurants and hotels throughout Europe, and the best way to get from Izmir to Aleppo. No doubt he knew about changing money in Port Said. Now he would be forced to work as a stock clerk or a Western Union messenger, or perhaps as some sort of trainee competing with another generation. The idea made us uncomfortable.

Margaret would soon find a job. Excluding the fact that Bunce was on the Board of Education, she was evidently an experienced teacher with the proper credentials. She could do private tutoring until there was a full-time position. But J.D. in his coat of many colors couldn't do anything professionally.

I have a suggestion, Zobrowski said to him on the telephone. This will sound insulting, but you've got to face facts. Your capacities, such as they are, don't happen to be widely appreciated.

I'm insulted, J.D. said.

Zobrowski cleared his throat before continuing: Fortunately, our postmaster is related by marriage to one of the cardiologists on the staff of Park Lane Hospital. I have never met this man — the postmaster, that is — but, if you like, I will speak to the cardiologist and explain your situation. I cannot, naturally, guarantee a thing. However, it's my feeling that this fellow might be able to take you on at the post office. It wouldn't be much, mind you.

Well, said J.D. from a great distance, please have a talk with that cardiologist. I'm just about broke.

I'm sorry, Zobrowski said, although not surprised. You enjoyed yourself for a long time while the rest of us went to an office day after day, whether we liked it or not. I won't belabor this point, but I'm sure you recall the fable of the grasshopper and the ant.

J.D. had never cared for lectures, and in the face of this we thought he might hang up. But we all heard him say yes, he remembered the fable.

If I sound harsh, forgive me, Zobrowski said. It's simply that you have lived as the rest of us dreamt of living, which is not easy for us to accept.

J.D. didn't answer.

Now, as we wait to greet him, we feel curiously disappointed. The end of his journey suggests that we were right, therefore he must have been wrong, and it follows that we should feel gratified. The responsibilities we assumed were valid, the problems with which we occupy ourselves are not insignificant and the values we nourish will flower one day — if not tomorrow. His return implies this judgment. So the regret we feel, but try to hide, seems doubly strange. Perhaps without realizing it we trusted him to keep our youth.

Arcturus

Verweile doch, du bist so schön.
Linger awhile, thou art so fair.
　　　　　　　　— GOETHE

The children, Otto and Donna, have been allowed to stay up late this evening in order to see the company. Now with faces bewitched they sit on the carpet in front of the fireplace, their pajama-clad legs straight out in front of them and the tails of their bathrobes trailing behind so that they look somewhat like the sorcerer's apprentice.

Outside the wind is blowing and every once in a while the window panes turn white; then the wind veers and the snow must go along with it. Automobile horns sound quite distant even when close by. Aside from the hissing, sputtering logs which are growing black in the fire, and the alluring noises of the kitchen, the most noticeable sound is a melancholy humming from the front door. Otto and Donna are convinced a ghost makes this dreadful wailing and no amount of explanation can disprove it. Their father has lifted them up one after the other so that they can see it is only a piece of tin weather stripping that vibrates when the wind comes from a certain direction, and they have felt a draft when this happens, but their eyes are dubious; wind and metal are all very well but the noise is made by a ghost. It is a terrible sound, as no one can deny, and upon hearing it Otto shivers so deliciously that his little sister must also shiver.

"What does company look like?" he inquires without lifting his gaze from the burning logs. And is told that company will be a gentleman named Mr. Kirk. Otto considers this for a long time, wiggling his feet and rubbing his nose which has begun to itch from the heat.

"Is he coming to our house?"

Otto's father does not answer. Lost in meditation he sits in his appointed chair beside the bookcase.

Presently Otto sniffles and wishes to know why the man is coming here.

"To visit with your mother."

A cloud of snowflakes leaps to the window as if to see what is going on inside but is frightened away by the weather stripping. How warm the living room is! Donna yawns, and since whatever one does the other must also do, her brother manages an even larger yawn. The difference is in what follows: Donna, being a woman, does not mind succumbing, and, filled with security, she begins to lean against Otto, but he is convinced that sleep is his enemy and so he remains bolt upright with a stupidly militant expression that tends to weaken only after his eyes have shut. Though his enemy is a colossal one he accepts without concern the additional burden of his infant sister.

"Why?" he asks, and looks startled by his own voice. It is doubtful he can now remember what he wishes to know, but why is always a good solid question and sure to get some kind of response.

"Because your mother wrote him a letter and begged him to come see her."

Again follows a silence. The clock on the mantel ticks away while the good logs crackle and the coals hiss whenever the sap drips down upon them. Otto is remotely troubled. For several weeks he has sensed that something is wrong in the house but he cannot find out what. His mother does not seem to know, nor does the cook, who usually knows everything. Otto has about concluded the nurse is to blame; therefore he does whatever she tells him not to do. Sometimes he finds it necessary to look at his father, or to sit on his lap; there, although they may not speak to one another, he feels more confident. He is jealous of this position and should Donna attempt to share it he is prone to fend her off until orders come from above.

In regard to this evening, Otto has already gotten what he wanted. He does not really care about Mr. Kirk because the value of a visitor lies simply in the uses to which Otto can put him, whether it be staying up late or eating an extra sweet. All at once Donna topples luxuriously into his lap. His hand comes to rest on her tiny birdlike shoulder, but through convenience only. At the moment he is careless of the virgin beauty; her grace does not intrigue him, nor does he realize how this tableau has touched the heart of his father across the room. Somberly Otto frowns into the fire; almost adult he is in the strength of such concentration, though one could not tell whether he is mulling over the past or the future. Perhaps if the truth were known he is only seeing how long he can roast his feet, which are practically touching a log.

"Is he coming *tonight*?" Otto knows full well this is a foolish question, but there lurks the fear that if he does not show a profound and tenacious interest in the whole business he will be sent to bed.

With ominous significance his father demands, "Why do you think you two are up this late?"

Otto stares harder than ever into the fire. It is important now that he think up something to change the subject in a hurry. He yawns again, and discovers that he is lying down. He sits up. He inquires plaintively if he may have the drumstick on Christmas.

His father does not reply, or even hear, but gazes at the carpet with a faraway expression somewhere between misery and resignation and does not even know he has been spoken to by the cook until she firmly calls him by name.

"Mr. Muhlbach!"

He starts up, somewhat embarrassed. Cook wishes to know at what time the guest will be arriving. Muhlbach subsides a little, takes a sip from a tumbler of brandy, and is vague. "Ah . . . we don't know exactly. Soon, I hope. Is there anything you want?"

But there is nothing; she has finished all preparation for the dinner and now is simply anxious for fear that one delicacy or another may lose its flavor from so much waiting. She looks at the children on the carpet before the fireplace. Otto catches this look; he reads in cook's stern face the thought that if she were their mother she would have them in bed; instantly he looks away from her and sits quite still in hopes that both his father and the cook will forget he is even there. Seconds pass. Nothing is said. Cook returns to the kitchen with an air of disgust.

Now the suburban living room is tranquil once again, much more so than it was two hours ago. At that time there were tears and reprimands and bitter injustice, or so the participants think. Otto especially felt himself abused; he was the object of an overwhelming lecture. He did not comprehend very much of it but there could be no mistake about who was in disgrace; therefore he rolled over onto his stomach and began to sob. Surely this would restore him to the family circle. No one, he thought, could refuse to comfort such a small boy. It was a fine performance and failed only because he peeked up to see its effect; at this he was suddenly plucked from the floor by one foot. He hung upside down for a while, gravely insulted, but found it imposssible to weep effectively when the tears streamed up

his forehead, so after a fit of coughing and bellowing he was
lowered to the carpet. On his head, to be sure, but down at
any rate, and for some time after he occupied himself with
the hiccups. He still believes that his punishment was not
only too stringent but too prompt; one appreciates a few
moments in which to enjoy the fruit of one's evil-doing.
Furthermore all he did was take a stuffed giraffe from his
sister. It is true the giraffe belonged to him; the trouble
came about because he had not thought of playing with the
giraffe until he discovered she had it, and when he had
wrung it away from her he put it on the table out of her
reach. So, following the administration of justice, he was
ordered to kiss his little sister on the lips, a penance he
performs with monstrous apathy, after which the living
room was turned into a manger for perhaps the twentieth
time and the father magically transformed himself into a
savage dog, growling and snarling, keeping everything for
himself. Donna and Otto are spellbound, so terrifying is
their father in the role of a dog. In fact he is so menacing and
guards the cushions and pillows with such ferocity that the
point of the fable is invariably lost. On occasion they have
even requested him to be a dog so that they might admire
his fangs and listen enraptured to the dreadful growls. But
perhaps they are learning, who can tell?

Now the lesson is ended and, as usual, forgotten. The
giraffe is clamped upside down beneath Donna's arm; it is
fortunate in having such a flexible neck. She no longer cares
that a visitor is on the way; she does not listen for the
doorbell, nor does she anticipate the excitement that is
bound to follow. By firelight her hair seems a golden cob-
web, an altogether proper crown. Blissfully asleep she lies,
despite the fact that her pillow is one of Otto's inhospitable
knees. Barely parted and moist are the elfin lips, while her
breath, as sweet as that of a pony, sometimes catches between

them, perhaps betokening a marvelous dream. She cannot be true, Botticelli must have painted her. Her expression is utterly pious; no doubt she has forgotten her miniature crimes. One hopes she has not dwelt too hard upon those miniature punishments which followed.

Now comes a stamping of feet just outside, an instant of silence, and next the doorbell, dissonant and startling even when one expects it. Company is here! Otto is first to the door but there, overcome by shyness, allows his father to open it.

Here is more company than expected. Kirk has brought along someone he introduces as Miss Dee Borowski, an exotic little creature not a very great deal larger than Otto although she is perhaps eighteen. One knows instinctively that she is a dancer. She is lean and cadaverous as a grey-hound, and her hair has been dyed so black that the high-lights look blue. She draws it back with utmost severity, twists it into a knot, and what is left over follows her with a flagrant bounce.

They have entered the Muhlbach home, Sandy Kirk tall as a flagpole and a trifle too dignified as though he will be called upon to defend his camel's hair overcoat and pearl-gray homburg. He has brought gifts: perfume for the woman he is to visit, its decanter a crystalline spiral. For the master of the house something more substantial, a bottle of high hard Portuguese wine. With a flourish and a mock bow he presents them both to Muhlbach. He apologizes for his lateness by a rather elaborate description of the traffic in the Hudson tube, and as if a further apology may bring a smile of pardon to Muhlbach's face he adds in an almost suppli-cating way that Borowski was late getting out of rehearsal. Immediately the dancer confesses that her part will be small; she is third paramour in a ballet production of "Don Juan." Well, she is feral enough and will probably mean bad dreams

for the young men in the audience, but there is something
ambivalent about her as though she has not quite decided
what to make of her life. Her eyebrows, for example, do not
grow from the bony ridge that protects the eye; someone
has plucked the outer hairs and substituted theater brows
that resemble wings. She pauses beside the lamp and a
shadow becomes visible high on her forehead — it has been
shaved. Now she has decided to take off her new mink
jacket; underneath is a lavender sweater that clearly intends
to molt on the furniture, and a pair of frosty-looking tailored
slacks. Quite rococo she looks, and knows it too. But to
complete this ensemble she is carrying a book of philosophy.

Replies Muhlbach, conscious that his own voice must be
a monotone, "My wife is upstairs. She will be down in a few
moments. This is our son and there asleep by the fire is
Donna."

Kirk has been waiting for this introduction because he
has presents for the children too. To Otto goes a queer little
stick-and-ball affair, a game of some sort. Otto receives the
device without enthusiasm but minds his manners enough
to say thank you. For Donna there is the most fragile,
translucent doll ever seen. It is not meant for her to play
with, of course, being made of Dresden china, not for years
yet. Kirk places it on the mantel.

Miss Borowski has stooped a little so that she and young
Otto look at one another as equals. Otto wishes to appear
self-sufficient but despite himself he likes what he sees; then,
too, she is considerably more fragrant than his mother, who
always has an odor of medicine. He decides to accept the
overture. They are friends in an instant and together, hand
in hand, they go over to inspect Donna, who has found the
carpet no less agreeable than her brother's leg. Otto does
not object to anyone's admiring his baby sister; there are
times when he discovers himself seized by the desire to tickle

her ribs or her feet. He does not know this is love. So much the better, for if he knew he might stop. Nor is he unaware that she is the beauty of the house, though he takes comfort in the memory of her astonishing helplessness. He fails to understand why, despite his instructions, she cannot learn to put on her shoes or even go to the toilet when necessary.

Sandy Kirk meanwhile has been appraising the home and he has learned something: the supper table has been set. Only then does he recall the invitation was for supper. Unfortunately he and the dancer stopped to eat before coming over. Muhlbach hands him a cocktail, which he accepts with a serene smile; he waits to see if there will be a toast, but there is none. He notes that Borowski is giving the little boy a taste of her drink and he sees Muhlbach frown at this.

Into the room, supported by a nurse, comes Joyce Muhlbach, and the attention of everyone turns to her. She is unsmiling, clearly suffering deep pain. She is dressed but there is about her the look and the fetid odor of someone who has been in bedclothes all day. Her eyes are febrile, much too luminous. Straight across the room she moves, clutching the nurse's elbow, until she reaches the invited guest. Kirk, who is about to tap a foreign cigarette on the back of his wrist, seems paralyzed by the sight of her. Her husband turns around to the fire and begins to push at a log with his foot. And the dancer, who is holding Otto by the hand, stands flat-footed with the prearranged expression of one who has been told what to expect; even so her greedy stare indicates that she is fascinated by the sick woman's appearance.

Joyce now stands alone, and while looking up at Kirk she addresses her son. "Isn't it about time for little boys to be in bed?"

Otto assumes that nasal whine which he feels the best possible for all forms of protest, but he knows the end has come. Still a token argument is necessary. He knows they expect one. He reminds his mother that he has been given permission to stay up tonight; the fact that it was she who gave the permission seems not especially cogent. With strangers present his pride forbids the wheedling and disgraceful clowning which is sometimes successful, so he is reduced to an obstinate monologue. He watches his father pick up Donna, who is quite unconscious; she could be dragged upstairs and would not know the difference.

All of a sudden Otto gets up from the corner where he has been stubbornly crouching since bed was mentioned, and the churlish whine disappears. He owns a rifle. It is on the top shelf of the hall closet where he cannot reach it; nevertheless it belongs to him, and if Miss Borowski has a fancy for rifles his father might bring it out. Otto has reasoned no further than this, indeed has done nothing but look crafty, when his father remarks that there will be no showing of the gun tonight. Otto instantly beseeches his mother, whom he considers the more sympathetic, and while his back is turned he feels himself caught around the waist by that inexorable arm he knows so well. His head goes down, his feet go up, and thus robbed of dignity he vanishes for the night.

There follows one of those queer instants when everything becomes awkward. Otto has taken away more than himself. Is it affectation that causes Dee Borowski to sit cross-legged on the floor? Time is running out on them all.

Joyce begins: "Well, Sandy, I see you got here."

The moments which follow are stark and cheerless despite the comfortable fire. A flippant answer could make things worse. One listens moodily to the poltergeist in the door. But Muhlbach re-enters to save them, re-enters briskly with a cocktail shaker and says, while filling the dancer's glass, "A month ago my father died." And he proceeds to tell about the death of young Otto's grandfather. Nothing about

Muhlbach suggests the poet—certainly not his business
suit, not his dictaphonic sentences, least of all his treasury of
clichés. His story unwinds like ticker tape, yet the visitors
cannot listen hard enough. Even Borowski has forgotten
the drama of herself, and if one should quietly ask her name
she might reply without thinking that it is Deborah Burns.

And the urbane Sandy Kirk, who has found his way
around half the world, by this recital of degeneration and
dissolution he drifts gradually into the past, into profound
memories of his own. Unlike the ingénue, death is not
unfamiliar to him, death is not something one mimes on
cue; Kirk once or twice has seen it look him sharply in the
eye and finds he does not care for that look. As the story
progresses he begins to empathize with Muhlbach; he is
gratified that this man does know some emotion, and he
wonders less why Joyce married him. When he read her
letter, read the sardonic description of her husband, he was
astonished to perceive that beneath the surface she was
utterly in love with the man, a man who until now has
seemed to Kirk like a shadow on the water. He did not much
want to come for this visit because he is afraid of Joyce.
Their relationship never brought them any kind of fulfillment, never carried them to an ocean, as it were, but left
them stranded in the backwash of lost opportunity. No
matter how many years have since intervened she has had
the freedom of his heart as now it seems he has had hers.
Kirk has not been able to resolve his feelings about Joyce; he
was never able to place a little statue of her in his gallery as he
does with other women. No, the letter put him ill at ease; he
did not want to see her ever again but there was in her appeal
such urgency that he could not refuse. However, he has
come prepared. He has thought everything out. He has
brought along this terribly serious little ballerina for protection. He has only to say the magic word, that is, he need

only mention ballet or the theater and Dee Borowski will take over, destroying all intimacy without ever knowing what she has done. It is a shrewd device, one Sandy Kirk has used in other clumsy situations; all the same he knows that Joyce will not be deceived.

Now Muhlbach, seated like the good merchant that he is, shaking up his trousers so as not to result in a bulge at the knee, continues in his oddly haunting style, telling how young Otto was invited to the sickroom but was not informed he would never see his grandfather again. And they talked a little while, did the boy and the old gentleman who was dying; they talked solemnly about what Otto had been doing that afternoon. In company with two other neighborhood gangsters he had been digging up worms. At the end of this conversation Otto received a present all wrapped up in Christmas tissue, though Christmas had hardly come into sight. It turned out to be a primer of archaeology, and while Otto held this book in his hands there beside the bed his grandfather sleepily explained that it was a book about the stars. After a momentary hesitation Otto thanked him. Muhlbach, standing on the other side of the deathbed, was carefully watching his son, and many times since that afternoon he has mulled over a curious fact, the fact that Otto could recognize the word "archaeology" and knew its meaning. Indeed the book had been chosen for him because he had sounded interested in the subject; furthermore Otto has always had fewer qualms than a Turk about displaying his accomplishments. What restrained him from correcting his grandfather? It was a marvelous opportunity to show off. The father does not know for sure, but he does know that the boy is preparing to leave the world of childhood.

And so Muhlbach, without understanding exactly why either of them did what they did, hurried out to buy his son a rifle. In a sporting-goods store he handled the light guns

one after another, slipped the bolt and examined the chamber, raised the sights, caressed the stock, and in fact could
hardly contain his rapture, for he has always been in love
with guns. To one side stood the clerk with arms folded and
a mysterious nodding smile. "This is a twenty-two, isn't it?"
Muhlbach asked, though naturally it was not a question but
a statement. However he bought no ammunition because
even pride must genuflect to reason.

From the bedroom comes the querulous voice of Otto,
who has been abandoned, and he wishes to know what they
are talking about.

"Go to sleep!" orders his father.

In the bedroom there is silence.

Every few minutes the cook has peered out of the kitchen,
not to see what is going on but to announce her impatience.
She has allowed the door to swing back and forth; she has
rattled silverware and clinked glasses. She cannot figure out
why people linger so long over a drink. She herself would
drink it down and be done with the matter.

Kirk is now obliged to confess that both he and the
dancer have eaten. Pretense would be impossible. He turns
helplessly to Joyce with his apology and she feels a familiar
annoyance: it is all so characteristic of him, the tardiness,
the additional guest, the blithe lack of consideration. How
well she remembers this selfish, provoking man who means
so much to her. She knows him with greater assurance than
she can ever know her deliberate and, in fact, rather mystic
husband. She remembers the many nights and the mornings
with a tenderness she has never felt toward Muhlbach. Thus
Sandy Kirk finds her appraising him and he glances uneasily
toward her husband: Muhlbach is absorbed by the snow
clinging to the window panes.

It is decided that the guests shall sit at the table and drink
coffee while dinner is served the host and hostess; there is no

other solution. And they will all have dessert together. The cook thinks this very queer and each time she is summoned to the dining room she manages a good bourgeois look at the ballerina.

Around the mahogany oval they sit for quite a long time, Muhlbach the only one with an appetite. Once Joyce Muhlbach lifts her feverish gaze to the ceiling because the children's bedroom is just overhead and she has heard something too faint for anyone else, but it was not a significant noise and soon she resumes listening to Sandy Kirk, who is describing life in Geneva. He says there is a tremendous fountain like a geyser in the lake, and from the terrace of the casino it is one of the most compelling sights in the world. Presently he tells about Lausanne farther up the lake, its old-world streets rising steeply above the water, and from there he takes everyone in seven-league boots to Berne, and on to Interlaken where the Jungfrau is impossible to believe even if you are standing in its shadow.

Muhlbach clears his throat. "You are probably not aware of the fact, but my parents were born in Zurich. I can recall them speaking of the good times they used to have there." And he goes on to tell about one or two of these good times. They sound very dull as he gives them, owing in part to his habit of pausing midway to cut, chew, and swallow some roast beef. It occurs to him that Kirk may speak German so he asked the simplest question, "*Sprechen Sie Deutsch?*" Conversation in German affords him a kind of nourishment, much the same as his customary evening walk around the block, but aside from his mother, who now lives in an upstate sanatorium, there is no one to speak it with him. Joyce has never cared much for the language and it appears that Otto will grow up with a limited vocabulary.

Kirk replies, "*Nein. Spanisch und Französisch und Italienisch.*" To Kirk the abrupt question was disconcerting be-

cause he had fancied himself the only one capable of anything
beyond English. He has come to this home with the expectation of meeting a deadly familiar type of man, a competent
merchant who habitually locked his brain at five o'clock, and
Kirk is trying to remain convinced that this is the case.
Muhlbach admits to not having traveled anywhere danger-
ously far from the commuter's line, south of Washington,
say, or west of Niagara, and it is one of Sandy Kirk's prime
theses that a stay-at-home entertains a meager form of life.
The world, as anyone knows, was made to be lived in, and to
remain in one place means that you are going to miss what is
happening somewhere else. All the same Kirk sports a few
doubts about his philosophy and so he occasionally finds it
reassuring to convince other people that he is right. He has a
talent for evocation and will often act out his stories, tiptoe-
ing across the room and peering this way and that as though
he were negotiating the Casbah with a bulging wallet. Or he
will mimic an Italian policeman beating his breast and slapping his forehead over the criminal audacity of a pedestrian.
Very droll does Sandy Kirk become after a suitable drink;
then one must forgive his manifold weaknesses, one must
recognize the farcical side of life. Thus he is popular wherever he goes; it is a rare hostess who can manage to stay
exasperated with him all evening.

He seems to present the same personality no matter what
the situation: always he has just done something wrong and
is contrite. He telephones at a quarter of eight to explain
that he will be a little late to some eight o'clock engagement.
"Well, where are you now?" they ask, because his voice
sounds rather distant, and it turns out he is calling from
another city. But he is there by midnight and has brought an
orchid to expiate the sin. Naturally the hostess is furious and
wishes him to understand he cannot escape so easily but her
cutting stare is quite in vain because he can no more be

wounded than he can be reformed. One accepts him as he is, or not at all.

Now he has taken them though the Prado, pausing an instant in the gloom-filled upper chambers where Goya's dread etchings mock the very earth, gone on to Fez and Constantine and swiftly brought them back to Venice, where a proper British girl is being followed by a persistent Italian. She will have nothing to do with this Italian, will not speak to him, nor so much as admit he lives, despite the most audible and most extraordinary invitations. Now a man must maintain his self-respect, observes Kirk with a dignified wink, so all at once the frustrated Italian seizes her and flings her into the Grand Canal, and wrapping his coat like a Renaissance cloak around his shoulders he strides regally off into the night. Such are the stories he tells in any of a hundred accents, and no one can be certain where truth and fiction amalgamate, least of all the narrator. He speaks incessantly of where he has been, what he has done, and the marvels he has seen. Oh, he is a character—so exclaims everyone who knows him. It is amazing that such a façade can exist in front of a dead serious career, but he is a minor official of the State Department and puzzles everyone by mumbling in a lugubrious way that his job is expendable and when the next election comes around they may look for him selling apples on the corner. Still, he travels here and there and draws his pay, rather good pay, no matter who is elected. It is suspected that he is quite brilliant, but if so he never gives any evidence of it: one second he is a perfect handbook of slang, the next he becomes impossibly punctilious. It is difficult to decide whether he is burlesquing himself or his listeners.

The Muhlbachs are content to listen, regardless, because there is little enough drama at home and this visitor floats about like a trade wind of sorts, bearing a suggestion of incense and the echo of Arab cymbals. His wallet came from Florence—"a little shop not far from the Uffizi," he will answer—and his shoes were made in Stockholm. They can hardly equal his fables by telling how sick young Otto was the previous summer even though he spent several weeks in a hospital bed and required transfusions. It was a blood disease and they were fortunate that one of Muhlbach's business partners had contracted the same thing as a child and could supply the antitoxin.

Nor can they explain the curious pathos everyone felt over a situation the doctor created. It happened on the worst day of the illness, when they had at last come to believe he could not get well. While the doctor was examining him Otto became conscious, and to divert him the doctor asked how he would like to attend the circus that evening. Otto thought that would be fine and managed enough strength to nod. So they agreed that the doctor should call for him at six o'clock sharp that they might have time to reach the grounds ahead of the crowd and secure the best possible seats. Otto then relapsed into a coma from which he was not supposed to recover, but one eye opened around five o'clock in the afternoon and he spoke with absolute lucidity, asking what time it was. There could be no doubt that the speaker must be either Otto or his reincarnation because he has always been fearfully concerned over the time. By five-thirty he was certain he should be getting dressed and by six o'clock he had begun to sob with frustration because the nurse prevented him from sitting up. When they sought to pacify him by means of a teaspoonful of ice cream he rejected it with pitiful violence. His father's promise of a trike when he got well was received with an irritated hiccup. In vain did they explain that the doctor had been teasing; Otto knew better. Any moment the door would open and they would all be dumbfounded. The clock ticked

along, Otto watching desperately. The hand moved down
and started up, and finally started down again. Then he
knew for the first time those pangs that come after one has
been lied to.

But perhaps it was not unjustified; they had thought he
would leave them and he did not, and scars on a heart are
seldom seen.

Meanwhile the cook has been acting superior. Around
the table she walks and pours fresh coffee with her nose in
the air as though its fragrance were offensive. She stumbles
against Miss Borowski's chair, does this sure-footed cook.
What can the matter be? And she is so careless in pouring
that coffee slops over the cup into the saucer. It is true the
cook apologizes, but her resentment is implicit and there
follows a baffled silence at the table.

Joyce Muhlbach perceives the cause. The cook is jealous
of the ballerina. But who can imagine the cook in tights? It
would take two partners to lift her. Here is an amiable
creature shaped like a seal, beloved of her employers and
playing Olympian roles to a respectful audience of Otto and
Donna, yet unhappy. She has found a soubrette at her
master's table and is bursting with spite. She too would be
carried across a stage and wear mascara. Rather great tragedies may be enacted in the secrecy of the heart; at this
moment something very like a tear is shining in the cook's
artless eye.

Joyce again is listening to a sound upstairs. She is attuned
to nothing with such delicacy as to the events of the nursery.
Donna will cough only once, muffled by the pillow, yet her
mother hears, and considers the import. Is it the cough of
incipient disease, or nothing but the uncertain functioning
of babyhood? Accordingly she acts. To her husband everything sounds approximately the same, but that is the way

with husbands, who notice everything a little late. Good man that he is, he cannot even learn how to tell a joke, but must always preface it with a hearty laugh and the advice that his listeners had better get set to split their sides. Of course it is all one can do to smile politely when Muhlbach, after ten minutes of chuckling and back-tracking and clearing his throat, gets around to the point. Kirk would tell it with a fumbled phrase and be midway through another tale before his audience caught up with the first one.

She surveys them both as though from a great distance and knows that she loves them both, her husband because he needs her love, and Kirk because he does not. She half-hears the dancer asking if Sandy has changed since she knew him.

Again comes a stamping on the walk outside, but heavier than were the feet of Kirk. This is the sound of big men thumping snow from their boots. Everyone hears and looks through the archway toward the front door — that is, everyone except Joyce, who has instantly looked at her husband. Kirk from the corner of his eye has taken in this fact and for the first time becomes aware of the strength of this marriage: no matter what happens she will look first of all at her husband and react according to him. There is something old and legendary about this instinct of hers, something which has to do with trust. Kirk feels a clutch of envy at his heart; when he and she were together she did not necessarily look to him whenever anything happened; he had always thought her totally self-sufficient. Now Muhlbach turns back to the table, frowning, and considers his wife, but when she cannot supply the answer he crumples his napkin, places it alongside his plate, and goes to the door. They hear him open the peephole, call someone by name, and immediately swing open the door.

Cold and huge they come in, two men. Duck hunters they

are. One is John Grimes and the other is always referred to as "Uncle." Muhlbach, appearing overjoyed, insists that they come into the dining room, so after a few moments they do, though "Uncle" is reluctant. Both men are dressed in corduroy and heavy canvas. Grimes also wears a brilliant crimson mackinaw to which a few flakes of snow are clinging, and while he stands there boldly grinning the snow melts and begins to drip from the edges of his mackinaw onto the dining-room carpet. His pockets bulge with shotgun shells. His gigantic hands are swollen and split from the weather.

Behind him, away from the circle of light, stands Uncle, who is long and solemn and bent like a tree in the wind. His canvas jacket is open, revealing a murderous sheath knife at the belt; its hilt looks bloody. Dangling by a frayed strap over one of his bony shoulders is a wicker fishing creel, exhausted through years of use, from which a few yellowed weeds poke out. He has a bad cold and attends to it by snuffling every few seconds, or by wiping his nose on the cuff of his jacket. Obviously he is more accustomed to kitchens than to dining rooms, nor would he seem out of place in overalls testifying at a revival. He grins and grins, quite foolishly, exposing teeth like crooked tombstones, and when he speaks there is always the feeling that he is about to say something bawdy. But he is considered a great hunter; it is a rare animal or bird that can escape from Uncle. At present he is gaping at Miss Borowski. Uncle recognizes her as an unfamiliar piece of goods but is not altogether certain what. Borowski returns the stare with contempt.

Both hunters smell acrid and salty. About them wells a devastating aboriginal perfume of wood smoke, fish, the blood of ducks, tobacco, wet canvas, beer, and the perspiration of three inchoate weeks. Sandy Kirk got up slowly when they came in. No longer the center of attention, he stands with his napkin loosely in one hand and watches what goes on, making no attempt to join the bantering conversation. Astutely he measures John Grimes. With one glance he has read Uncle's book but this Grimes is anomalous: he might be a politician or a lawyer or some kind of professional strong man. Above all this duck hunter is masculine. The cumbersome mackinaw rides as lightly on him as does the angora sweater on Borowski. His very presence has subtly dictated the terms of the assembly: he rejects the status of guest and demands that he be distinguished primarily as a man; therefore Joyce and the dancer find themselves reduced to being women. By way of emphasis there looms behind him that sullen scarecrow known as Uncle with a few whiskers curling under his chin, in his awkwardness equally male.

The duck hunter feels himself scrutinized and swiftly turns his head to confront Sandy Kirk. For an instant they gaze at each other without pretense; then they are civilized and exchange nods, whereupon the hunter smiles confidently. Kirk frowns a little. Whirling around, Grimes makes a playful snatch at Uncle's chin as if to grab him by the whiskers. "Try to kill me, will you?" says he, and turns up the collar of the mackinaw to display a tiny black hole caused by a shot. At this Uncle begins to paw the floor and to protest but at that moment is petrified by an oncoming sneeze which doubles him up as though Grimes had punched him in the stomach. He emerges with a red beak and watery eyes and begins hunting through his filthy jacket for a handkerchief, which turns out to be the size of a bandanna.

John Grimes snorts and grins hugely, saying, "Missed the duck too!" This further mortifies Uncle. The two of them look as though they can hardly restrain their spirits after three weeks in the forest and may suddenly begin wrestling on the carpet.

The cook has pushed open the kitchen door and is having a necessary look. Everyone is aware of her; she is not subtle about anything. She seems particularly struck by the fact that both men are wearing knitted woolen caps—John Grimes' is black as chimney soot and Uncle's is a discolored turtle green. It is curious what a cap will do. A cap is like a beret in that when you see someone wearing it you can hardly keep from staring. Cook has seen these men dozens of times but looks from one to the other in stupefaction. She is not unjustified because the headgear causes Uncle to appear even taller and skinnier and more despondent than he is; if ever he straightens up, the pompom of his cap must certainly scrape the ceiling. At last, conscious that she herself is beginning to attract attention, though she knows not why, cook allows the kitchen door to close.

But another rubberneck is discovered. Near the top of the stairs a pinched white face looks through the railing, and of course it is Otto come out to see what this is all about. He resembles a lemur clutching the bars of some unusual cage, or a tarsier perhaps, with his impossibly large ears and eyes wide open for nocturnal prowling. Like the cook, Otto finds himself on display; he becomes defensive and starts to back out of sight, but is asked what he thinks he is doing up there.

"I want a drink," says Otto piteously, and quite automatically. He has been on the stairs for ten minutes listening without comprehension to a description of the camp in the forest. He comes part way downstairs, holding on to the banister, and as the chandelier light falls upon him it may be seen that if there is anything on earth he does not need it is a drink: his belly is so distended with water that the front of his pajamas has popped open. Unconscious of his ribald figure he asks, "Who are all those men?" He cares who they are, more or less, but the main thing is to turn the conversation upon someone else. While his mother is buttoning up his front he is trenchantly introduced to the hunters.

"Are they company?"

They are. The lack of repartee following his question implies he is unpopular, but Otto scintillates.

"What are they *doing*?"

It should be clear to anyone that the hunters are standing at the mahogany sideboard where the good cook has poured them each a cup of coffee. They are too wet to sit down anywhere. Otto studies them from top to bottom and says he thinks Donna needs to go to the toilet. Will someone come upstairs and see? The nurse is upstairs. If either of them needs anything the nurse will take care of the matter. Otto feels the balance of power swinging away from him; unfortunately he cannot think of anything to say, anything at all. He stands on the bottom step with his belly out like a cantaloupe and those dark eyes — the gift of his mother — wondering. There is nothing special on his mind when he complains that he wants to see the ducks; in fact he hardly knows what he said and is startled that it has gotten a reaction.

Grimes and Uncle have bagged a few over their legal limit, to be sure, but that is not the reason they have brought some to the Muhlbachs. At any rate two fat mallards are lying on the front porch and Otto is allowed to watch through the closest window while Uncle goes outside to get them. Otto mashes his hot moist face against the chilled glass and is quiet. They do not look like ducks to him, but that is what his father said; therefore they must be ducks.

Uncle stoops to catch each mallard by a foot. Already the birds are freezing to the step and when he pulls them up they resist; Otto sees that a few feathers remain on the concrete. The front door opens for a second while Uncle comes in, each bird hanging by one foot so that its other yellow web seems to be waving good-by. The heads swing underneath. The male looks almost a yard long — it cannot be that big, of course, but Grimes and Uncle, who is still snuffling, agree it is the biggest mallard they have ever seen. Around its green neck is a lovely white band; Otto reaches out hesitantly to discover if it is real. The neck feathers are cool and soft. The female is a mottled brown and buff, a small one, not much more than half the length of the male. They are dead, this Otto knows, but he is not certain what death is, only that one must watch out for it.

John Grimes takes each bird around the middle and everyone is a little surprised when the heads rise, just as though they had finished feeding, but the reason is simple : the necks have frozen. Grimes holds both mallards up high; he cracks the cold orange beaks together and smiles down at Otto.

"Quack! Quack!" blurts Uncle.

Otto knows who made the noise and pointedly ignores Uncle, but he cannot get enough of staring at the refulgent bodies. He has never seen anything so green, or of such tender brown. The breasts are full and perfect; to find out what has killed them one must feel around in those feathers, parting them here and there with the fingertips, until the puncture is suddenly disclosed.

Otto is subdued, and when the episode of the ducks is ended, when they have been taken roughly into the kitchen and nothing more can be said of them, he must struggle to regain his plaintive tone. Now there is not a chance it will be successful but he says he thinks Donna would like a drink. It is not successful. However, there are two big guns that Otto always keeps in reserve; one is that he believes he is getting a stomach ache and the other is that he is afraid the stars are falling. He is no fool, this Otto, and realizes that if he tries them both on the same evening he will be found out. He studies his bare feet like a politician and estimates which question would be more effective, considering the fact that there are some ducks in the house and that his mother has been in bed all day. He begins to look wonderfully ill at ease.

"Are the stars falling down?"

Always that is good for an answer, a long melodious one, always. But tonight it is met by a grim stare from his father. He looks hopefully at his mother; she is not so ominous but equally firm. There is about the atmosphere something that tells Otto he might soon be turned across his father's knee. He elects to retreat and backs toward the stairway, wondering if he could reasonably ask for the dog-in-the-manger again. His father places both hands flat on the table, which means he is going to stand up. Otto abandons all hope, and, wearing a persecuted face, goes up the stairs as rapidly as possible, which is to say in the manner of a chimpanzee.

Almost immediately there is a crash in the upstairs hall followed by the unmistakable sound of Otto falling. Once again he has forgotten about the hall table. Originally there was a vase on this table but after he destroyed it while hurrying to the bathroom they reasoned that sooner or later he would take the same route; hence there is nothing but a lace doily on the table. In fact, Muhlbach finds it a senseless place to put a table, but his wife wants it there though she cannot explain why. Otto is bellowing. To listen to him one would be convinced that in all history no individual has ever experienced such pain. He varies pitch, rhyme, and tempo as he recalls the tragedy; it is a regular Oriental concert. The footsteps of the nurse are heard, and the mutter of her scientific soothing, but he will have none of this professional.

Joyce gets up from the table, but in passing behind Muhlbach's chair an expression of nausea overspreads her face and she almost sinks to the floor but recovers without a sound. Kirk started to cry out, and upon seeing her straighten up he emits a weird groan. Dee Borowski and Muhlbach gaze at him very curiously.

Otto can still be heard, although the sincerity of his dirge may now be questioned. At any rate he has been carried to bed, where the nurse swabs his bumped forehead with mercurochrome and covers it with a fantastic bandage that he seems to enjoy touching. Still he is so exhausted by the hour, the splendor of the ducks, the strange men, and the accident in the mysterious hallway that it is necessary to continue whimpering. This self-indulgence halts the instant he becomes aware that his father has entered the room. Otto prepares himself like any rascal for he knows not what judgment, and cannot conceal his apprehension when his father draws up a chair and sits wearily beside the bed. They talk for a while. Otto does not know what they are talking about. Sometimes they discuss his mother, sometimes himself, or Donna. He industriously maintains his end of the conversation though he feels himself growing sleepy, and in time he is neither displeased nor alarmed to feel the hand of his father stroking his head. Somewhat groggily he inquires if the stars are falling. In addition to being a useful question Otto is moderately afraid of just such a catastrophe. He did not come upon this idea second-hand, but thought of it himself. The first time it occurred to him he began to weep and though a number of months have gone by so that he trusts the sky a little more he is still not altogether confident. One cannot be sure when a star is falling. Clearly there is nothing to hold them in place. Why should one not suddenly drop on his bed?

Countless nights, in winter and spring, autumn and summer, have Otto and his father gone out of doors, or sometimes driven toward the country far enough that the city lights were less obtrusive, and here, with the boy on his father's lap, they have considered what was above. At first there was a certain difficulty in communication. For example, Muhlbach discussed the planets and stars while Otto listened with profound concentration. Muhlbach was impressed until Otto, after a period of deep thought, inquired if Donna was a star, a question that might be answered in various ways, of course, depending. But with practice they began to understand one another so that after several months Otto grew familiar with the elementary legends and was apt to request his favorites, such as Andromeda, or The Twins. Or he might ask to hear that wonderfully euphonious index to the Great Bear, which goes: Alkaid, Mizar, Alioth, Megrez, Phecda, Merak, and Dubhe.

"What does the bear eat?" he asks, and this is certainly a question packed with logic. His father's faith is renewed; the lessons continue. Not far behind the bear—do you see?—comes Arcturus, its warden, who follows the animal about. This happens to be the father's personal favorite among the stars because it was the first one he himself ever learned to recognize, and was taught him by his own father, the very same who gave young Otto the archaeology book. Muhlbach hopes that Otto will learn Arcturus before any other. This is the reason he points to it first of all. He directs the flashlight beam toward this yellow giant, so many times larger than the sun, and though Muhlbach has searched the heavens with a flashlight numberless times he is yet amazed that his light appears to reach all the way.

We can never go there, Otto. It is too far. Muhlbach includes a few statistics and is again deluded by his son's intelligent expression because it develops that what Otto wishes to know is whether or not Arcturus is farther away than downtown. Still, hope springs eternal, and after smoking half a cigar Muhlbach has recovered from the blow enough to try again. Once upon a time—yes, this is the right approach—once upon a time Arcturus came flying straight toward the earth! What do you think of that? Otto is shaken by the premise; in his father's lap he sits erect and anxious, no doubt pondering what will happen when they meet, or met, since it is all in the past. Half-a-million years, for that matter, and Muhlbach, now savoring parenthood to the utmost, adds with a sportive air that the sole observers were troglodytes. Otto lets this pass. Now Muhlbach hesitates because he has pumped up his story; the full truth is that Arcturus was also drifting a bit to the side as it approached and even now is passing us so there is not to be a collision after all. Fortunately Otto considers the telling of greater value than the tale. He is not much gripped by explanation or hypothesis; he would as soon just look. One would think he was gazing into a mountain lake. According to his father they can see perhaps three or four thousand stars in the sky; Otto again looks up and is stunned, though for a better reason. He is a pure voluptuary, a first-rate knight of the carpet. Sidereal time, relative motion, and years of light are all very well — astronomy, in short, can come or go, so Otto feels — but stars are magnificent. Briefly he is held by the constancy of Arcturus, then he loses it. There are a great many things in the sky. How shall he hold fast to one? When he is older he will distinguish more clearly but now a light is a light, each about as effective as its neighbor. Now he has been seduced by Mars. It seems bigger and more suggestive. What could he not accomplish if only he held it in his hand! As there is no moon, and Sirius is down, nothing can be more glamorous. How red it is! How wondrous bright! In vain does Muhlbach point out Pollux and Castor, Procyon, Regulus.

In his bedroom the little boy sleeps with one arm raised and a fist clenched as if in triumph, on his helpless face a stubborn look, his forehead all but invisible under the preposterous mercurochrome-soaked bandage. Muhlbach sits beside his son, watching and thinking. The bedroom is silent but for the breathing of the two children. The nurse has gone downstairs. After a while Muhlbach rises and walks soberly across the room to stand above his daughter; her pink jade lips are parted and it is clear her dream is a serious one. Muhlbach wonders if she will sleep until spring. He longs to pick her up, somehow to unfold himself and conceal her deep within, and he bends down until their faces are an inch apart.

He hears the front door close, the faint after-knock of the brass lion's head on the outside of the door. He moves on tiptoe to the window and looks down at his two friends, the duck hunters, who elect to tramp across the snowy lawn even though the walk has been shoveled. He looks at his watch to discover he has been up here almost a half-hour. He very much wanted to go hunting this year, possibly more than ever before; each time this thought comes to him he feels unutterably disgusted with himself.

Uncle and Grimes leave dark symmetrical prints on the snow and as always Uncle is one step behind. There is no reason for this; it is just the way they are. It comes to Muhlbach that John Grimes is leading his afreet by a chain round the neck. He watches them get into Grimes' car, sees the headlights flash and thus notices that the snow has stopped falling, and moodily he looks after the burning red tail lights until the street is again deserted. That snowy rectangle over which they walked oddly resembles the eight of spades; and now the half-moon comes floating above the rooftops as if to join in this curious game. Much higher— well along in the night—kneels the father image, Orion. While Muhlbach stands at the window the moon's light descends calmly upon his troubled face and reaches beyond him into the nursery past Donna's crib to the wall poignantly desecrated by paste and crayon scribbles. There a swan is in flight. Otto has seen fit to improve this wallpaper swan. What could be gained by telling him its elegance is perhaps impaired by the measles he has added? Muhlbach thinks over the shards remaining from his own childhood, but is conscious mostly of how much has perished.

Some time longer he stands there steeping himself in this restorative moonlight, and looks around with approval at the knotty pine toy shelf he has knocked together and varnished, and again remarks the silence of this night which is counterpointed by the breath of his children. An unimpressive man he is, who shows a little paunch and the beginning of a stoop, though otherwise no older than forty warrants. People do not ever turn around to look at him on the street. At cocktail parties no feminine gaze lingers on him. When it comes to business there are men who find it worthwhile to seek out Muhlbach for an opinion; otherwise he is left alone.

Quietly but without disappointment he leaves the nursery, shuts the door, and descends the staircase hopeful that his wife has recognized the futility of this evening. It strikes him as incredible that she can maintain interest in a man she has outgrown.

When he enters the living room the nurse slips back upstairs. Sandy Kirk and Joyce are making no attempt to communicate; they sit side by side on the sofa but behave like strangers seated together at a movie. Borowski appears hypnotized by the embers; she has taken off her shoes and placed them neatly like an offering on the marble hearth. Muhlbach finds her naïveté wearisome and he thinks that if she does anything else ingenuous he will lose his manners and become rude. She does not even blink when he strides past; she does nothing but dully watch the subsiding flames, her mouth idiotically open. From his chair beside the bookcase he glowers at her, and it suddenly occurs to him that he is sick of the cook, too, and sick of the relentless nurse. He is sick to death of life itself, and of solicitous neighbors, and he has forgotten whatever is not despair. Too much is happening to him, whereas all he wants is to be left alone that he may regain some measure of his inner strength. Even one hour, uninterrupted, might be enough. He thinks he cannot pretend much longer. His thoughts turn upon Goethe, from whom he is remotely descended, and he visualizes that man interminably searching himself for power while playing to his sycophants a stiff-legged excellence.

All at once his wife trembles; she bites her lip over some private thought, and looking at him she remarks, just loud enough to be heard, that John Grimes and Uncle left a few minutes ago.

Muhlbach, struggling against disorder, allows himself a few seconds before replying, "I know, I know."

Sandy Kirk rouses himself, picks up a magazine and fans his cheek as if only now he realizes how suffocating the room has become. Muhlbach, watching Kirk, is filled with hatred; it seems to him that never before has he encountered a man he despises as much.

"They missed you," his wife continues, "but I told them you'd go hunting again next year."

In this speech there is a note of self-pity that causes Muhlbach to shut his eyes and throw up his hands, though he does not say a word.

"I told them I was being selfish but I want you with me every minute of the time. Next year they'll have you the same as before." Having started she cannot stop; she turns swiftly upon Sandy Kirk and presses one of his limp hands to her breast. Her eyes fill with tears but except for this she appears peeved, resentful, and she talks compulsively. Words pour from her nerveless mouth without meaning and Kirk is obviously terrified. He stares at her out of the corner of his eye like a trapped animal; he is powerless to recover his hand. Muhlbach scowls at Dee Borowski who has turned around to watch, and he knows that she is aware of him, but she cannot get enough of the nauseating scene; she must look and look. Muhlbach springs out of his chair and rushes into the kitchen.

Sandy Kirk turns his head this way and that to avoid looking at Joyce. All the precautions he took, they were no good. She has not respected any convention; she has lunged through every defense and taken him. Even under the circumstances it was not decent of her to do that. She has always shocked him one way or another, even the first time they met. He had been a college student then and one afternoon was standing on a snowy bluff overlooking a river that had frozen close to shore. He had brought along a sled and was wondering if he dared coast down because the slope was studded with pinnacles of rock; furthermore, if he could not stop in time there was a very good possibility of crashing through the ice and drowning. Then he noticed this girl trudging up with a sled. When he warned her it was unsafe she replied, "Mind your own business," and without hesitation flung herself upon the sled, hurtled down among the rocks, and reappeared far out on the ice, wriggling to a stop not five yards from the water. That was the way she did everything. Now she is twenty-nine years old — an aged, wasted old woman who can scarcely walk without assistance. Her arms have shriveled to the bone and the veins are black.

Kirk is furious that Borowski has not reacted the way she was supposed to. When at last he had gathered the will to speak, to interrupt the horrible monologue, and pointedly mentioned Don Juan, the dancer only looked at him in stupefaction. So he has not distracted Joyce, she has still got him, hanging on; but then he recovers his voice, that familiar ally, and all by itself his voice starts to tell about something funny that once happened in Switzerland. Kirk waves his free arm and rolls his eyes comically toward the ceiling until at last, thank God, Muhlbach comes out of the kitchen. It is over. Joyce loosens her grip and he begins to pull his fingers away one at a time.

With an ingratiating tone Sandy Kirk addresses Muhlbach, who gives back a clinical stare and stretches out his hands to the fire. Seeing this calm gesture of self-assurance, seeing as it were, a true Hofmeister, Kirk suffers a familiar malaise, for among diplomats and intellectuals, or artists of any description, he feels established, but faced with a solid pedestrian he loses confidence in his own wit and commences to doubt the impression he is making. It has always been so, though for the life of him Sandy Kirk fails to understand why. And this Muhlbach is indestructible, a veritable storm cellar of a man. No catastrophe will ever uproot him or confuse him, this man of the flatlands with a compass on his forehead. Kirk is envious, and also contemptuous. He is a little afraid of Muhlbach. He has finally managed to draw the captive arm away from Joyce, yet she clings mutely with her eyes. He feels sorry for her and wishes he could feel more, but there it is: she seems to him unreal and distorted, not the girl he once knew. This sick woman is distasteful. In the future he may feel some compassion but this evening she has driven him backward till he has begun to grow violent. If she does not soon release him altogether he will throw a fit. He cannot stand being forced this way, being accustomed to having what he wants only when he wants it. During intolerable situations Sandy Kirk always envisions himself in some favorite locale thousands of miles away. It is a form of ballast. And now he decides to imagine himself in Biarritz seated regally on the hillside on his favorite bench. From there he would contemplate the Atlantic sun shining on red tile rooftops, and after an expensive supper he might wander into the casino to luxuriate in the sound of clicking, rattling chips and the suave tones of croupiers.

Otto has wakened; he can be heard talking to the nurse about something, no doubt vital. A jack-in-the-box will go down for the night more easily than will Otto. Recently he has taken to singing in the middle of the night; he disturbs everyone in the house with his pagan lament. "What are you singing about?" he will be asked, but he always refuses to answer.

Just then the telephone rings. Who could be calling at such an hour? Sandy Kirk, like a doctor, must always leave word of his whereabouts, and so does the dancer, though with more hope than expectation. As usual the actual message is less exciting than the suspense. Joyce, whose call it was, returns to the living room almost immediately. She seems more vexed than she has been all evening and after resting for a minute she mimics the inquisitive neighbor.

" 'I saw your lights were still on and simply thought I must find out if there was anything I could do.' She got a couple of ducks, too. Your friends are dreadfully generous."

Muhlbach makes no attempt to reply. He shakes his head as if he can endure nothing more.

Joyce Muhlbach's voice begins to rise unsteadily. "I told her not to telephone! I told that woman to let us alone!"

Borowski has emerged from her private reverie long enough to gobble this up and Muhlbach, who was watching her, is again filled with loathing. Little by little everyone in the room becomes aware that a group of carol singers is approaching, and finally, in passing the Muhlbach home, their song is clear. The voices are young; most likely a group of students.

After they have gone Joyce slowly resumes twisting her wedding ring; it is loose on her finger and slides off easily, hesitating only at the knuckles. She takes it off and puts it on and all at once remarks that she has received an ad from a mortuary. In this there is something so ghoulish that it is almost impossible not to laugh. Her husband of course knows about the advertisement but the guests have a tense moment. Joyce glances from one to the other in a malicious way, twisting her ring and sliding it off, waiting to see if either of them dare smile.

Borowski becomes flustered. "Sandy has told me everything about you." This gets no response at all. Borowski turns red, and says that Joyce meant a great deal to Sandy years ago. Neither was that the proper speech so Borowski glares at Sandy Kirk because it is his fault she has gotten into this situation.

Joyce is suddenly aware that Donna has wakened, and though not a sound comes from the upstairs nursery this same knowledge reaches Muhlbach a second later. Both of them wait. He glances across the room to her and she catches the look solidly as if she had been expecting it. Kirk guesses they have heard one of the children and he recalls that earlier instant when they reacted as a unit, causing him to sense how deeply they were married. He is a little injured that they mean this much to each other; he feels that Joyce has betrayed him. He knew her long before Muhlbach ever did. It is as if something valuable slipped away, disappeared while he was preoccupied. Now he thinks that he intended to come back to Joyce. They would have gone well together, and he knows that whatever Muhlbach may have brought her he did not bring something she has always needed— excitement. This intelligent, sober, prosaic man escorted her into a barren little room, a cool study where she has withered. Kirk feels himself growing embittered over the way life has treated him. This woman was rightfully his own, even if she refused to admit it. There were instances, it is true, when she became tyrannical, but later she would always repent; and if he should abuse her he had only to hang his head until her eye grew milder. To his mind comes the observation of one of those lugubrious Russians: that from the fearful medley of thoughts and impressions accumulated in man's brain from association with women, the memory, like a filter, retains no ideas, no clever sayings, no philosophy, nothing in fact but that extraordinary resignation to fate, that wonderful mercifulness, forgiveness of everything.

The longer Kirk sits in the room with Muhlbach's wife the more does he perceive how terribly he is still in love with her. He has been afraid this would happen. She is one of those legendary creatures whom the French have so astutely named *femme fatale*. One does not recover. Kirk permits himself a furtive look at the husband. Yes, he has been stricken too.

What kind of a woman is she? One talks to her a little while of this or that, nothing remarkable is said, nothing in the least memorable, and one goes away. Then, all uninvited, comes a feeling of dreadful urgency and one must hurry back. Again nothing is said. She is not witty, nor is she beautiful; she is in fact frequently dour and sullen without cause. Periods of gloomy silence occur, yet no sense of emptiness, no uneasiness. She seems to wait for what is about to happen. It is all very confusing. Sandy Kirk broods, puzzles, gazes hopelessly into space for vast amounts of time thinking of nothing, unable to formulate questions worth asking himself, much less answer, feeling nothing at all but a kind of dull, unhealthy desire.

He steals another look at Muhlbach and discovers in that stolid face a similar misery, which makes Kirk feel better. He remembers with embarrassment certain phone calls during which he was unable to speak. "Hello," he will mumble, already despondent at the thought that she is listening. "Is that you?" And when she replies, sounding stubborn, or irked that he has telephoned at such an inconvenient hour,

then every single thought explodes like a soap bubble. He
waits anxiously to hear what she will say next, which is
nothing: he is the one who has called, it is up to him to
manufacture a little conversation. But he is destroyed by
aphasia, he finds nothing humorous about life, not a thing
worth repeating. What has he been doing? Well, quite a lot
but now, thinking about it, what is worth the effort of
describing? He summons all his strength: "What have *you*
been doing?" He has just managed to mutter this. She
replies in an exhausted voice that she has not done anything
worth mentioning. This is impossible! He mumbles something about the fact that he has been thinking of her and
called to find out what she was doing — what a stupid thing
to say, he realizes, and discovers to his amazement that he is
clutching the telephone as if he were trying to strangle it.
The wire has been silent for five minutes. He prays no
operator has decided to investigate this odd business or he
will be locked up for insanity, and in a voice more dead than
alive he demands, "Are we going out tonight?" He is positive she will say no, and that is exactly what she does say.
Instantly he is filled with alarm and wants to know why not;
she replies callously that she doesn't want to see him ever
again, but offers no explanation. He subsides. He leans
against the wall with his eyes closed. He has not eaten all day
but is not hungry. Minutes pass. Neither of them speaks. It
is raining, of course; water splashes dismally on the window
ledge and life is implacably gray. One cannot imagine sunshine, laughter, happiness. He staggers and understands
that he was falling asleep. He whispers good-by and waits.
She immediately answers good-by. Neither hangs up. Love
is not supposed to be like this. He announces his good-by
again with renewed vigor just as though he were rushing
out to the golf course, but the mummery sickens him. There
is no significant click at the other end of the line. What is she

waiting for? Will she never release him? Can she possibly expect him to hang up first? Life is a wretched joke. He cannot abide the sound of his own name. Still she refuses to hang up the receiver, and it goes on and on, a long, dreary, stupid, inconclusive affair. These calls have on occasion lasted a full hour or more though neither of them said a good minute's worth. How desperate was the need to communicate, how impotent the message. So when he sees her he wants to know why she does not talk to him over the telephone, and she looks at him without a smile.

Kirk decides he is losing his mind. Has Muhlbach, that barn of a man, disgraced himself in a similar manner? Because normal men do not ignore their pride. Yet look at those tormented eyes! It is clear that he, too, has fallen apart in front of her. There could be no other explanation.

Kirk will never forget one night he went shambling through the streets without enough energy to lift his head until all at once, as though he had been handed a telegram, he started rapidly across the city, rushed through Times Square with his eye fastened on Forty-fourth Street, and just around the corner there she was! What fantastic perception could account for this? And she seemed to be waiting— expecting him! Yet she was anchored securely to the arm of some nondescript man in a bow tie. As they passed each other he nodded curtly and stalked into the crowd. What a lover does he make! What happened to the celestial phrase? He is the sort of man who would address the wrong balcony. Even his agony is fraudulent because he is hoping everybody on the street notices his tragic face. He thinks he could not be more obvious with the stigmata; still, nobody paused when he strode somberly toward the river. Well, he has been through no grimmer night than that one. It might have made sense if she had been a famous beauty, but even in those days no one ever picked Joyce out of a group. She never was quick on her feet, or had a musical voice, nor did her skin ever take the light as the artists say. And how did they know—both of them—that they were destined to meet just around that corner?

At this instant the cook appears, not in her black uniform but in a rather shocking dress. She has finished every dish and emptied the garbage and now she would like permission to go home. Muhlbach calls a taxi for her. Cook bids good night to everyone, to everyone except the ballerina, and then she returns to the pantry where she will sit like a monument on her favorite stool to brood until the taxicab arrives. All have noticed her going upstairs a few minutes ago with a sweet for the children. She wakes them up to feed them something that will ruin their teeth; nothing can break her of this habit. Neither explanation nor threat of dismissal deter this cook, not even the formidable nurse. Cook is of the opinion the children are her own and it is clear that her heart would fall open like an overripe melon if Muhlbach ever made good his threat. The nurse and the cook look upon one another as hereditary enemies and neither questions that this should be so. Nurse dislikes going into the kitchen and while there is apt to sit with arms crossed and a severe expression. Cook feeds her without a word, stinting just a little, and afterward scrubs the dishes quite fiercely. She has never seen this nurse before; who can tell how reliable the creature is? Cook believes this nurse is neglecting the babies and thus it is she sneaks upstairs at least once a night. That is why, when Muhlbach calls for something, there may be silence in the kitchen.

All at once comes the sound of a shot. Conversation stops in the living room. There are no cars on the street, so it could not have been a backfire, and besides it sounded as though it were in the house. Muhlbach is about to investigate when at the head of the stairway appears the nurse, dreadfully embarrassed, to explain that she has been listening to a gangster story on the radio. She hopes they were not alarmed. She just now looked into the nursery; the children were not awakened. No, they are accustomed to sounds like that. Machine guns and bombs are natural toys nowadays.

Well, so much for the shot; cook has not committed suicide after all.

Presently the taxi may be heard crunching up the street. One expects it to climb the little drive, but it does not, even though Muhlbach has sprinkled rock salt from the street to the garage. Cook expertly flickers the porch lights but this taxi driver is leery of hillsides and does no more than blink his headlights by way of announcing that if she wishes a ride she must take the risk. That is the way of cab drivers nowadays; one must bow to their high-handed manner or simply do without. And should you fail to tip them they may slam the door on your fingers. Cook often tells about the friend of a very good friend of hers who lost a thumb just that way and almost bled to death. Oh, it is a gruesome tale indeed and always concludes with the cook nodding darkly, hands folded severely over her white apron. She believes in a day of reckoning with as much faith as she attacks her Sunday hymns in the kitchen. These hymns have made her a neighborhood celebrity; whenever she is mentioned someone invariably adds, "—the one who sings in the kitchen." The cab driver, ignorant of the future, states his position by lighting a cigarette, and at this the cook capitulates. She lets herself out the screen door—so useless in winter—and is heard walking cautiously down the icy steps. One can see her getting into the back seat of the cab. The door is closed and she is taken away, unhappy woman.

The children—"my babies," she calls them—are undisturbed that she has left. They are never sure whether they dream of her nightly visit or whether they really do wake up and eat something. No matter, they will see her the following morning. Just before noon she will arrive, lumbering and scolding without even waiting to learn what they have done wrong. If they have been really bad she will frighten them by saying she is going to California. Their eyes open wide. It is the word alone that Donna has come to fear; the sound of it is enough to make her weep. Otto knows it is a place far off in the direction of downtown where people go when they are angry, and he knows that no one ever returns from California, so he too begins to sob. Oh, there is no punishment worse than when cook starts packing her suitcase.

But they are sleeping now. Otto is a little boy, there can be no question of that, but Donna, what is she? She is so small! Can anything so tiny be what she will one day be? Will there come a time when she would abandon her father and her brother for the sake of someone they have never seen? Someone perhaps as impossible as Otto, or even more so? Surely no one more obstinate and militantly ignorant than Otto can lay claim to being human. Only wait and see! He will come for Donna with biceps flexed and a hat crushed on the back of his head. Most likely he will be chewing gum. He will converse like a cretin, yet how accomplished will he think himself. Will Donna think as much? Will she peer into her mirror and suffer anguish over the shape of her chin or the cut of her gown? She could not be more perfect yet she will despise herself because of him. Perhaps he will even be tattooed! He is so clever and so handsome, she thinks, how can it be that her father pokes fun at him? Well, her father has grown old and does not know about the latest things. In fact Donna is mortified that he chooses to wear the kind of collar and necktie he does; it might have been very well in Mother's day, but that was twenty years ago. "How just positively incomparable!" she cries at the sight of her girl friend's new dancing slippers. By next month, though, every thing has become "beautific." Her father mulls over the expense he has gone to in sending her to a decent university. All in vain. She might as well have been educated by comedians. Yet how lovely she is! Muhlbach feels tears surging to his eyes, but of course nothing shows. Why not? Why is he unable to weep for beauty that is positively incomparable? And he thinks of her mother, and when Donna twirls about the living room for him with flushed cheeks Muhlbach cannot trust himself to speak.

Who can say whether this will all come to pass? Is that the way it is to be, or will panic annihilate them all? Perhaps such horror will occur — bombs and irresistible rays not yet invented, a holocaust even the comic-books have not conceived — that Donna will never be stricken by this ludicrous young god. In view of the damage he is sure to inflict perhaps it would be just as kind if she died in the wreckage of war. Well, they will all find out.

Now, this starry night, she lies serenely sleeping, a Botticellian morsel, the cook's beloved, an altogether improbable object, cherished above life itself.

Otto, being masculine, cannot afford to be so complacent as his sister, not even in dreams. His fists fly back and forth, he cracks his skull against the wall and does not feel a thing, he thrashes, mutters, climbs mountain peaks, vanquishes his enemies in a second, and above all else he frowns. Not for him the panacea of Donna's rag doll. A gun may be all right for a time, a puppy is even better, a picture book is good too, and attempting to climb the willow tree is a worthy project, but there seems to be no final answer. He must investigate one thing and then another, and in each he finds something lacking. Here he is scratching at the screen door again though he wanted to go outside not five minutes ago. His nature is as restless as the nose of a rabbit. No one can be certain what he is seeking.

He is wakened by something happening downstairs. The voices have changed. There is the sound of coat hangers rattling and of people moving around. Company is going. Otto looks groggily at the ceiling and tries to stay awake although he does not know just why. He would like to get up and look out the window but the room is cold; then too the nurse would probably come in and he does not especially like her. He has thought up some grisly tortures that he intends to try on the nurse, such as flooding the bathroom and when she runs in to turn off the water he will lock the door so that his father will think she did it. Otto has a great bag of schemes for the nurse. He is certain to drive her away. Meanwhile he must concentrate on the noises and so understand what they are doing downstairs. Donna is breathing passionately at the moment and Otto is annoyed by this interference; he props himself up on both elbows.

The front door opens and people can be heard talking outside. This is really too much; Otto is wide awake and out of bed, creeping to the window. There he crouches, his brilliant eyes just above the sill. The winter air makes his eyes water so he grinds his fists into them, the best remedy ever. And he shivers without pause. He has come unbuttoned again.

Muhlbach is following the guests down the icy walk to Kirk's car. Its windshield is a mound of snow and while the guests are getting into the car Muhlbach reaches out and brushes off the windshield. This is no instinctive action: for the past hour he has been thinking about this gesture. When he opened the door for Grimes and Uncle he noticed the snow still falling and saw that it was about to cover the other car. Not long after that he hit upon the proper method to end the evening, a simple act not only cordial but final. It should express his attitude. Now he has done it but too fast; Kirk was not even looking.

The engine starts up. The diplomat has fitted on his elegant gray gloves, settling each finger, and now pulls the overcoat across his knees while waiting for the engine to warm. Beside him the dancer is already beginning to look snug; she has drawn her rather large strong feet up onto the seat and tucked her hands deep inside the mink sleeves of her jacket. She is only waiting for the instant the wheels begin to turn, then she will lean her head against his shoulder and like the wheels she will roll toward a conclusion. She is always touched by this moment when the acting is done, the curtain comes swaying down, and life takes over. Each time, however, she is a little frightened, a little doubtful that she can survive.

Muhlbach, standing soberly beside the hood, brushes more snow from the edge of the windshield and receives a faint shock when Kirk acknowledges this by glancing out at him; for an instant the man looked older, much different, the hair on his temples appeared silver. Muhlbach is well aware that Kirk is eight or ten years junior, yet he cannot escape the eerie feeling that he saw a man distinctly older than himself.

Throughout the evening these two have avoided each other, and so it is destined to end. Circumstances have set the limit of their association. They must be neutral forever. Sandy Kirk has divined the truth of this while Muhlbach was thinking it through. They nod. The car starts forward but immediately slips sideways into a rut where the wheels spin ineffectively. Kirk, tightening his grip, presses the gas pedal to the floor and Muhlbach realizes the man is a poor driver. The tires are screaming on the ice. Muhlbach waves both hands, shakes his head, goes around to look, and sees that he must get out his own car to give Kirk a push. In a few minutes it is done; they are safely away from the curb.

The visitors have gone. Muhlbach eases his car once more

into the garage and closes the door, but despite the extreme cold he cannot bring himself to go inside the house right away. While he stands forlornly gazing down at his shadow on the moonlit snow he hears the voice of his son crying timorously into the windy night.

Muhlbach lifts up his head. "Go to sleep, Otto."

And the apprehensive Otto, peeping down from the nursery window, hears this faint reply. It is the voice of his father saying everything will be all right.

Otto and the Magi

In the pallid March sun that leavens her patio Helen Chong reads a ladies' magazine. Muhlbach, having greeted her as a neighbor, nothing more, merely commenting on the weather, keeps his eyes averted from the hedge over which he has seen the chaise lounge, the eloquent Oriental figure in Capri pants and a diminutive blue halter which has caused him to think, inexplicably, of twin bluebirds. From somewhere nearby comes an odor of burning leaves, the scent of spring returning, dark loam newly spaded, life resurgent. The sky has not yet cleared, however; winter retreats but slowly, trailing its ghostly haze. The sun obtrudes, strange fruit in the western quadrant, viable, promising an end to these brief, metallic days. And Muhlbach, his winter-long project almost complete, feels himself mystically stirred, restless, absorbed and yet dissatisfied, anxious for whatever is to be. Is it the attenuate hint of spring? — this early season without his wife? Lately the children have not mentioned her; Muhlbach hopes they are forgetting those last months and, when they do think of their mother, recall only what she once was. For himself, there is no forgetting.

Underground once again, he pauses to contemplate his work: the room is functional, which is its purpose, yet not uncomfortable. He reflects that he might spend summer evenings here; it should be cool and quiet. He reaches up, cautiously touches the ceiling. Good. The paint has dried. What remains to be done? — purchase a shade for the lamp, some additional batteries, gravel to spread across the roof. What else? There are a dozen chores, none vital. The retreat is finished. Muhlbach, having draped a rag over a can of paint, hammers the lid shut, gathers the brushes and turpentine, turns off the light, goes out the door and climbs the narrow steps.

Helen Chong is sitting up, legs crossed, petting an English sheep dog that each afternoon comes wandering through the neighborhood. She glances at Muhlbach and winks, as though there were something to wink about. It is a habit which irritates him; a habit she has copied from her husband. It is, indeed, one of the things about the Chongs that he quite actively dislikes.

"I simply love you to death!" she exclaims, and promptly buries her face in the sheep dog's gray fur. Thus, as she leans forward, the sheer cloth flattens across her thigh and Muhlbach during this moment cannot turn away.

"When are you and Bob to go trout fishing?" she calls while her long fingers, supple and jeweled, fondle the body of the dog. "I've heard about this trip for months!" She laughs. Her laughter is not mellifluous; it is slightly coarse.

Muhlbach replies that he has been looking forward to the fishing trip and hopes it can be arranged before much longer. He adds that the weather should be improving. Saying this, he wonders how she can spend hours on the patio dressed as she is. That voice, the gaudy clothing; she might at one time have been a chorus girl. He considers going over to talk with her. After all, they are neighbors. And if Bob Chong should return — well, what difference would that make? The Chongs have lived next door for a year; both he and they often have told one another they must get acquainted.

Across the dividing hedge he remarks, "I've not seen your boy today." To his own ear this sounds commonplace; she must think him insufferably boring.

Helen Chong glances up in mild surprise. "Isn't he with Otto? I was sure Cecil told me . . ."

"Otto has gone hiking with some older boys. He left quite early."

"Oh?" She is not alarmed, squeezing and stroking the animal.

Muhlbach turns away, repelled by this casual affection. The situation, he thinks, is absurd, although no one else is aware of it. He covets his neighbor's wife; it is as simple as that. Every night he imagines himself with her, acting once again the role of a husband. He wonders how long they have been married; they both must be older than they look, because their son is nearly Otto's age. If a perceptive neighbor discerns no hint of domestic friction, does that mean there is none? Bob Chong appears less than passionate, unless baseball and bow ties and intellectual acrostics may be so considered. He is a graduate of UCLA — summa cum laude, Helen has let it be known. Still he is a poseur, for all his fine credentials. The cigarette holder, offhand gestures, habits unexplained. Curious, thinks Muhlbach, that love of baseball. Friday night does he go bowling? Does he belong to a lodge? — this highly paid chemist from the California wastes, who speaks of skin diving and of surfboarding at Santa Monica, who in expensive and sporty attire, laughing, confident, is rumored to be in line for an important government position. And this wife of his, this empress with lips so pale they are almost white, and Asiatic eyes blacker than Chinese ink, with her immense diamond ring and coiled hair. . . .

She has risen from the chaise lounge, is gathering her things, preparing to go inside. She sees him looking over the hedge. She hesitates, but then: "We're having a few people for cocktails a week from tomorrow. Can you make it?"

Angered with himself for staring, embarrassed that she has noticed it, he replies, "Thank you. I believe I don't feel up to such an evening." But how foolish to reject the invitation! God knows he has been too much alone these past months. Solitude enough, and more. To have accepted would please everyone; friends and neighbors would say that finally he was starting to recover. One must begin again, and cocktails next door would be an easy, inauspicious step. But still, it is easier to say no, to vegetate. Five days are fully taken, caring for themselves and so for him; it has been the evenings and the weekends that needed occupation. Possibly it had been a mistake to employ Mrs. Grunthe as mother surrogate; without her, the children would have used his time. But of course she was necessary, martinet that she is, efficient and scrupulously clean. Otto and Donna do not love her, of this Muhlbach feels certain; however, they are afraid of her, and so order is kept in the home. Yet the concomitant of order has been leisure, and soporifics lose their power. How many books has he read since August? How many magazines? How many times has he listened to the Bach Passions? — the phonograph records have been reduced to strident mimicry; even in appearance they are used and exhausted, as though such comfort as they might proffer is wearing through. And now what? Miss Eula Cunningham? — she of the pink and buoyant shape, adequately dusted, fragrant, reminding him of last week's bouquet. Eula. Is she next? This would please the Forsyths, who plucked her from a sunken garden. Past thirty-two, twice divorced, childless, eager—oh, *anxious!*— to try again. Eula. And she *is* an exciting woman, Muhlbach reminds himself. Men do turn to watch her, this is a fact, indeed more than that— something of a joke. The young men and the old, they turn in their tracks; even small boys are impressed.

"Perhaps you'll change your mind."

Muhlbach, startled, glances across the hedge, wondering if his silence has been too deep, his expression too abstract. He does not want to appear eccentric, unbalanced by the loss of his wife. He manages a neutral smile, thanks her for the invitation. Has she said anything else? If so, he failed to hear. Has another silence marked the distance of his thoughts?

"We're always home. Drop over." She is examining her arms to discover what effect the feeble sunshine might have had.

The Chongs are not always at home. Indeed, fairly seldom. Muhlbach finds himself resentful, though he cannot be sure whether he resents the casual hypocrisy of her statement or the fact that so frequently they go out, leaving their son alone.

Now she has gone, with an indifferent wave of the magazine. Such an informal, bland, Occidental salutation seems to him grossly incongruous; she has gone, leaving a perceptible hint of lilac through the barren hedge of winter. Muhlbach contemplates the tin can of paint he holds, a spattered rag, some brushes that might as well symbolize his present estate, thinking of a life that used to be, a life he knew must end, and did, yet how bitterly! And he remembers, too, a phrase of music, crumbs of madeleine, since these are common properties, the gynandrous quality of a woman's limbs — well, these and more. And how does it conclude? What is it, after all? Children, a quiet neighborhood, a funeral not too ostentatious. Surely, he thinks, there must be more.

A sparrow hops across the frozen flower beds; Muhlbach gloomily oversees this petty search, half impressed by the absence of despair, a ritual less convoluted than his own. Soon enough it will be time to wash and dress himself as expected. The Forsyths, with Eula, are due at seven o'clock. Two drinks, the usual conversation, and away to supper. What is the point of this foolish affair? Eula, no more subtle than the next, pretends to seek nothing except his company. So will he pretend, and she, and the Forsyths, and yet they all four know better. Marriage is her heart's desire. This evening she once again will cultivate the children, more especially Otto, the recalcitrant one, attempting to persuade him of her good intentions. Otto will not be deceived; he suspects. He may not know precisely what he suspects, and he will be civil, but that is all; Eula's voluptuous blandishments bring to his foxy face an expression of studied cordiality, nothing else; he knows that his every word and gesture is supervised by adults. This evening she will exclaim with simulated delight at finding him here, where he lives, as though she expected him to be somewhere else. Otto, in turn, will glance upward, shiftily, from Miss Cunningham to Dr. and Mrs. Forsyth, estimating the situation, perhaps formulating a marvelous idea such as kicking Miss Cunningham in the bottom. But it can't be done, however appealing the thought.

Muhlbach lifts his head. Shadows cover the yard. The sparrow has disappeared. How long ago? The sun provides no warmth, retreating, beyond the tangled housetops, beyond the hooks, ropes, and wires of civilization. Evening comes on. This day is nearly finished. Tomorrow will be Sunday, next comes Monday, Tuesday, the comfortable tedium. Once, he reflects, work seemed vital; now it is the means to fill a day. Suppose he should import Greek amphorae, sell wool, speculate on munitions, design cathedrals, would it be much different?

The voice of Mrs. Grunthe is heard. She is annoyed over

something, which is usual. Muhlbach listens. Ah!—the
scouts have completed their hike, the aspiring trooper is
home. Yes, that is the tone she reserves for Otto. When
Donna has contrived to displease Mrs. Grunthe the repri-
mand is less vehement. Well, Mrs. Grunthe is right, however
often one may disagree with her; she is right when it comes
to dealing with Otto, whose skin would spoil the edge of a
scalpel. The mighty, two-handed sword of a Crusader is the
appropriate weapon to convince him of error, and wielded
with heroic strokes may even bring a trace of blood. So,
Otto has come home. Muhlbach listens to the sounds of
discord. Whatever the argument is about, Mrs. Grunthe will
win.

Chill as any stone, the sun sinks through cloudy folds,
through antennae and chimneys; and Muhlbach after a few
minutes enters the kitchen.

"If I'm not mistaken, the prodigal has returned," he says.

"Oh, yes! Look at him, now, would you, sir?" Mrs.
Grunthe opens for the prosecution. "Claims he doesn't need
a bath! He won't spend the night under this roof without a
bath, I can tell you!"

Otto speaks. The defense. He commences to recite a
formidable list of reasons for his uncouth appearance. The
ice was thin, the ice looked thick; unfortunately the ice was
thin. Thus we account for Otto having stepped into the
creek—warped shoes, dried over the campfire. They are dry
enough now, true, with a crusty look that no polish will
soften. One pair of shoes ruined, or at least less serviceable
than they were. Yes, yes, the water was cold, no doubt, Otto.
Neither Mrs. Grunthe nor I will dispute this statement,
thinks Muhlbach. One learns, my son, not to walk on ice
until one has tested it with heavy rocks, with the recollection
of yesterday's temperature, et cetera. There were no rocks
near the stream? Well, we must doubt that. And what has

yesterday to do with it? The scoutmaster himself walked on
this ice? Indeed? Ah, along the edge of it! Now, what about
these gloves? They got wet when you stepped into the creek
because you lost your balance, all right. Under the circumstances, all right, but why do the gloves no longer have
finger tips? Would you be good enough to explain? Here are
the gloves, so called, consisting of cuffs, palms, and the
beginning of fingers. Only one question: viz., where are the
finger tips? Being wet, yes, we understand, because you
were in the creek, yes, please continue. It was very cold, you
already have informed us of the fact. As to the gloves,
please? You dried them. Commendable. How did you dry
them? By the fire, of course. How close to the fire? You don't
exactly remember. Not really very close? No? Then why, at
the point where the fingers vanish, does the wool exhibit
this charred appearance? Charred? Yes, meaning burned.
The gloves have been burned. But you don't know how this
happened? Suppose you take a moment to reflect.

Silence.

Mrs. Grunthe, arms crossed with Teutonic certitude,
awaits the confession.

Well, Otto?

Possibly, that is to say, there might just possibly be a
chance that the gloves, while being dried, were hung an inch
or two closer to the fire than necessary. Immediate qualifica-
tions follow; Muhlbach cuts them short. One pair of shoes,
one pair of gloves. What next? The pedometer, lost in the
woods at the age of seven months. The pedometer, faithfully
logging the distance covered this Saturday, now is resting in
one of two places—in the underbrush or in the creek. Otto
is of the opinion it is in the creek. Because the ice was thin.
Everything is the fault of the ice. It seems the ice should have
spoken up. So, the list is increasing. Anything else? A hatchet.
A hatchet is missing. Where is the hatchet? The leather

sheath is produced. Excellent, the sheath is safe, in good condition. But where is the hatchet?

Silence.

Otto? Speak up.

Otto is not positive that he took the hatchet on this hike; perhaps the hatchet is in the basement? No, the hatchet started off this Saturday morning hooked to Otto's belt. Mrs. Grunthe distinctly remembers. Now where is it? Quite obviously it is keeping company with the pedometer. These artifacts will serve as museum pieces for some future society. Now, is there anything more? Shoes, gloves, pedometer, hatchet. According to Mrs. Grunthe this is merely a beginning. Consider, for instance, the mess kit. The canvas cover is filthy—did it fall into the bean soup? Otto resents this. One David Guckenheim, it seems, having allowed his shoelaces to become untied—David Guckenheim is a big fat slob—all right, never mind, we can do without that. Continue. David Guckenheim, in short, tripped himself, and as he, Guckenheim, happened to be carrying a cup of stew at the time—well, all right, all right. The mess kit cover is not important; it can be boiled and scrubbed. So that's it? No? The compass, too, has been lost. Succumbing to irony, Muhlbach points out the function of a compass, which is to prevent the woodsman from becoming lost, whereas in this case the compass has been lost. Ha ha!

Otto does not grasp the irony.

Never mind, let it go. The list of equipment destroyed, lost, mutilated, or forgotten, becomes almost unbelievable. Add to the shoes, gloves, and so forth, the following: waterproof matchbox, good-luck charm—a magnesium horseshoe from a box of cereal—and, among numerous other items, the chipmunk tail. It is this loss which sorely grieves Otto, his most grisly possession. Mrs. Grunthe, not unexpectedly, is relieved to learn it will be seen no more.

The chipmunk tail. Muhlbach thinks of it for the first time since last summer. He thinks of Otto's triumphal return from four weeks at camp in the Alleghenies, full of marvelous accounts of wild life, carrying a bronze medal—third place in the archery competition—a collection of fishhooks, a broken canoe paddle. What use is a broken canoe paddle? No one knows, even the owner, but still it stands in a corner of Otto's room, a relic not lightly discarded. And the chipmunk tail?—ah, the woodcraft instructor, he who teaches survival in the wilderness, teaches the building of traps—in this case a heavy wooden box, overturned, propped up with a peg, a string attached, bait underneath the box, and the hunter concealed behind a nearby boulder. Enter the rodent. The rest is foreordained. But the tail? Enter the camp physician, a young and ruddy resident from uptown Manhattan. How did he get into the Alleghenies? How did he learn to extract the bone from the tail of a chipmunk? And what then?—it is packed with salt, and thus, up to a certain age, remains pliable. This, therefore, is the trophy whose loss Otto regrets so bitterly.

Otherwise, apart from having lost or destroyed an impressive percentage of your belongings, Otto, how was the excursion? Excursion, yes. That is to say, an outing, a trip, a brief journey, usually for pleasure. In this instance, a hike. What did you eat? Excepting the inevitable chocolate bar. What did you cook for lunch? Well, there was a minute steak, tenderized by the butcher. Times have changed. Muhlbach remembers his own camping trips, and the minute steak, remembers buying them from the grocer, the price was ten cents. He does not know how much they cost these days, that being Mrs. Grunthe's concern.

So you ate a minute steak. What else?

Stew, naturally, and something known as bean-hole beans. No doubt everything was liberally seasoned with ashes and dirt, twigs, insects—or perhaps it was too early for insects. And did you have a good time, my son?

What a question.

For now, for this Saturday, the hike is over. Details of it we will hear later. The time has come for a bath and clean clothing. And a word of advice: stay away from Donna, because it appears she is coming down with a cold, or some such. She has been in bed since noon, and seems listless. Mrs. Grunthe not being concerned, Muhlbach is not. Despite certain antipathies, certain reservations about Mrs. Grunthe, he has utter confidence in her female powers of divination. If Donna were in the first stages of a serious illness, Mrs. Grunthe would know. Just how she would know, Muhlbach cannot imagine; it is enough to believe that in this respect the housekeeper is infallible. He muses on this, recalls having watched Mrs. Grunthe tuck in the covers of Donna's bed, has observed the clean, capable, plump, lentiginous hands at work. He compliments himself for having the wisdom to select Mrs. Grunthe from among the applicants.

Off to the bath, Otto, off with you! And pick up your room! Mrs. Grunthe has enough to do without—yes, yes, all right, all right. Otto heads for the stairs, shirttail dangling, warped shoes creaking. It would not take an Indian to follow his trail; indeed, the odor would be enough.

And as his son is tramping out of sight Mulbach remembers when the shelter plans were delivered, how strangely Otto responded to them—how he seemed to withdraw. From what? That was months ago, but still there is a sense of cross-purpose, a dissatisfaction, a lack of rapport persisting between himself and his son. And he falls to thinking of this, and does not listen to Mrs. Grunthe complain of one thing after another, of a universe poorly ordered—she is well-paid, she will stay. He thinks of that Saturday morning when the plans arrived, in an outsized manila envelope, with a handsome seal embossed in the upper left corner, the word RUSH stamped in red on the front and back, with a Washington postmark. There was a look of authority to that envelope. Otto had stood by, attentive but inscrutable, wearing a new sweatshirt, respectful, knowing that envelopes from Washington may be significant.

Yes, and he had been wearing the ill-starred pedometer, having just received it for a birthday. The pedometer had been worn each day for about a month, then less frequently, and now appeared only on special occasions such as the hike. But at first it was always evident, attached to a sock where it attempted to register every step. Muhlbach, on the assumption he should display some interest in its calculations, used to ask. But the answer, customarily, was Otto's favorite; that is, he didn't know, wasn't sure, or had forgotten how far he had gone that day. Then of what use is a pedometer, if you don't know, or already have forgotten? Well, having thought this over, of course, he didn't know. Victory belongs to the ignorant, a variation of Gresham's law. At all events, there he had stood, the solemn Philistine, on the day the plans arrived, dressed in sweat shirt and baseball cap, the pedometer noncommittal and yet somehow malevolent, dangling from a white wool sock on which several burrs were lodged — a surly little machine, bloodless and efficient, ready to click the instant its owner moved a foot.

Eying it from time to time, Muhlbach had been almost overcome by an urge to take advantage of this instrument, to deceive it, to hold it up and swing it back and forth until it died of exhaustion. Indeed, very late one night he did take it up from the bureau where it lay surrounded by marbles and Indian-head pennies, but quickly set it down, for the thing was curiously repellent, seemingly aware of him, and might cry out in a thin metallic voice, crying "Otto! Otto!" in the depths of the night. Then what? How should he explain if Otto should waken and sit up stiff with alarm?

So, if he has not commented on the loss of the pedometer, Muhlbach nonetheless is vaguely relieved that it is gone. It cannot, of course, return of its own volition; it was a ghastly totem, nothing more, inanimate, not a conscious and motile automaton — it only seemed to be.

Thus accoutered, in sweat shirt and pedometer, Otto had watched the opening of the manila envelope, watched the unfolding of the blueprints, examined the drawings in the booklet, looked speculatively at a photograph of a pretty young woman, obviously a professional model, smiling and displaying her personal dosimeter, weight one ounce and a half, compactly and attractively designed as a locket. Like Grandmother's cameo, it hung about her neck to measure both the rate of radiation and the amount absorbed. Otto inquired about the dosimeter, whose function puzzled him, radiation being something he does not comprehend. And he looked long at a picture of someone's basement recreation room, so called, with murals of primitive bison, and a television set recessed, its gray elliptoid screen waiting. Is it this he finds so absorbing? — a television set in the basement? No, nor the mural. And how unconsciously droll, thinks Muhlbach, that the family should be contemplating paleolithic art. Could this be deliberate? No, impossible. Irony presupposes a feeling for humor; there is none here. None. How bizarre, in fact, are these ferruginous animals eternally poised in apocalyptic gloom. Is it the bison which fascinates Otto? No. *Ah!* — it is, of course, the exercycle. Yes, a bicycle without wheels. Of course. And, for the sake of realism, this contrivance has a speedometer attached!

What else have we? What else in this basement? One spade neatly pegged upon the wall, a long-handled pick — what for? A pick looks anachronistic, relevant to the Punic

Wars. But still, who knows? The pick appears confident that it will be used. A wrench, too. Well, wrenches are convenient, and screwed down close enough may be employed against a reluctant toothpaste cap. And next to the wrench a battery-operated hot plate. A hand-crank phonograph, records, a book or so. Not many books; television is more direct, opportune, demanding adherence. Who doubts the graven image?

And on the shelf is a rag doll! Muhlbach, prepared to turn the page, scarcely can believe what he sees. Yet there she lies, appealing to every little girl, stuffed legs outstretched and hair of colored yarn. She wears a jumper. Her eyes are buttons. How anachronistic, Muhlbach thinks; he has not seen such a doll in many years. The children of our time amuse themselves with plastic robots which squeal and periodically stain their garments, deliver monologues, walk, throw fits of temper. The marvels of realism. Why was not one of these hideous creatures included, rather than an old rag doll? Why?

Otto has had enough of this page, what comes next? Architectural sketches. Muhlbach is interested, Otto is not. Turn the page. Photographs. Charred steel, smashed concrete, the ruins of a warehouse at Nagasaki Medical College, meaningless to Otto. Roof trusses twisted like dental braces, a streetcar flung off its tracks and lying on its side. What have we next?

A portrait of "Fat Man," sixty inches in diameter, length one hundred and twenty-eight inches, weighing just over ten thousand pounds. He is painted black, stands on some sort of trestle, a box guidance system affixed to his rear. He it was who rode unannounced into the heart of the city, a gift from America, riding bloated with the knowledge of triumph through Persepolis. Otto asks if it is a submarine. No, it is not. We'll talk about it later. That is, in a few years.

And here, cradled, is "Little Boy," the predecessor, the

original. Muhlbach stares at this thing which has altered history. It is so recent, yet it has an antique look, primitive, rusty. It appears to have been made by hand. How strange! Conventional bombs of that era had a sleek, well-fed aspect. Why should this appear so crude? It looks as though two boys had built it in a garage with a hammer and pliers and parts from some abandoned generator. It has the look of a device submitted to the government patent office but rejected. So much for that. Turn the page.

Aerial photos, before and after, with concentric rings superimposed. Yes, even the untrained eye can note the difference. Here the bend of the river is the same, otherwise nothing. A city, not unlike Paris, with its rivers and bridges, constitutes Exhibit A. Exhibit B is merely an area. Muhlbach fingers his lip, frowning; this is how the state of Arizona must look from high above.

Otto is impatient. Turn the page.

Grids, screens, additional views of Sodom and Gomorrah. Maps, statistics, drawings — a man dressed in a double-breasted business suit! He appears to be standing in a strong breeze, his hat has just hopped off his head, he is covering his face with both hands in order to protect himself from an explosion. Muhlbach skims the explanatory text, bemused by the double-breasted business suit. How very odd, such attention to fashion, but still a fashion out of date.

Next we have a photograph of a Mr. Wheeler Rosenbaum, a grocer from Sioux City, Iowa. Grocer Rosenbaum is pictured lifting the lid of his shelter garbage can and, at the same time, drinking something from a paper cup. Curious, to say the least. Otto, too, seems puzzled. What is the grocer drinking?

It occurs to Muhlbach that there is about this booklet a feeling of insanity. And the people whose pictures appear, are they inhabitants of an asylum? A grocer, ostensibly, from Sioux City, a portly, self-satisfied grocer stands beside a garbage can. Yes, with one hand he lifts the lid of the receptacle and he soberly drinks from a paper cup. Someone is mad. Surely this pamphlet was composed by the unfortunates of a madhouse.

But let us see what the grocer does next. Surrounded by his five children and his wife, and a neighbor — Miss Holloway, she is called — the grocer is shown seated at an oilcloth-covered table. He is waiting, this is quite evident. Everyone is looking at him. Presently he will do something, or something will happen. Perhaps the others will join him at the table and they will eat scallopini. We cannot be sure.

Grocer Rosenbaum also is pictured out of doors enjoying the sunshine. It would be October in Iowa, to judge from the trees, a few leaves on the ground. The photo has an October feeling. Rosenbaum stands, hands thrust into his pockets, smiling at the camera, beside the emergency exit which, like some prairie rodent, he has most prudently burrowed. For unknown reasons this exit has been camouflaged — a piece of garden statuary adorns it, a concrete cherub holding in its arms a birdbath half filled with water. Would not this hinder the escape? Presumably not. One must suppose the statuary tumbles aside when the grocer and his family and Miss Holloway emerge from beneath the sod.

And we are shown pictures of the Rosenbaum food cache, adequate, more than adequate, which is to be expected.

We have a picture of Doris, the eldest, who is eating what is called a Survival Ration Cracker. It resembles the common graham cracker, we are informed; however, the taste is slightly different. This cracker is composed of 8.4 per cent protein, 8.5 per cent fat, 79 percent carbohydrates, and 1 per cent sodium chloride.

Muhlbach cannot help himself; he knows he must total

these percentages. Something is missing. Impossible! 96.9 per cent. What has become of the remaining 3.1 per cent? Protein, fat, carbohydrate, sodium chloride, yes. What could it be?

Otto asks what the girl is eating. A cracker, Otto. It is a cracker, as you know quite well.

What next? The two Rosenbaum boys, on their knotty pine bunks, pretend to read, eyes carefully averted from the camera in order to give the impression of candid photography, life as it truly is.

Next, our grocer once again, appraising his groceries. Peaches, spinach, peas, jam, soup, cocoa, candy, et cetera. Splendid. Turn the page.

Consumption as well as production, we learn, will be government-controlled. We will not be allowed to purchase food. Therefore the list for stockpiling, calculated to the ounce. How many government employees, loyal and trustworthy, using how many computers, for how many months, have arrived at this conclusion: 448 ounces of sterile whole milk will suffice one child for a period of fourteen days, provided said infant is not more than eighteen months of age? But if he should be nineteen months and sickly? If he has a large appetite? Never mind, let us continue.

A serving of diced carrots in a plastic bag — are you listening, Otto? — subjected to Gamma radiation 2×10^6, has been kept at room temperature for almost three years! One cannot help wondering if the carrots are tasty. We have also a bag containing five — why *five*? — "frankfuters" — yes, that is the way it is spelled — five of these revolting edibles subjected to higher irradiation.

Ah! — here is the famous bottled water, the taste of which, our government informs us, the taste of which may be restored by pouring from one container to another in the same fashion as the Lion's Club magician entertains us. See the water? Otto sees the water.

Mrs. Rosenbaum now enters the activities. She, with one foot on the pedal, has raised the lid of yet another disposal unit. In virtually every picture there has been one or more waste containers. Well, the implications of this are not pleasant. Back to Mrs. Rosenbaum, immortalized with a foot on the pedal. She wears an everyday sort of dress. Her hair, it would seem, has been curled by a Sioux City beautician. Malloy's Beauty Parlor? Gertrude's Beauty Shoppe? One cannot help wondering what things are like in Sioux City. In regard to Mrs. Rosenbaum, we cannot tell too much about her, the photograph being grainy, except that her waist is thicker now than it once was, and her curls appear to be gray. She is fifty, and after five children she is what we expect. Does she doubt that when the moment comes she will once again place her foot on the pedal? Now she only simulates her chores. Can she doubt that everything will function? It is wise to be prepared.

Consider the chemical toilet, privacy afforded by a decorated bamboo screen. Precisely how many rolls of tissue will be consumed by a family of seven, plus one neighbor, during a period of fourteen days? Has this been calculated? What if the government broadcaster, after fourteen days, informs Mr. Rosenbaum that, unfortunately, because of certain unexpected and regrettable conditions, he cannot come upstairs? Well, we are working on these problems, of course. We do the best we can. A start must be made somewhere. A stitch in time, et al.

Thus we leave our good grocer and, having turned the page, receive lessons in first aid. Muhlbach scans the instructions. Eye drops are sold by druggists under various trade names. True. One does not quarrel with such a statement. A one-ounce bottle, with dropper, is recommended. Very well. For eyes irritated by smoke, dust, or fumes it is advisable to use two drops in each eye. Apply cold compresses every twenty minutes, if possible.

If possible?

A forty-page newspaper folded to dimensions — *what* dimensions? — pieces of orange-crate sidings, or shingles cut to size. Read this again. Oh! — yes, yes, splinting. But a *forty-page* newspaper! Muhlbach attempts to recall the size of his daily, and cannot. He doubts it is forty pages. But suppose it is not only that, but larger. Are the extra pages to be thrust into one of the disposal units? Could a forty-*eight*-page newspaper be folded to these mysterious, unspecified dimensions? However, let us proceed.

In case of shock, dissolve one teaspoonful salt and one-half teaspoonful baking soda in one quart of water. Have patient drink as much as he will. Yes, under the circumstances it is safe to assume there will be a number of rather shocked individuals. But will they enjoy this potion? Will they agree that it is good for them? How much will each victim drink? What if he refuses? Otto, for example, is hostile to unfamiliar liquid; he resists, as a matter of course, whatever is said to be beneficial.

Do not attempt to give anything to the patient by mouth, Muhlbach reads aloud, if the patient is vomiting. Has such advice spewed out of a computer? The booklet does not give us the name of its author. But let us go on. Let us read further. Who can say what fascinating information will be revealed?

Do not use a tourniquet unless you know how to use one.

That is the recommendation.

When bleeding stops, bandage firmly but not tightly.

The mind boggles before such wisdom. Firmly. Tightly. What can be said? So much for first aid.

Here comes Mrs. Rosenbaum again, serious, farsighted, even a bit truculent, on the exercycle. Onward the grocer's faithful spouse! Underground she rides magnificently nowhere. The enemy so high above, will he plot her bearing and speed in order to calculate the destination? Do not worry, Mrs. Rosenbaum. Ride faster. Faster.

Turn the page.

Ace Electronics now has on the market — what is this? Advertising? Collusion? Ace Electronics is marketing a high-quality, yes, it is so described, a high-quality radiation meter, portable, sturdy, battery-powered, selling, mind you, for a mere $59.95. Less than sixty dollars, so long as one does not count the tax. On the eve of Armageddon the precepts of Madison Avenue have not been neglected. The consumer is of the opinion that $59.95 is less than $60. That is true. So it is, indeed. Furthermore, this handy device is pictured. It has a convenient knurled grip and would be a joy to carry through the countryside. The gauge resembles that of a voltmeter; the needle is long, red-tipped, extremely sensitive. When one discovers that one is entering an area of intense radiation one turns around and goes back.

Next we see a photographic enlargement of some chromosomes that have been badly confused by what is happening. One chromosome has sought to trifurcate rather than bifurcate itself, as is the custom.

Finally the check list. Muhlbach runs through this — Otto long since having become bored — turns the page and discovers an essay on morale. Games, crafts, home movies, and so forth, in consequence of which a deep, quiet satisfaction is promised. There is the government promise in black and white — "a deep, quiet satisfaction."

This is a good time to strike out on new paths which have lured you through the years but which have never been taken or have only been briefly tried because of lack of time.

Ah, now! — don't we know that voice? Consider the limpid, persuasive style! We can almost see you in the fury of creation, scribbling on sheets of foolscap, impatiently crumpling them, one after another. The carpet of that little

Washington office is littered. Or could we be mistaken? Do you lean back, comfortably dictating immortal suggestions? Dust and flapping shades, toppled columns, garlands and scepters, prince of scribes, we know you. Could anyone be deceived? Could we mistake the hairy mammoth? Does one confuse the stegosaurus with the pterodactyl? Yes, yes, we are listening. Pray continue.

To throw away your own life through lack of preparation for survival is suicide.

Wait, permit us to interrupt. But no! Go on.

To throw away the lives of your family through negligence is murder.

Maxims, apothegms, dicta, precepts, epigrams, cabbages. Memories of Aesop. Shades of the French salon. What next?

If derision is thrown at you for your efforts, just don't talk about them.

Thrown? *Them?* Plural of derision? Oh!—now it becomes clear. Our friend speaks of the efforts. Do not talk about the efforts. Very well.

The care of birds is relatively simple.

Birds?

Actually, it might be wise to put the bird in their cages into the shelter area now but if that area is in a cellar or basement or in another building just make a note of the fact that you must get the bird and post this where you can see it.

Suppose we try that once more. Ready? Begin. Actually, it might be wise to put the bird (singular) in their (its?) cages (singular or plural?) into (yes, in*to*) the shelter area now (no comma) but if that area is in a cellar or basement (where are we?) or in another building just make a note of the fact that you must get the bird and post this where you can see it. When an alert or warning sounds you won't forget.

In quintuplicate. Well, there it is. Government advice. Onward.

Do you like to dance? Get records or take advantage of music which you might get over short-wave stations outside this country or over Conelrad stations broadcasting morale-boosting melodies.

Muhlbach, somewhat stunned, gazes at what he has just read. It cannot be true. Nevertheless, it is. Morale-boosting melodies. The exact phrase. Can this be some ghoulish parody?

If you have family diaries and scrapbooks, heirlooms such as journals and photograph albums and letters, put them in a box and in the shelter.

The box, that is. Put the box in the shelter.

You might find them intriguing as reading material and they might also serve as an inspiration to start you on the road to writing such a journal of current events of your family's experience from day to day.

Oh, how easily we recognize that style! Muhlbach, hypnotized, reads on.

Why not write letters? Of course they won't be mailed as they normally would, but when they are mailed you will have given those who receive them reassurance as to your well-being, your thoughts, your daily problems and your solutions to them.

Unless, of course, the problems turn out to be insoluble. Never mind. Engrossed by this document, this runic dream which might well be preserved on slate tablets, he cannot stop reading.

Otto is restless.

Go outside and play, Otto. Go outside and dance. Take along your heirlooms. Start a journal of current events for purposes of inspiration, by all means, as our favorite author would say.

Thus the booklet accompanying the plans, marked RUSH, from the nation's capital, that bulwark of sanity and prudence, cynosure of all eyes in the midst of these troubled times. Let us repose our confidence in the perspicacity of our nation's leaders.

And the image that has lingered in his mind's eye — a very good phrase, that! — is a sketch of a happy family enjoying their deep, quiet satisfaction after the Event. We behold the earth above, devastation absolute, and the triumvirate below. On the divan Mother takes her ease. Smiling, she holds a letter she has just received. Father, casual in slacks and windbreaker, as though he has completed a round of golf, selects a phonograph record. He, too, is smiling. Susan, let us call her, wearing her school sweater, lounges on the carpet where she works at her arithmetic. We are not astonished that she, too, is smiling. On the wall are four large, beautifully framed prints — early American sailing ships. There are many pillows, triangular, elliptical, the latest thing in pillows. We see also the grocery shelf, the generator, the disposal unit, yes, there it is, right next to the shovel. But where is the pet? Surely such a family would not be without a pet! We must conclude the siren caught the miserable beast away from home. That is to say, Rollo is now a shadow on the pavement.

When the chips are down — ah ha! Here is our author again. We promptly identify that prose. When the chips are down — yes? yes? — you will want to live. The premise. How does one refute such fearsome logic? Impossible.

Insane? This is not insanity, for there is meaning to insanity. And yet, is there not meaning to everything? Muhlbach cannot forget this drawing; and each time he thinks of it he must ask himself if, by spading up his own back yard, by constructing a similar refuge, by implication and association he therefore has committed himself to the company of these placid cretins.

What is the answer?

Unable to reply to his own question, he thinks he might as well ask Otto. Still, he reflects, because I have chosen this road I will go down it some distance further, and we shall see what we shall see.

Again his thoughts turn upon Otto and the indifference, the all but overt hostility, his son displayed toward these plans. Here arrived from Washington a set of blueprints, accompanying it a treatise on living underground with pets, family, and friends, with pictures of explosions, flaming houses, devastated cities—and Otto withdrew! He is fascinated by tree houses, caves, fires, catastrophe of every description, and has demonstrated his affinity for a wilderness wherein one eats out of tin cans. Then why should he view so coldly this exciting prospect?

Why?

He asked very, very few questions about the shelter. This, of itself, is odd. And the questions were unlike his usual queries, which customarily are noted for a certain lack of distinction. Why are trees green? — and so forth. Demotic questions. In short, however capable or ingenious Otto might be, and though he is one's own flesh and blood, it would be excessive to pretend that he is remarkable for his intelligence.

Well, then, how account for the surly bite of his questions regarding the shelter? There was, Muhlbach remembers, a vesicant quality to them; it was as though Otto had been transmogrified and, full of *Weltschmerz,* proposed to doubt everything. Will the roof fall in? This is a question he once asked about the house, but he was then half his present age and it seemed not unreasonable. But that he should ask such a question now! He knows better. He knows, thinks Muhlbach, he knows damn well that the shelter roof will not collapse. He knows what a blueprint is for; he understands. What was the purpose of that question? The boy is growing up. Yes, it will pay to listen more closely. We may ignore the duplicity of the infant, only take care as he grows older.

At any rate Otto now is out of sight, rinsing away the creek water. That hike was rather expensive. One doesn't think of hikes as costing much. Well, so be it. Muhlbach sighs — and is startled by the noise. Perhaps there is time for a nap. But, no, the Forsyths will be coming over, with Eula. What has been planned? — he cannot remember. Oh, yes, cocktails here, then out for the evening. They are all four to go out for dinner. He wonders if he might cancel the evening. Women make use of the sick headache and no questions are asked. What does a man do? Ordinarily nothing; he puts up with the situation. And here comes Mrs. Grunthe.

Yes, yes, he replies, I know — they'll be here in a little while.

So, like Otto before him, Muhlbach trudges up the steps, conscious of the housekeeper's eye upon him, as though he too were a small boy.

In the shower, steaming the March wind from his bones, he leans against the warm tile wall and shuts his eyes. It seems so long since Joyce died. It seems so long ago. Times change, we are told, and we with them. How lonely it has been, these past months.

Dressing, he regards himself in the mirror, manages a smile, not that there is much to smile about; the smile is for practice. He will be expected to smile this evening. Everyone wonders to what extent he has recovered from the death of his wife. Well, that is something he himself can wonder over. He walks and talks, goes to the office as expected, eats, sleeps; it is only that life is senseless, as though he had been mildly drugged all this while. Nothing is of much consequence. As to the shelter? — who knows? He has built it not because it was something to do; he could as easily have spent these weekends painting the house with a small brush or picking up autumn leaves one at a time. But because the shelter might possibly succeed, because of the children, on their account, he has built it. And because of his own perversity — yes, that is the true reason. I accept the madness of our time, he thinks. Each age does produce its folly — some scheme, project, or fantasy toward which the blood drains — economic, political, religious. Always. Panniers of mold from the hill of the Crucifixion, flagons of water from Jordan. There is testimony to the madness of an earlier age, but is ours more sapient? Compare us to the men of Urban's time, those that listened, rich with devotion, while he communicated his madness till Europe boiled and the meadows of France were covered with tents. How have we grown? Here am I, dabbling in an art that may soon be lost, the building of shelters against total irruption; one might as well have faith in the power of shrunken heads. But I acquiesce in the name of prudence, which is a sort of wisdom.

So, carefully drawing the noose of a quiet necktie, having been fastidious since he can remember, drawing and placing the knot, Muhlbach somberly contemplates his image.

At last he blinks and draws a breath. His thoughts turn to the present evening, to the curious solicitude of friends. How tentative each suggestion, each invitation. No doubt the Forsyths and Eula discussed this supper before proposing it. Eula, anxious to begin the assault, probably protested nonetheless, out of sham modesty, with Margaret countering, women not wanting other women to go to waste. And Lewis, to whom death is as common as a radish, seeing it approach and seize his patients despite his most valiant efforts — quite probably Lewis ignored this female intricacy. Is it, in fact, too soon? What will the neighbors think? Muhlbach speculatively taps the mirror with a fingernail file as though to elicit some response. The face in the mirror does not speak. Come now, my familiar friend, show a reasonable countenance. This evening we must be genial, we two.

Downstairs again, the night has taken on a winter look.

The Volkswagen is parked next door, Bob Chong is home, the sound of jazz is heard, a tree filled with black-birds. Every night this charivari, this unspeakable bobbery, emanates from their house in concentric rings, thrusting itself upon the neighborhood, Bob Chong's voice shouting intermittently to some nonexistent personage — *"Bix!* Do it, man! Muggsy, go! *Go!"* Muhlbach cannot separate them. Who is Bix? Is he also Muggsy? Perhaps they are brothers. Are they figures of speech? Symbols of distress? They cannot be real, only the uproar which is promulgated in their name.

With hands locked behind his back he stares at the lighted window, at the shadows bouncing back and forth across the half-drawn shade, and hopes it will not last much longer. He had thought there might be time for some music of his own choosing, perhaps the Brandenburgs, but nothing — surely not the Stuttgart chamber group — could compete with Muggsy and Bix. Patience, therefore. Goths and Vandals passed away, so must these individuals, whoever or whatever they are.

Guided by his nose, Muhlbach enters the kitchen. Mrs. Grunthe, it is true, resents his presence there. He may be the employer but the kitchen belongs to her; which of course is a proper reason to enter now and again, to impress upon her the fact that it is he, not she, who is the captain of this sloop. Besides, he wishes to know what she is cooking for such a chilly night. He does not inquire; he lifts the lid of the kettle, sniffs, peers, nods, replaces the lid. For all her faults, she most certainly is a cook. He cannot say what is on the fire, but his mouth waters; he is tempted to call the Forsyths and plead a sick headache. How satisfying to spend the night at home with the contents of this kettle, a slice of pie, and coffee, brandy and a cigar; and, once the atmosphere has purified, once the cacophony subsides, to sink into the green leather chair, close his eyes, and keep company with Bach and Vivaldi and whoever else might come to mind. Patience. Patience. There are more ways than one of looking at a blackbird.

The doorbell. Muhlbach goes to welcome his guests. But there stands a young man, a stranger, who thrusts out a hand and begins to talk. No, I'm sorry. Go away. No. No, whatever it is, no. And as he shuts the door, courteously but firmly, he thinks there should be an ordinance against this sort of peddling. It is not the principle, really, quite so much as the deceit—the insincerity of that outstretched hand. The footsteps beat down the walk and Muhlbach reflects that as he nears forty he has conquered his need to be considered a friendly man. The wasteland roils about us. I refuse, he announces to himself, to shake each hand. And yours, especially, whoever you were. I do not know you, I do not believe you came in friendship but only because you wanted something of me; it is not that I was averse to helping you, or your cause, but you offended me, insulted my intelligence, by your dissimulation. That smile was unctuous. Am I some address, a potential source of profit? Would you have smiled such a beaming Christian smile and proffered that hand if you had known that I never would buy your product? Therefore I rejected the overture. The door is not so easily opened these days. I am not what I once was.

Minutes later the doorbell rings again; he composes himself, pulls the lingering annoyance from his features, and, to be sure, here are the Forsyths and Miss Eula Cunningham. Ah?—not quite. Margaret Forsyth and Eula Cunningham. Where is Lewis?

"He got a call as we were leaving." Margaret expresses her resignation, her understanding, her years of being the physician's wife; this and more she can express in a single weary sentence. Another minute, she says, and they'd have escaped. Pretend you don't hear it, she advised him, but of course he wouldn't. Some child had found a firecracker left over from last year and had set it off in his ear, of all places. Honestly, it does make you wonder about people.

Mrs. Grunthe is summoned to take the ladies' coats. Muhlbach, already bored by the sound of Margaret's voice, pours her a glass of ginger ale, mixes a drink for Eula, and thinks about the boy — it could not possibly have been a girl — with the wits to set off a firecracker in his ear. It is precisely what might be expected of Otto.

As though materialized by his father's reflections, Otto becomes visible at the top of the stairs. He is en route to the kitchen for supper, but in order to get there he must pass by the living room where he will be subjected to the guests. He knows them well enough, and though he has expressed no opinion about them, except to say that he likes Dr. Forsyth, it is plain that he does not care for the women. Each time he encounters them there is a horny, medieval restraint to his amenities.

How do you do, Miss Cunningham? How do you do, Mrs. Forsyth?

He cannot get away with less than this, and he will volunteer nothing more. He glances sharply about, expecting to see the doctor, but does not ask.

Mrs. Grunthe has your supper ready, says Muhlbach.

"Okay."

However, as long as you are here, make yourself useful. Muhlbach holds up the two cocktails for delivery, ginger ale and ice for Margaret, which, as a drink, is fair enough if taken on its own merits. For Eula — this is what she wanted — bourbon mixed with a commercial preparation whose taste is as noxious to the tongue as its name is to the ear, a magenta-colored syrup symbolic of the aesthetics of America. That is what she ordered, that is what she gets. Each society must endure the crime it deserves. Here you go, Otto, and be good enough not to spill them.

"Okay."

The only living Philistine. My father, thinks Muhlbach, would have rapped me across the skull if I dared answer him that way. Times change. Language deteriorates. The absence of culture becomes a culture.

He sees that Eula deliberately has blocked Otto's line of retreat. She is attempting to — well, seduce him. She is using her female body to overpower him, to win him, and through the son to obtain the father. It is a crass maneuver. And I, he reflects, the ultimate prey, somehow find myself obligated to observe this scene as though indifferent to its significance, to say nothing of its immorality! Can this woman presume I am not aware? If so, if true, the famous intuition of women is a myth.

He watches, silently.

Otto, young Ganymede, you and I know that your desire is merely to reach the sanctuary of the kitchen. I could extricate you, but you are growing up, my son, and soon enough must manage these affairs by yourself. We will observe your performance now. See if you are able to outwit the gross female.

"I'll bet you just hate Saturdays, don't you? No school."

She is being arch. Riposte, Otto. Riposte!

"They're okay."

Outwit her? With such a response? It will be years yet before Otto is capable of outwitting anybody.

"What'd you do all day? I'll bet you played games with your little friends."

"I went on a hike with some guys."

Eula leans plumply nearer and at this instant Muhlbach decides that he will not marry her. He has known, of course,

how narrowly she has been calculating, has noted her
shrewd, appraising glances at the furnishings of his home;
and various oblique questions, ostensibly innocent, have
not been lost on him. But until this one moment, seeing her
bend that body against a boy, he had not realized how cold
she was. There will be no marriage. Miss Eula Cunningham
now is wasting her time, exuding spurious warmth, one
hand resting with simulated affection on Otto's sleeve. She
smiles in what she believes to be a confidential manner;
meanwhile she is plotting, unaware that she has no future in
this house.

"My! How exciting! Where did you hike to?"

Otto gestures, easing himself away from the clutching
hand. "Nowhere. Just sort of out that direction."

"I'll bet you cooked your own lunch, didn't you?"

He nods. "Yes, ma'am."

Muhlbach is startled. Yes, ma'am. That is not Otto speaking. There is some mockery here. Eula as yet has not perceived it, but she will, assuming Otto plays this tune a little
longer, which he most certainly will, if he thinks nobody is
on to him. Muhlbach clears his throat, and again.

Otto, however, has gone mad with success. He pays no
heed to this warning — a malignant gleam has lit his eye, he
is set to make a fool of Miss Cunningham. This is slightly
incredible. Otto is not that subtle. Muhlbach gazes earnestly
at his son, wondering if he has misinterpreted.

"What fun!" exclaims Miss Cunningham. "Then what did
you do?"

Otto is insufferably casual. "We went ice skating on the
creek."

This leads to something, Muhlbach does not know what,
but he is sure that Otto is about to overplay his hand. In a
moment Otto will make some curved remark and there will
be a deadly silence; both women will perceive the ape, and

Otto himself will perceive that somehow he miscalculated. Muhlbach sets down his glass, not too loudly, yet loud enough for communication. This time Otto hears.

He says that he guesses Mrs. Grunthe wants him to come and eat. And as he goes out he directs one brief, inquiring glance at his father, not quite convinced that he has been detected. Muhlbach returns an ominous look, and Otto, to judge by a suddenly altered expression, is convinced; no further verification is required. Exit Otto. In the future perhaps he will tread more softly.

The doorbell again. This would be Lewis. But there, both of them together on the horsehair mat, clasping hands like children, stand Bob and Helen Chong.

"Oops! — Oh!" Helen exclaims, pretending astonishment that he is not alone. "You're entertaining." However, they make no move to leave. The visit, therefore, is not accidental. This would have been her idea, thinks Muhlbach; no doubt she has learned about Eula Cunningham, sensed the machination, and could restrain herself no longer. What is the candidate really like? A neighbor can deduce only so much by peeping from a window corner.

Do come in, have a drink. What a nice surprise. Permit me to introduce you. Margaret Forsyth. Eula Cunningham. Yes, Helen, this is she, this is the one to evaluate. Tell me, what do you think? Is she acceptable?

"We can only stay a moment."

Of course, of course. Now, quickly, manage another look. Shoes, stockings, hands, accessories. What about it? Will she do?

"I was just telling Bob how you seemed so deserted this afternoon, so we thought we'd drop over to say hello."

Very glad you did. For a year, now, we've been promising each other, et cetera. Is she a bit heavy, do you think? A trifle ripe? How about her perfume? Rather challenging, isn't it?

And is her suit tailored to your demands, or does it fit too closely across those alarming billows of rubicund flesh? What of her earrings?

"We're headed for the ballet," Bob Chong explains, and goes on to say they will grab a bite at a lunch counter somewhere. Muhlbach understands that this is so; unequivocally it has the ring of truth. It is a clumsily offered, masculine truth, doglike in its honesty; he cannot help smiling, and feels at the same time a surge of affection for this man whose wife is now attempting to conceal her displeasure. She imagines the other women smiling at her, secretly, and quite probably they are. From lunch counter to ballet. Will this anecdote spread throughout the neighborhood? Helen Chong does not look at her husband.

Margaret has asked if Cecil Chong is their son. Yes. Well, it appears that Margaret's boy, Duncan, is a classmate of Cecil Chong. Conversation, such as it is, grows out of this.

Muhlbach, studying Margaret Forsyth, half listens to her talk. In a polka-dot dress that is much too large, limp colorless hair knotted at the base of her neck, she is prim and flat, a married spinster with steel-rimmed glasses and a nasal Midwestern voice. It seems to him that she gives off an odor of something stale and sour. He tries to recall if he ever has seen this woman excited, animated for any reason. She does not gesture. At thirty-one she is humorless and old. Is it not remarkable that she has four lively sons? Her eyes are vacant, her body does not exist. She is, he reflects, the most tedious creature he ever has met. Then how is it she happens to be here? Why must he regard this woman as a friend? Why is it necessary to entertain and to pretend affection for someone who bores you? The answer, of course, is that she comes with Lewis. That is the answer, but it hardly seems enough. Why doesn't she stay at home? Why doesn't she recognize what she is?

Muhlbach, having asked himself these questions, begins to wonder if perhaps he has not been drinking too much, or at least too quickly. He adds a squirt of soda to his glass, rattles the diminishing ice, and turns his attention to the Chongs. They seem to him a curious pair, overly American, determined to prove their Occidental sympathies. For instance, how could a man so obviously intelligent and worldly as Bob Chong be obsessed by the sport of baseball? Baseball is the sport of truck drivers and, these past few years, of effete and balding young men who scream with joy — neither of which pertains to Bob Chong, who is not aggressively masculine any more than he is epicene. With his crew-cut hair and Argyle socks, his casual slang, and a preference for pastel shirts with French cuffs, with the mien of an Elks Club loyal, he is somewhat bizarre, more than a little contradictory. His attitude is so fraternal. Confidence is implicit in the manner with which he strips cellophane from a pack of cigarettes, taps one into space, and in the ease of long accomplishment flicks the flat gold lighter, cleverly chatting — each insuperably normal remark following another. He was, as one might guess, a pilot during the war.

Muhlbach studies him, not without admiration for the man's intellectual and imaginative achievement. He is, as the saying goes, a brain — the consequence of which, Muhlbach suspects, may have a profound influence on the lives of many people. Infrequently, hardly perceptible even then, Chong seems to reveal a further self, differing from this outer, visible man — chill, withdrawn, imperturbable, insistently at work behind the good-fellow mask. It is a little frightening, somehow. One could not say just why.

Muhlbach suddenly gets out of his chair, draws the emptied glass from Chong's delicate, blue-veined hand and fills it with liquor until it looks like a glass of German beer. He notes with amusement Chong's sharp, questing expression, which instantly vanishes. Yes, another man lives somewhere in back of this chortling neighborhood *bon vivant*. And this mysterious personage whose face so seldom shows is the one to estimate more carefully; it is he who decides, who directs the gesticulations and inane mouthings which the world assumes are representative. Santa Monica surf rider, indeed! Grab a bite at the lunch counter, indeed. Muhlbach revises his estimate. Even this man's apparent lapses are calculated, decorations on the mask. Toward what end? That by seeming innocuous he may go about his business undisturbed?

And as Chong recounts that dramatic ninth inning, ostensibly for himself and Muhlbach as the only males, for their mutual pleasure — women not being interested in that sort of thing — the narration is, yet, directed toward these women, although he evidently is ignoring them. Thus, deviously, most subtly, the fox doubling across its tracks, he believes himself undetected on the hillside, from which vantage point he will observe the hunter hunting him, not aware of a second hunter at his back. Or is he aware? And by this apparent ignorance perform a further arabesque?

Muhlbach all at once has the sensation of half a dozen eyes peering at him, coldly, through the pupils of Bob Chong, and feels his stomach tighten. This is how the suspect feels, guilty or innocent, helplessly illuminated while the inquisitors remain in darkness. But of course it is his own probing that has alerted Chong, has brought to life the recessed intellect. And at this realization he smiles, and is more at ease; after all, not himself but Robert Chong has been examined. Now it is Chong who must venture forth, must reconnoiter, simply because he has no choice.

Muhlbach tips his glass, nods, clears his throat pedantically and remarks that he has been intending to go to a baseball game. So many people, he says, seem to enjoy it.

For one moment he is almost able to believe that baseball defines the full extent of Chong, so convincingly does the man approve this statement. But their eyes have met, long enough. No, there has been no mistake.

So, this initial evening will not be the last. Bob Chong will come back again. Surprised in the course of a pointless neighborhood visit, himself tracked down, he must learn how this happened; he cannot help himself, it is the nature of the scientist. He cannot rest until he knows. Thus, inaudibly, invisible to any but the narrowed eye, a relationship is born. Muhlbach permits himself to laugh aloud, and does not explain; he turns his attention to Helen Chong, deliberately, boldly. Each look and gesture, henceforth, and the response each calls forth, will be slipped beneath the husband's microscope. Helen Chong, he notes, is not drinking. She is here on female business, no doubt of that, lured across the intervening hedge by the presence of Eula.

Margaret licks her lips. She has finished her drink and studiously is examining the empty glass. He takes it from her. Then, just as he begins to fill it up again, he understands that she is alcoholic. He almost drops the glass; at this same instant he feels Chong's eyes like pincers hook the back of his head. The sensation is not pleasant. Nothing will escape Chong's attention from now on. Nothing. No one else has noticed. He takes the glass more firmly in hand, pours the ginger ale, adds a cube of ice, and returns it to her. She accepts with a look of wan gratitude, lusterless, exhausted. She gazes remotely at the bubbles. Is she imagining champagne?

A car draws up outside the house.

Yes, this time it is Lewis. Muhlbach opens the door and waits to greet him, thinking meanwhile of his wife — those pink-rimmed watering eyes, the weary voice. Strange he had not thought of it before, but there can be no doubt. How

well-kept a secret! And for how many years? Always, when
visiting, she asked for ginger ale, always more than one, as if
the very act of swallowing was vital. And, waiting for Lewis
Forsyth to reach the door, he is fascinated that such a
woman could possess depths enough to ruin herself.

Well, Lewis, it's about time, I should say. How are you?

Forsyth stamps his feet on the mat, as though snow still
covered the walk. It has been a long winter; habits persist.
He removes a glove to shake hands. "I suppose Margaret
told you why I'm late. Somebody dared that kid to set one
off in his ear. Frankly, I don't hold out too much hope for
the human race."

The record isn't encouraging. At any rate, come in. Bob
and Helen Chong, Dr. Lewis Forsyth.

The men reach forward, grasp one another by the hand,
the ageless mistrust of the male. Having disarmed each
other, they withdraw a step. The women smile. There follows a pause.

How's that shelter coming along?

It is almost completed, a few details remain. One could
say, really, that it is complete. As a matter of fact, perhaps
everyone would like the grand tour? Open house, so to
speak. By the way, Lewis, I should appreciate your opinion
of the sanitary facilities. Everything is in accord with government specifications, but nowadays one can't even trust
the government. Least of all the government! And at this
there is a certain amount of laughter. Remind me, Lewis, to
tell you some of the things which appear in the booklet of
survival instructions. At any rate, I've been thinking I might
spend tonight in the shelter. I thought it should be chris-
tened! Now, smile.

"Oh?" Forsyth hesitates, glances around.

Muhlbach suddenly is aware of his own loquacity, and
that whenever the shelter is mentioned, no matter under
what circumstances, everyone grows ill at ease. Why? As

though he had mentioned that he intended to sell his business and become a poet, or that he planned to walk from New York to Seattle.

Bob Chong, authority on batting averages and earned runs, the suburban husband, jumps to his feet, ready for the grand tour.

Anyone else? asks Muhlbach, attempting levity. Admission free.

Yes, the others will come along; they scarcely can do otherwise.

Muhlbach beckons, leads the way. Through the kitchen they go; Mrs. Grunthe does not bother to conceal her displeasure.

"Oh, doesn't something smell divine!" This is Eula.

"Good evening, Mrs. Grunthe."

"Good evening, Dr. Forsyth."

And so out the back door into the light of early stars. Across the lawn. Careful. There should be a lantern of some sort.

Muhlbach feels in his vest pocket for the key, descends the steps and with a flourish inserts the key in the lock, installed only last week, swings open the door and switches on the light. There is an odor of cement, of paint, the unmistakable knowledge that one is underground.

Without a word the guests walk in like refugees from the plague. Here is a castle hidden in the forest; here they shall occupy themselves with drinking and telling stories until Death has gone from their land. Here they will be safe, and those outside must die.

"What is this?" Chong asks. He, alone, has observed the poem lettered above the door.

> N'en déplaise à ces fous nommés sages de Grèce,
> En ce monde il n'est point de parfaite sagesse;
> Tous les hommes sont fous, et malgré tous leurs soins
> Ne diffèrent entre eux que du plus ou du moins.

"It is from Boileau," Muhlbach replies, and waits.

Forsyth now has scanned the lines, but shrugs. "I read very little French," says he, and indicating the shelter, goes on: "Frankly, I dislike such precaution, yet I suppose it is only sensible."

"It is, I guess," says Muhlbach, and Chong, nodding, seems to agree.

Here we stand like Gaspar, Melchior, and Balthazar, thinks Muhlbach. We are stuffed with holy wisdom. Who is there to contradict us?

"A fine sense of irony you have," Chong remarks. "After going to all this trouble you ridicule your work."

"Not the work so much as myself," Muhlbach answers without a smile. Then, in an altered tone of voice, he announces to the women that he has ordered a Navajo rug which should make the room somewhat more cheerful and will soften the noise. He demonstrates by advancing, and his footsteps echo on the unpainted concrete.

Eula exclaims with pleasure; one would think she has always wanted to live in such a place. But then the oppressive nature of this room descends upon her. She cannot sustain her attitude of delight. It is, beyond doubt or concealment of the fact, a dungeon. A colorful rug will not enliven it. Dart boards, lemonade, phonograph records — no, this is a crypt. It speaks of evil, of misery, destruction, violence, life without hope. Eula apprehends this, gradually. Her face is stricken.

Muhlbach observes how she falters, gazes desperately around; then he becomes conscious that everyone is looking at him. Are they wondering why he has brought them here? This terrifying room is of itself meaningless; the evil it represents is of his own construction. They are looking at him. They seem to be waiting for some explanation.

"I'm sorry," he begins, embarrassed. He does not know what to say next. "I must have been asleep," he adds. What a thing to say! He cannot imagine why he has said that.

Murmurs, vague condolence. They assume he has not yet recovered from the death of his wife. They think he is distraught; they are being kind.

"What time is the ballet?" Chong asks his wife, pretending not to know.

"We should be leaving, too," Forsyth suggests, and turns to Muhlbach. "Well, my friend! Ready for a hamburger?" This is Forsyth's familiar joke. He is a gourmet, former president of the wine and food society. It has been twenty years since he ate a hamburger.

Muhlbach nods; he does not trust himself to speak. Already he is weary of this evening and longs to be alone, to meditate. But they are going out and he must go with them. All right.

Mysteriously, as though he had been subject to teleportation, he finds himself seated in Forsyth's car, talking with him, answering the women who are comfortably arranged in back. He cannot recall what he has been saying or what anyone else has said; but evidently the habits of a lifetime now preserve him. He listens and responds, that is enough; and sinks again into the dream he has dreamed these passing months.

Death and transfiguration. Meters of time, distance counted. We are like medieval figures dancing and capering across the hill.

He hears himself chatting with one of the women and knows that he is looking at her, yet for an instant it is difficult to think of her name, difficult to recognize the features. He discovers himself patting his lips with a napkin. Supper is ending. Lewis is about to light his usual cigar. At any moment the two women will excuse themselves to visit the lounge. Or have they already gone and returned— Muhlbach looks at them wonderingly.

Soon he is lost again among his thoughts, the body's presence of little consequence. Interesting that Chong should so quickly have noticed the Boileau poem. He, too, must be concerned with the perpetual madness of men, there's no better explanation. Yes, that would be it. Out of his smoking alembics have drifted the weird gases of our time. His robe may be a trifle new, no writing tools in a pouch at his belt, nor the right sleeve pushed back to his shoulder and the hood half lowered around his neck with a long cowl hanging very low. Caged birds, ox hearts, prostrate angels. Red copper, basilisk eyes, human blood, and vinegar. Whose decoctions are more marvelous, or more horrifying? What protection have we? Infatuations and delusions increase, they do not diminish, as the world grows older. It is wisdom to retreat, but madness to face each day. Let us seal ourselves behind seven doors. With the aid of curious devices and varicolored powders of projection we shall make great metals and all manner of substances. Let us form a famous triumvirate, wizard, physician, and digger of graves, typical of our age, deep in correspondence with the capital. Less ignorant than our neighbors, we must diagnose the time in which we live and albify the shadow that now has fallen across the earth.

Muhlbach coughs and gazes about with a feeling of mild astonishment, aware that he is rubbing his hands together as he often does when deeply troubled. He notes that his hands are gloved, that he is wearing an overcoat and a hat. He is standing in the street in front of his house, and dimly he recalls that he has said good night to the Forsyths and to Eula. In fact they are just now leaving—the red lights of the automobile diminish, turn a corner, and he is alone. To judge from the position of the stars it is after midnight. He listens to the sound of the night wind through wires and bushes. The neighborhood is dark, silent. There is one light, far down the deserted street. Perhaps a child is ill. Or someone works late.

He has walked halfway to the corner. Why? Where he was going, he does not know. A few blocks further and the street will conclude in a circular drive; whoever goes that way must come back again. He stops, tucks the muffler more closely around his throat. The silence is profound. The night will be long and hollow. He contemplates the sky. If the stars showed some slight compassion, he could weep. But the stars pay no attention; they offer nothing. They return his gaze.

He finds he has walked around his home and is standing in the back yard staring at the entrance to the shelter. He realizes that he is frowning, and wonders without the least sense of alarm if he is going mad, truly and publicly mad. Would it matter? The insane, we presume, are not unhappy, having made peace with their awful problems. If, he thinks, Forsyth should come waltzing around tomorrow, bright and early, followed by two hulking attendants, and, with his most affable smile, explain that he believes I need a rest, how would I respond? Possibly I would agree. There should be no trouble, Lewis, just call off the dogs. I understand. Nor do I care, especially. Only tell these secondary persons not to touch me, not to put their hands on me, not ever. Never. That is the one thing that could make me violent. Well, but then there are the children. You will see to them, Lewis, will you not? Of course. Now for Mrs. Grunthe. She is a virago of sorts. Who would employ her? Still, she is not helpless; it *is* madness to worry on her account. Concern one's self over Mrs. Grunthe?

Muhlbach startles himself by laughing aloud. He looks

around uneasily. Is anyone observing him from a darkened window? Here he stands by himself in the middle of the night braying like an ass. He coughs against his fist, turns abruptly and goes into the house.

From the linen closet he pulls out sheets and a pillow and a blanket. Will one blanket be enough? The shelter might be cold. This March night is almost freezing. Well, there is an electric heater; that will do.

Outside again, he crosses the yard, goes down the steps and into the shelter and switches on the light. The bed has already been made — Mrs. Grunthe must have made it while he was out to supper. Fancy that! Mrs. Grunthe is a gem, an utter gem. He drops the linens across a folding camp chair and turns down the cover of the bed, then hesitates, pinching his lip. Isn't it a little odd that Mrs. Grunthe should have prepared the bed? She is not usually so thoughtful. She ought to have done just what she did, to be sure, considering that she is paid to keep house; and this is, in a manner of speaking, part of the house. Yes, it was her job, no doubt of that, but still it is peripheral. At any rate, it was decent of her.

Muhlbach removes his coat and looks about the room. There are no coat hooks, no hangers. Somehow this becomes amusing. That he could have forgotten such a thing! He laughs again, then drapes his coat across the extra linens, pulls off his necktie and sits down. It occurs to him that he has not brought along his toothbrush. Every night — for how many years? — he has brushed his teeth before going to bed. Every night. Not once has he neglected to do so.

He sits for a long while, his chin resting on his fist, wondering whether or not he should make the trip back to the house to get the toothbrush. He cannot decide. Just how important is it? What is the good of all this toothbrushing? Really, when one comes to think about it, what good has been accomplished? The dentist continues to fill the visible teeth with porcelain and plug the concealed teeth with gold. So what good is all this scrubbing?

Muhlbach pulls off his shoes, which drop to the linoleum with an unfamiliar noise. He reflects that always before tonight he has dropped his shoes on a carpet. This business of dropping his shoes rather than setting them down — this always annoyed Joyce. How could he explain that he needed to do this? There was never any way to explain. It is all a consequence of working at the office and of obeying traffic signals, of being married, domesticated, and so forth and so forth. No, there never could have been an explanation. He recalls that after a year or two she quit objecting. He picks up a shoe and drops it again. Truly, the sound is different. And the air in the shelter — that has a different odor. All in all, this is quite unreal. There is a perception of dampness, of earth just beyond the walls. He holds his breath in order to listen. One almost could hear worms burrowing, and the distant rushing noise of space, the revolution of the planet and the passage of time.

The door has opened! There, with sleep-drugged eyes, wind-blown hair, pajamas giving him the aspect of a badly wrinkled bird of paradise, stands Otto, splayfooted, anxious, the final result of love. What are you doing up at this hour? Where are your bedroom slippers and your robe? You'll catch cold! But most of all, exactly what are you doing here? You are supposed to be asleep.

Otto, it develops, does not want his father to spend the night in the bomb shelter.

Nonsense! There's nothing to be afraid of; there won't be any burglars sneaking into the house simply because I'm out here. And, come to think of it, should one do so, it is a certainty that without warning Mrs. Grunthe would materialize in wrapper and nightcap, more terrifying than a squad of policemen. Go back to bed, Otto. Avaunt!

Blinking, yawning, Otto militantly repeats his request.

Back to bed, at once! It's the middle of the night. Off you go, friend. Muhlbach looks at him sternly, the look that heretofore has been sufficient, the look that puts an end to argument.

But on this occasion Otto ignores the gathering cloud, though its implications are not lost on him. His lip trembles. Muhlbach, quite amazed, calls the boy and takes him in his arms. What is the trouble? He thinks Otto must be lonely for his mother. He waits to discover if this is it. Otto never mentions her, but of course memories may be the source of grief, however mute. Well, Otto, what is it? Tell me. That's what fathers are for, you know. Tell me, did Mrs. Grunthe hurt your feelings? No. Well, then, what?

Otto has only one thing to say, a simple request.

Muhlbach becomes puzzled, then annoyed. Perhaps, Otto, if you can explain *why*, we might come to an understanding. A compromise, even a concession. Tell me.

Otto cannot explain.

What possible difference does it make, Otto, whether I spend the night underground, or in the house?

Otto, with tears streaking down his chin, remains defiant. Furthermore, it is quite obvious that he has no insight into his problem. There is, figuratively, a big black bear in the woods. What this bear is up to, no one can say. But he is there, he is in the woods.

Perhaps Otto would like to sleep in the shelter? — a bed can be fixed up, and the two of them will sleep underground.

That is not satisfactory, either. In fact, if anything, this idea has compounded the difficulty. Only one thing is clear: Otto does not want his father to sleep in the shelter, nor does he want to sleep there himself. That is final. It is unmistakable.

Well, my friend, you're behaving like your little sister, who seldom has a reason for anything. That may be all right for little girls, but it just won't do for a man! Men must give reasons for what they do. They know what they are doing, and why. Or, if not, they should. Do you understand? No. Well, anyhow, that's the way it is. That's all there is to it. So when you decide to come up with a proper reason, then we can discuss this matter. Until that time, mister, nothing doing. Sorry. Now you get back into that house and climb into your bed and don't let me hear one more quack out of you until the sun shines. Is that plain enough? Any questions?

Otto staggers out, more asleep than awake, and bangs shut the door. As the shelter is airtight, the concussion is something of a shock. Muhlbach gasps; he considers going after Otto to put a more definite end to this foolishness. But banging the door that way could have been accidental. Let it pass.

He switches on the blower which will draw fresh air through a pipe that sticks up into the garden. In the summer this pipe will be concealed by flowers; now it stands out of the barren ground like a submarine periscope. And, having finished undressing, he turns off the light and rolls into bed.

As minutes go by it seems to him that he hears Otto singing. How very strange! Otto always has loved to sing, and many were the nights past when Muhlbach and his wife had been wakened by a pagan lament, a dirge full of meaning, no doubt, signifying something. But again, who could tell? What are you singing about? they would ask. I don't know, he would answer. Then kindly don't keep us awake. Remember, you are not a young animal, a wolf or a coyote who is privileged to howl at the moon; you are a human being, civilized, and we wish you would stop this nocturnal serenade and go to sleep. Thus it would stop for the time, perhaps for the night and the night that followed, but eventually Otto again would favor them with his ability. Had he showed some promise they would not have minded, but the operatic stage, it is safe to say, will not ever be graced by the presence of that renowned tenor, Mr. Otto Muhlbach. Not in the lead, not in the chorus. His best notes are indisputably canine.

And now, thinks Muhlbach, he has taken to singing once again. Or is this all a dream? Am I asleep? Can this be a warning? Is there a rustling overhead? — and he believes he is seated at a sumptuous table in an immense dining room and is holding in one hand a heavy linen napkin. There are many diners, and severe waiters dressed in tuxedos; and almost everyone, while eating, is listening to the news over portable radios. Something terrible has happened, that is why they are listening. He is paralyzed with horror; and he feels, too, an imperial sense of rage because this occurred despite every precaution. His hands tremble and he looks at them but cannot decide whether they are shaking from fright or anger. He stands up, thinking he will tell everyone what has happened. No one pays any attention to him. He wonders what is going on. He rushes to the window and looks down. The street just below is filled with police busily directing traffic. Something lands suddenly in the street, very near the middle, like a spear — the heavy point pierces the pavement and the object stands almost upright, but does not explode. The night sky is filled with streaks of light and a furry creature has fastened itself to his throat, attentively sucking his blood. Batlike, with bony wings trailing, rising and falling — he feels them drawing across his chest — the creature is fanning him with its wings as though to console him and persuade him to keep quiet. He struggles, bends backward, but cannot make a sound. He is standing quietly in cold moonlight. Around him are scattered crumbled stones and mortar, statuary, marble pillars half concealed by withered grass. He does not know where he is, but this may be the ruin of Baalbek, or Uxmal. He feels no emotion. He looks at the shattered columns, chipped faces of forgotten heroes. He shivers, perspires, turns from side to side and tries to sit up, but cannot; then finds himself awake — alive on the marble steps of the ruin. They are cold and rough. They are real, made of concrete. Once more he attempts to sit up. His arms do not support him. He believes he is going to vomit, but after a while the nausea passes. He notices that he is outside the door of the shelter, staring up the steps toward the night sky. The night is very cold and this seems wonderful. He thinks that he will sleep awhile.

How much time slips past before his eyes open again? Who can say? The stars are less brilliant, fewer. He turns his head, languorously, toward the dark opening, the rectangular Egyptian entrance, knowing that within are blankets and musty linens. He feels that he has accomplished some immortal act; he has renounced the gods, outwitted them, and survived.

On his knees he crawls up the steps, uncertainly, out of the tomb. Overhead the stars seem to withdraw until only one or two remain; and while he gazes at them they disappear. It is nearly dawn. There must be sunlight on the ocean to the east.

He gets to his feet, awkwardly, not certain that he will be able to stand. Having achieved this, he feels encouraged. He walks halfway to the house. Just then he hears the jingling of Mrs. Grunthe's alarm clock; it stops immediately, throttled by a brawny hand. She sleeps in a tidy room with the shades drawn, with a broom as a weapon posted beside her bed in the event of an amorous prowler. The question as to whether she would flail the intruder or merely sweep him right back out the window has yet to be resolved. Muhlbach, continuing his careful journey toward the house, smiles at the thought of Mrs. Grunthe; however, the smile is tentative. He feels himself to be a patient only now beginning to recover from an almost fatal accident. But given a few hours to get over the shock, and a good hot breakfast, he thinks he should improve.

All at once he stops. He looks at the periscope in the garden. It protrudes to a height of twenty-four inches, just as it is supposed to, a steel intake pipe, and there it stands among the dead leaves of autumn. On the ground beside it, no longer attached, lies the protective screen. Nearby is the little conical cap that makes the pipe resemble a water tower. The cap and the screen have been dismantled. The orifice of the air intake is plugged with a potato.

Muhlbach, even before he has reached the pipe and bent down to inspect it, fully understands, but cannot let himself believe the truth. There is a look of wonder on his face as he examines the potato. How forcefully it has been stuffed into the pipe! How absolutely it has sealed the shelter. One potato. Nothing more was needed. One potato.

He straightens up. He continues to gaze at the potato. There it sits, not quite half visible to the spectator, ensconced like a diadem in the spiky crown of an underworld deity, this fruit of the earth, seed of Pluto. One potato. Muhlbach, staring at it, cannot quite accept the fact. It is a trifle difficult to admit that someone undertook to murder you.

Who could have done such a thing? And why? As to the first, several names present themselves. Helen and Bob Chong. Absurd. Next, the Forsyths. Can one imagine them returning in the dead of night? Hardly. Eula? Mrs. Grunthe? But Muhlbach can proceed no further. He knows who has attempted to destroy him. There is no possibility of mistake. Why seek to blame the innocent? And yet, he thinks, just suppose—still not willing to acquiesce. Dark rivers rise inexplicably from the depths of the soul. It *could* have been Mrs. Grunthe, could it not? No. No, it could not. Her weapon is a broom, together with a vigorous tongue. But it

might have been Helen Chong. Yes, yes, it might have been.
No, it could not. Women, young and seductive, do not
murder for the sake of a concept, an abstraction; they kill
out of jealousy, from a nourished grievance, frustration,
fantasy, rage. It is not probable that the empress could have
become unbalanced over the cause of a somewhat academic,
fortyish gentleman who scarcely has spoken to her—has
spoken across a hedge, rake in hand, conscious of his paunch,
remarking on the weather. A pity, in fact. One might not
mind being assaulted by such a woman. Well, her husband,
then? Assuming a motive, however implausible, discretion
enters. This man is not a simpleton; he knows the consequence of imprudent acts, even when justified. He is far too
brilliant to risk his own destruction over a fancied cause.
Consider, then, the Forsyths. And Eula—with hopes of
marriage, Eula. Later, in disappointment, she might never
hesitate. But not now, not before the ceremony. Which
leaves only Margaret and Lewis. But why go on? If we
discount the unknown, that mysterious Mr. X so beloved of
trivial thrillers, there remain but two possibilities, both
children—a very little girl, very little indeed, and her elder
brother. The little girl has been in bed with fever. She is wan
and listless, dependent. She does not halfway comprehend
the structure buried in the back yard.

Muhlbach realizes that he is weeping. Tears are rolling
down his cheeks. He has not wept since—since when? And
now these tears, as though he were still a child! How odd!
He wipes his face on his pajama sleeve. He reprimands
himself. Be reasonable. There are no problems that do not
have solutions. The question to ask is not who, but why.
What could be simpler? Why? Why has this thing been
done? Let us choose to regard the individual as an abstract,
the Victim, of no significance. From this let us proceed,
objectively, as scientists. There is no crime without a motive.

Pragmatic, empirical, the contemporary man must inquire.

Having encouraged himself to take a few deep breaths, Muhlbach announces to himself that already he feels somewhat better. The tears are drying up. Once more he resembles a man. He will go into the house. If he should encounter Mrs. Grunthe—well, pretend that nothing is wrong. Truthfully, it may be that nothing is wrong. This problem can be solved; one need only ask logical questions in order to receive answers, which, if not rational, at least are instructive. Soon Otto will be awake. An explanation should be sought immediately.

Yes, of course. Logic. Questions, answers. Surely the boy cannot reject this age of reason.

Saint
Augustine's Pigeon

Too late loved I Thee, O Thou Beauty of ancient days, yet ever new! too late I loved Thee! And behold, Thou wert within, and I abroad, and there I searched for Thee! deformed I, plunging amid those fair forms which Thou hadst made . . .

Muhlbach closes the book sharply. How long must this continue? he asks of himself. Everywhere and always this theme recurs, spirit opposing flesh. I'd thought I would escape, but as Augustine would say, Alas! Yes, indeed, alas. Here am I dressed up for the twentieth century, affluent, reasonably affluent, stuffed with trivial comforts, with a home in a borough, two children, and my wife is dead. The pain of deprivation subsides neither more nor less quickly, I suspect, for me than it did for him; and the body's flesh does not care for sentiment more now than in past millenniums, conscious only that it has been deprived. What is more selfish than the body's appetite?

He taps the book with his index finger, a bit didactically, and puts it on the shelf. Rising from the depths of his green leather reading chair, he walks to the window; there he stands for a long time with a meditative and dissatisfied expression. From across the river Manhattan confronts him.

It's possible, he says aloud, that I ought to acquire a

mistress. I've said to myself that I should live moderately, which I have done, but too long. My spirit is suffocating. I've all but forgotten the taste of pleasure. It's as though I'd eaten plain bread for a year. What is ordinarily sweet and natural to other men seems as exotic to me as frangipani or a glimpse of Zanzibar. My senses are withering. My finger tips have memorized only the touch of paper. I need to court an Indian dancer with bells strung to her ankles, I need to go out shooting tigers, smoke hashish, explore the Himalayas. God knows what I need.

He turns from the window and looks critically at the room where he spends so much time. It is a comfortable room, this study he has established, a sanctuary, a rectory filled with books, a few photographs, records, a humidor, the substantial chair — yes, and it has become odious.

Muhlbach suddenly clasps his hands as though he were about to drop to his knees before an idol and offer up some passionate supplication. There are times a man must liberate his soul, otherwise he's in for trouble.

If I do not, he says, but persist in guiding my life, the reins of it beneath my thumb — well, who knows? It is not moderate or reasonable to live as immoderately as a demented anchorite plucking thistles for a shirt, suffering voluptuous hallucinations. A woman could save me from myself. And surely it should not be difficult to find one, not if I proceed logically.

Just then Mrs. Grunthe, that paragon, that archetype of sense and logic, brusquely raps at the study door.

Eight o'clock. Supper's on the table.

Whereupon she departs, muttering. But Mrs. Grunthe always mutters, whether the day has been good or bad. The plink of mandolins sounds no different to her than the crash of lightning; in fact it would be alarming, thinks Mulbach, if her disposition improved.

Eight o'clock, he says softly. I'm sure it is. Exactly eight. This, too, is my own doing. How many times has Mrs. Grunthe laid out supper at eight? The hour does suit me, the emanations of the day are gone, it all seems natural. The children are ravenous by six and I'm never home by then, so we eat separately. It's as though I have no family any more. Yes, I'm exiled from delight, he thinks, opening the study door.

And what do we have for supper? Chicken à la king with peas. Hardly a banquet. Mrs. Grunthe for some reason likes to prepare chicken à la king. We have it too often, I wonder if I should let her know. The problem is, she's not good at taking hints. What was last night's supper? He pauses, napkin half unfolded, and tries to remember what he was given to eat twenty-four hours ago, but cannot.

I believe I'll have a little wine, Mrs. Grunthe.

This isn't Sunday, she answers, Sunday being the day he is in the habit of opening a small bottle; nevertheless she plods off to fetch it.

This isn't Sunday, he remarks when she's out of hearing. Has my life sunk to such a pattern? I ask for a bottle of wine on Saturday night and my housekeeper comments. She may even tell her friends about this strange occurrence. Next thing you know, Bertha, he'll take to drinking on Monday and Tuesday and Wednesday and every other blessed day of the week. You can go a long way to hell with little steps.

And furthermore, Mulbach announces silently when she re-enters with the wine, I intend to go to hell, Mrs. Grunthe — very quickly, if I may say so. I'm planning to catch myself a little something, Mrs. Grunthe. What d'you think of that, eh?

Will you be wanting anything else?

Muhlbach is startled. The wine, of course, that's what she means. Will I be making any other odd demands, that's all.

She wasn't reading my mind. And he is tempted to ask: Why? Are you going out? For a moment the thought has come to him that Mrs. Grunthe is about to take a lover. She's going to slip away from the kitchen and run barefoot through the night, one hundred and eighty pounds of nymph, to the eager arms of Salvador, the mechanic. Salvador has been seen drinking coffee in the kitchen when he should have been flat on his back on a dolly beneath an automobile at Sunbeam Motors; God knows what intrigue has been prepared.

No, no, nothing else, Mrs. Grunthe. How are the children?

Both quiet. Donna's gone to sleep. Otto is in his room building a model airplane.

That's fine. Oh, by the way, Mrs. Grunthe, I'll be going to the city for a little while this evening.

No response.

Muhlbach feels a trifle let-down; after all, when one is setting out to discover a mistress, and gives a hint, it's justifiable to expect some curiosity. He pushes his fork at the creamed chicken and eats without appetite. It is not the stomach that's hungry.

When he has finished eating he doesn't linger with a cigarette but immediately goes upstairs to Donna's room. She is thoroughly asleep, too beautiful to be real. No doubt she is dreaming of princes and castles and white horses with flowing manes.

Otto in his room is just as quiet; he is gluing an insignia on the airplane and cannot be distracted by much conversation.

I'll be going out for a while, Otto.

Okay, says Otto.

I won't be late. If you want anything, Mrs. Grunthe will be here.

Okay, I know it, says Otto.

Incidentally, have you finished your homework?

At this Otto looks bemused, as though he has never heard of any such thing.

Speak up. Is it done?

Practically, says Otto, and quickly adds that he can do it tomorrow. But the rule is that he does his weekend homework on Saturday because he tends to disappear on Sunday.

I think, says Muhlbach, you'd better do it now. A short, fierce, querulous discussion follows, which ends with Otto sighing heavily.

Okay, but it's nothing except some stupid decimals and junk that any moron could do with one hand tied behind him.

In that case, my friend, if you are such a mathematical prodigy, why did your last report card show a C minus in arithmetic?

But to this there is no answer. Muhlbach does not insist. The horse has been flogged enough. Otto is on his feet with a gloomy expression rummaging about for a textbook.

So the house is in order, the inhabitants making their usual rounds, and Muhlbach considers himself free to do what he pleases. He heads for the shower, thoughtfully, fingering his bald spot. I'm going out to attract a woman, he thinks, and not by the use of my wallet; that may not be easy, I do look a bit professorial, but still it's true that women aren't so fussy about appearances as we are. And I'm not ugly, it's just that I look uncommunicative, as though I had a briefcase full of government secrets. I wish I didn't always look so stiff, but what can I do? Maybe I should try to smile more often, my teeth aren't bad. Well—step up, ladies! One insurance expert in average health, slightly bald, slightly soft at the hip, more perceptive than most, but also more constrained than most, seeks passionate and exotic companion between ages of eighteen and—now really, let's not be absurd! Begin again. Between ages of twenty, no, twenty-three, for instance, and, ah, thirty-five. Thirty. Twenty-six. Must be, ah, sophisticated and, umm, discreet. Abandoned. Lascivious. Dissolute. The more dissolute the better. Everything that I am not but would like so much to be. A young lady experienced in each conceivable depravity, totally intemperate, unbuttoned, debauched, gluttonous, uncorked, crapulous, self-indulgent, drunken and preferably insatiable. Never mind if it is an adolescent dream, never mind. There may be no such woman this side of Singapore, but I won't settle for less. Not for a little while. What about Eula?

Thank you, I believe not, he says to himself in the mirror, cautiously parting his hair and frowning. Eula Cunningham is comfortable as a pillow is comfortable, which at times is quite enough, but sometimes is not. Eula is yesterday's bouquet. Eula is a loaf of bread, unleavened and thirty-eight years old, if I'm any judge. Thirty-two, she claims. Maybe. She gives me the feeling of thirty-eight. I don't say she's stale or hard, no, no, it's just that she's like any domestic beast, or a geranium on the window sill, and let the metaphors fly where they choose.

Straightening up, he draws a long breath and studies his chest. It is not impressive. He exhales. No, it is not impressive at all.

He turns the shower handle, tests the water with one hand, shivers and wraps a towel about his pale shoulders. There he stands meditatively naked, curling his toes into the fluffy blue rug while he waits, a sight to inspire terror in nobody, the image of no feminine dream. He thinks again of Eula. Madame Everyday, that's what she is. Eula has the instincts of Mrs. Grunthe and fifty million others. Proper sisters, all of them. Eula won't be pinning an orchid in her hair or shimmying across the room, not now, not ever, because she never has, because it would attract attention, would be rather flamboyant, cause eyebrows to lift. She won't fly away to Las Vegas to play roulette, she won't practice the Lotus position. She is, in fact, just like me, reason enough to catch a cat of another color.

Muhlbach flings away his towel and thrusts himself beneath the shower as though he were plunging into a waterfall.

Mrs. Grunthe is downstairs waiting, arms folded, when he descends. Miss Cunningham has telephoned. What about? Mrs. Grunthe didn't ask, obviously doesn't care. I'm expected to call, he thinks, Eula's hoping I'll return that call, but I won't. I have other plans. Tonight I hope for the taste of Hell.

Good night, Mrs. Grunthe. If Miss Cunningham calls again, you can say that I'll get in touch with her soon.

Ten minutes later, underground and attached to a metal loop, it seems that he is already halfway to Hell. Rocking through the tunnel, he reflects once again that the professional aestheticians have been wrong, utility does not equal beauty. Some opposite dictum may lie closer to the truth. What is most useless or inefficient, say, is most appealing. What is more wasteful and extravagant, for example, than that epitome of sexual allure known as the chorus girl? But again, how is sex identified with beauty? It's a knotty problem.

Emerging from the subway, he sees just ahead, or thinks he does, a familiar profile. It's difficult to be positive, the crowd is gathering, shoving through the turnstile, and she is gone. He hurries a few steps further, stands on tiptoe, looks and looks, then turns around, searching every ramp, but she's disappeared. He goes to the phone booth.

Yes, she's listed in the book. In fact, she is listed twice. Blanche Baron on East Seventy-third, Blanche Baron on MacDougal Street. Which Blanche is real? Which is the red-haired Blanche with the poise of a lacquered mannequin whose husband killed himself? Chances are that she would not be living on MacDougal, not with her taste for elegance. He studies the number on Seventy-third. Here is the opportunity. Of course, the opportunity is not new; it is just that he's never thought of calling her, she has seemed so Continental and gelid, distant and expensive and bathed in rumor, a mistress of shadows. She is a figure in a French novel and he could not visualize himself with her. She must think of him — if ever she does think of him — as an office grub who has yet to recognize the exceptional perfumes of life. Persuading a woman that she has been mistaken can be a tedious process. Muhlbach hesitates.

If it was indeed Blanche getting off the subway, then *ipso facto* she can't be at home and therefore to call her now would be a waste of time. On the other hand, she probably doesn't ride the subway, ever. She might be home. Still, it's Saturday night, very unlikely that she's there, she's more apt to be at somebody's penthouse.

He cannot make up his mind. But then suddenly he puts a dime in the slot and dials. The telephone rings just twice. A male voice answers.

I think there must be some mistake, says Muhlbach. What number do I have?

The voice reads off the number he has dialed.

I'm calling Blanche Baron. Is she at home?

The voice asks who is calling Blanche.

It occurs to Muhlbach that this would be a good point at which to hang up. Something is wrong. If a man answers, hang up, that's the classic advice. But it has never happened to him — he has never called a woman without knowing the circumstances — and he finds that the idea of simply hanging up the receiver is both rude and cowardly. It smacks of being in some woman's home and dashing out the back door while the husband comes in the front. It's a bit farcical. He wants no part of it. Blanche is single, so far as he knows, a widow with whom he is acquainted and whom he has every right to call. He cannot bring himself to hang up, although he is certain that he has the correct number and also that Blanche's situation has changed. That male voice has such a proprietary sound.

He introduces himself to the unknown, explaining that he is acquainted with Blanche. Then he listens, expecting a congenial response, and hears nothing but hoarse breathing.

Is this by any chance her husband? he inquires, for it's possible that she has remarried.

The owner of the voice evidently is too confused or annoyed to speak. The receiver at the other end of the line is clumsily dropped in its cradle; Muhlbach, at once a little surprised but yet not too surprised by this treatment, is left holding a dead instrument. He feels insulted by such tactlessness and for a few moments does not hang up. However, there's nothing else to do. Nor would there be much point in calling again. Does Blanche have a new husband or a lover? He suspects it is the latter, and this is oddly gratifying. All right, she has found someone, so will he.

Out of the phone booth, he pauses to settle his hat and straighten his tie before the mirror of a chewing gum machine, then briskly walks up the steps toward the surface world. Blanche might not have been an appropriate mistress in any case. Probably she wouldn't. It's just as well. He feels a bit relieved. Talking to her could have been quite awkward; no doubt she would have thought he was calling in regard to her policy. And for a woman she's tall, close to being a flagpole. She's graceful and sensuous, true, her movements are feline — she knows what men are all about. Isn't it a pity that this experience couldn't be housed in the satin corpulence of Eula Cunningham — that amiable Venus

of Willendorf, steatopygous as an Upper Paleolithic figure.
Now there would be a woman, thinks Muhlbach, there
would be something!

Exactly what sort of a mistress should a man have? The
possibilities are infinite. A ballet mouse, agile and quiet and
seldom noticed? Or a more heroic piece of goods? One of
the great madams, say, regal and unforgettable, with a cold
eye and a bank account and scattered parcels of real estate,
supporting her amplitude behind black corsets like a formidable gift from faraway provinces. Or an actress dressed up
in hats and veils. A society girl?—somebody you could
introduce to senators. Well, he thinks, who or what's waiting for me? My shoes are polished and there's money in my
pocket. Not a great amount, but enough for tonight. I'm
ready for adventure. Now, let's see, where shall I find it?

He stops walking and looks around, for it occurs to him
that he doesn't have a plan in mind and has allowed himself
to be carried half a block by the crowd. Well, the logical
place to begin hunting for an available woman is in the
middle of town, is it not? Yes, all right. What happens next?

I'm going in this direction because of the people alongside me, he reflects, but this is foolish. Suppose I work my
way into the contrary stream, where will that lead me? What
should I do? I ought to do something, I ought to make a
positive gesture. Take the ferry to Staten Island? That
doesn't seem appropriate; if I should meet a strange woman
on the ferry she'd be apt to have a book tucked under her
arm. She'd wear spectacles and her hair would be a tidy bun.
No, no, I've come to Carthage for the sizzling and frying of
unholy love. I won't go to Staten Island.

He studies a billboard advertising a musical comedy on
which there is a chorus girl fifteen feet tall. The corner of the
billboard is streaked with birdlime. This does not add to her
appeal, but it can be overlooked. What sort of mistress

would she make? Avaricious she is, there's that look in her wickedly tilted eye. But also there's little doubt that she is passionate, probably given to illegal practices. This, he thinks, is the sort of woman I'm after, the question being merely how she's obtained. Must I buy ticket after ticket to the same seat and sit through this absurd entertainment for God knows how many weeks until she can't help but notice me? Is she worth all that? Six dollars for each performance. It would cost a hundred dollars before she so much as recognized my face.

If not a chorus girl, what? A cigarette girl, possibly. That would not be so glamorous, but after all I won't be taking her to Sun Valley or the Riviera where she would need to be introduced. And philosophers tell us that one's like another, attraction is where we find it. What about a model? A Tintoretto creature living in a cold-water flat, whose friends are intellectual and consumptive? That might be stimulating, a substitute for the youth in Paris that I never had. It's not too late. I'm just past forty, and artists and their kind are notoriously indifferent to age, among other things. Yes, that might do. Well now, I could pay a visit to Washington Square and see what's going on. I don't want a receptionist or a secretary or a teacher or a female executive or Eula Cunningham. What I require is something in spangled tights — a cocktail waitress, for example, who works at some extraordinary place with a shadowy reputation, where they ring a bell and girls come sliding down a fireman's pole. That sort of thing. Something on that order. Yes, or a flamenco dancer from Valencia.

Where does one meet these women? They exist, one sees them on the stage, sees their pictures in magazines or in the Sunday supplement as a result of some affair under the most bizzare circumstances, hears of them having leapt naked into the Tivoli fountain. But otherwise, where are they concealed? Why are they not more available? Are there not enough of them to go around? Do they live secluded in Hollywood harems and in Fifth Avenue apartments with gold plumbing? Occasionally one does see them on the street near the entrance to Saks, say, or in the lobby of an elegant hotel. But they are unapproachable. They are guarded by watchful eyes, by the very mystique of their existence. They are not for the man who works conscientiously in his office at Metro Mutual, now and then removing his glasses to pinch the bridge of his nose and wonder where life has gone. They are not for him, they are not seen with men who carry briefcases and who ride the subway hopefully reading the *Wall Street Journal* for news that a moderate investment is prospering.

I have forty-five shares of General Motors, says Muhlbach to himself, and I have sixty — thanks to the split — of Allied Potash, plus several bits of this-and-that. It's a tidy egg, for years I've watched it hatching, but there's a certain type of woman who'd gobble it up. I must remind myself to be careful. Yes, I'll be cautious.

It seems to him that already he has compromised his security, and quite possibly Mrs. Grunthe suspects him of squandering funds that must be kept safe for Otto and Donna. But Mrs. Grunthe, he reflects, has assumed more significance than she deserves. A housekeeper she is, that's all, yet she functions like a guardian of virtue, implacable, honest, devout in her brutal Anglo-Nordic way, and a terror to every spot of grease, every germ that seeks to invade the house. Mrs. Grunthe is priceless, of course, but her rectitude is stifling. No doubt the germs expire as much from guilt as from the incessant and terrible roar of Mrs. Grunthe's vacuum cleaner.

It occurs to Muhlbach that he needs a drink. At home he customarily has a daiquiri before supper, and because he did not have one this evening he thinks he will have it now. There is a nice place that he remembers on Lexington so he turns in that direction, and presently is seated at the bar with the daiquiri between his fingers. The place is busier than he remembered, he has not been here for almost a year, and it has been remodeled. He observes the comings and goings through a gilded mirror and sips his drink. Then, because nobody is looking at him, he has a look at himself. It is luxury for a man to gaze at himself in public; women are allowed the privilege, men are ridiculed. Well, he decides, women are also ridiculed, but with affection. There's a difference.

He glances from side to side. Nobody's noticed, so he continues to study the image in the mirror: it appears to be that of a man who is either ill or exhausted. The lips are compressed. The eyebrows lean toward each other. And at this moment, Muhlbach thinks, I could not possibly smile. My head feels molded, each feature set. I do believe I'm made of papier-mâché.

Just then two Hollywood people walk directly behind him and are ushered to a table. The woman's face and body are recognizable, although he cannot recall her name and does not think he has ever seen one of her movies. She is wearing a white leather trench coat open halfway to the navel and may not be wearing anything else. Of course it's impossible not to stare at her and inevitably their eyes meet. She looks at him boldly, for so long that he feels the blood rising to his face and is relieved when she looks away. Was there some meaning to this look? Can it be that she is tired of the pudgy director or producer, or whatever he is, and has issued a discreet invitation? Could it happen?

Muhlbach again stares into the mirror; the actress obviously is bored, she is yawning. Her lips are tinted not red but white, and have been outlined with a pencil; there is something inordinately sensual about this, the hollow of her mouth is suggestive.

She is offered a cigarette. She leans forward, the leather coat bulges, parts at the breast, two broad soft globes of flesh come pouring into view and rise slowly rather like poached eggs against each other. Down that phenomenal bosom the crease deepens and lengthens until, thinks Muhlbach, one could mail a letter in the slot.

Desperately he watches her preposterous body. She is not amusing, however ludicrous. Grotesque she may be, but amusing she is not; only fools, hermaphrodites and jealous women pretend to find her so.

Quickly he steps down from the bar stool and avoids glancing at her while he makes his way to the street. She will have nothing to do with him; if she stared at him with such insolence and challenge it was merely what she had taught herself to do; she would return any man's gaze.

But what he has seen cannot be forgotten and he strides along angrily, sober and baffled. It seems to him unjust, unjust that he must spend his life and energy among women such as Eula, ordinary women — unimaginative, average, modest women. It is not right. He feels obscurely cheated; it seems to him that if he were given the chance he could prove himself with the half-mad actress in a way that he has never proved himself before. He clenches his fists, halted by a red light at the corner.

Indemnities, cordial handshakes, briefcases, promises, raincoats, percentages, statistics, a drink before supper — too many years of it, too many years, he thinks bitterly, and discovers that he is walking along Fifth Avenue. There's a bus approaching; he realizes that he has been intending to get on this bus and go to the Village. All right, why not? He has not been to the Village in years.

He rides down the avenue with a fixed, irritable expression. He sees nothing. He does not know who is sitting next to him. He thinks again of the actress, of her flesh and the white leather coat. He has been on the periphery of another kind of existence, one infinitely more exciting, one that he is not privileged to share. He has not enough money to buy himself into it, does not have any creative talents that might win a place for him, nor friends who already belong. He is excluded, he can come no closer to this actress than imagination will take him; it is no good saying to himself that she is stupid and vain, that within a decade she will be meaningless. It is dry comfort every night to turn a book's thin pages.

He is surprised that the bus has stopped. The driver is looking at him strangely. Everybody else has gotten off.

Muhlbach steps down and brushes against a young girl in black leotards and a turtleneck sweater who is dismounting from a motor scooter.

Alors, she cries, *prenez garde, s'il vous plâit!* But the accent is American.

I'm sorry, says Muhlbach, I should have watched where I was going.

Just then an odd-looking youth appears, dressed in a cape and a plumed hat, takes the motor scooter and wheels it away; apparently it belongs to him and she had borrowed it for a ride around the square.

Sale cochon! exclaims the girl, snapping her fingers at Muhlbach.

He looks down at her with annoyance. The insult is nothing, the fatuous expression of youth, but he is irked by her pretense. She's not French, he doubts that she has been farther from home than the Cloisters. She is not more than seventeen, undeveloped, with delicate rebellious features. On her flat breast hangs a chunk of turquoise at the end of a leather thong. Very well, she has chosen to play at being what she is not, so will he.

Et vous-même, ma petite? Est-ce-que vous êtes si propre? he answers crisply, gratified that he has not forgotten everything learned in school. He sees at once that she is startled; her assumption had been that he would not understand. Now she gazes at him respectfully and he guesses that she has exhausted her knowledge of French. Her Village sophistication is badly torn, she may be even younger than she looks.

Are you a Frenchman? she asks, a bit derisively; but it's plain that she wants to know. She wants to believe that he is. She wants to believe that he has just arrived from Paris.

I'm twice as French as you, says Muhlbach.

Dad, you're too much! she replies, suddenly at ease. I mean, like, you're making the scene!

Muhlbach flinches slightly at being called Dad. It's true there's considerable difference in their ages. Well, it is true that chronologically he might be her father, but still she shouldn't call him that.

As a matter of fact, yes, says Muhlbach, since you put it in those terms, I am making the scene.

Well, dig, dig, Daddy. I mean, go!

This doesn't make sense. Is she suggesting that he leave, or what? Maybe she's wishing him a pleasant evening.

Comment t'appelle? he inquires.

Je m'appelle Rouge, she grins. Too much, Pop! You're the most!

Rouge? That can't be your name.

She shrugs, very French. That's the bit. You want to paint the top, I'm Rouge.

Is this an invitation? What does she mean?

Rouge settles the question. You got some wherewithal? I mean, that is, you want to stand this chick to a little spread, let's make it. I mean, *por exemplo,* they chop the grooviest cheesecake at the Queen's Bishop, dig?

Fine, says Muhlbach. She means to take him somewhere. He will be expected to buy her a piece of cheesecake. All right, fine, why not? He feels exhilarated. He is being picked up. A tough little Bohemian in Greenwich Village has picked him up. For the first time since leaving the house he smiles. Let's go, Rouge, lead the way. Take me to the Queen's Bishop, whatever and wherever it is. I'll buy you a wedge of cheesecake, Rouge, I'll buy you the whole pie if you want it.

Across the square they go. Muhlbach glances at each passerby to discover whether or not he is making a fool of himself, meanwhile half listening to Rouge, who's more talkative than he suspected. He cannot understand everything she says; she speaks an ephemeral dialect. If he could recall the patois of his own youth, which at the moment he cannot, would she comprehend? He thinks that when they are settled in the Queen's Bishop he will try to remember a few expressions and will try them on her.

The Queen's Bishop, what sort of place could that be? And then, as they walk by the last benches in the park he notices the chess tables. Of course! Coffee, cheesecake, sandwiches, interminable discussions about God, Communism, Art, Free Love, and a chessboard for the asking. That's the sort of place it will be.

Rouge, talking enthusiastically, as though they had known each other for at least a week, leads him down one street and up another and finally down a flight of worn stone steps to a basement with a brightly painted door.

In they go, and the emporium is quieter than he'd anticipated. There are no loud discussions, no arguments. It's like a library with everyone bent over chessboards instead of books. There's an Italian coffee urn on the counter, a case of pastries, a door leading into what appears to be a little kitchen, travel posters on the wall, and the proprietor — a dwarf wearing an apron and a checkered vest — carefully sweeping the floor with a broom taller than himself.

Bonsoir, Rouge, says the dwarf, grinning.

Bonsoir, Pierre, says Rouge.

Good evening, says Muhlbach, and takes off his hat.

Monsieur, the dwarf replies courteously, but goes on sweeping the floor.

So, the Queen's Bishop is very much as I guessed, he thinks, pleased with himself; and though he is not hungry he joins Rouge in a slice of cheesecake — which is, as she claimed, delicious. He tells her so.

The most, Pop.

Muhlbach looks about the Queen's Bishop and wishes that he had not worn his business suit. With an old pair of slacks and a sweater he wouldn't feel so out of place; he might even have passed for an artist. But it's too late now, and if Rouge does find his suit rather bourgeois she has not yet commented on it. Anyway, this is the Village where unnatural couples are common enough.

How about a game? he asks.

She hesitates, glances narrowly across the table at him, and Muhlbach's heart beats heavily. What has he said? Does "a game" have special significance?

Man, says Rouge, nobody's going to believe this! You mean you really cross the board? What I mean is, like, I tell myself this cat's flaky, dig? I mean, you pulling me around?

I'm not a bad player, Muhlbach answers. How about it?

Oh, ah! says Rouge, making a face, you are just the rookiest! You're greater than pot!

Yes, she's very young indeed; but it seems that she is willing to play chess, at least she has not said anything altogether negative, so he signals for the dwarf, who brings over a board and a cigar box filled with chessmen.

The game's not free, however. Thirty cents per hour, per

player. Muhlbach pays, amused. One hour with Rouge for sixty cents, change that one might leave for the bartender uptown. Has he ever found a better bargain?

He takes a pawn in either hand, shuffles them, holds out his fists side by side, and Rouge taps one.

White.

She arranges the white pieces while Muhlbach, having glanced about the Queen's Bishop and found no one watching, begins to set up the black.

Rouge opens King Knight to Rook 3.

Highly unorthodox. What has she in mind? He bends his attention to the board, fingers in a steeple.

Hey wow! she whispers. Great claws!

He discovers that she is staring with admiration at his hands. They are strong, neat, graceful hands; he is proud of them and has himself often looked at them and thought that he should have become a surgeon. These sensitive hands of his seem wasted when they have nothing more to do than shuffle papers, zip and unzip a briefcase, button a stiff white collar. Yes, it's a waste. They're the hands of an artist, of a musician, of a philosopher.

You do tricks? she asks, and he realizes that, incredibly, she is wondering if he is a magician. A magician! If only I were, Rouge, if only I were.

I sell insurance, fire insurance mostly, he says, and waits.

Too much, she answers.

Muhlbach opens his defense with pawn to King 4.

That figures, she remarks, nodding.

Does she know me so well? he wonders. Am I that conservative? He's tempted to recover the pawn and start again, but too late. She moves quickly, Queen Knight to Rook 3, and Muhlbach stares at the board. What's the significance of this curious ploy? An expert counterattack would make short work of such a beginning; its weakness will soon be quite evident. But he hopes that she will somehow strengthen her position. He is indifferent to winning or losing, so long as the game lasts—it's playing with her that counts; and while he pretends to concentrate on the board he imagines a crumbling apartment on Bleeker Street where roaches climb up and down the rusty pipes and the odor of gas seeps from a blackened stove, and the blankets on a sagging iron bed are worn through and frayed. Late Sunday morning, he thinks, we'd have orange juice, coffee, and croissants, if that would please her. Read the *Times,* listen to Mozart. If I seem elderly and repugnant, Rouge, I'll give you a present.

She has moved again; he answers.

The game proceeds, pieces deploy, are taken and dropped in the cigar box. But Muhlbach does not play with much enthusiasm. He is depressed by lecherous fantasies of Rouge; and that she resembles his niece is mortifying. Furtively he stares at her. She doesn't notice. She squints and glares at the board, savagely gnawing her lips.

He has felt, meanwhile, crawling over and around his feet, a small living object that demands attention. Rouge's foot? Could that be? With infinite tact beneath the table, concealed from the rude eyes of other chess players, has she sought him out? Her little foot, slipped loose from its sandal, creeps across his shoe, rubs affectionately against his ankle. He feels a gentle tug at his trousers, deft and knowledgeable, not the blind, clumsy tug of a human foot— there's a beast down below! He bends down to look. There is a hamster nibbling at his cuff.

Does this belong to you? he asks.

Rouge doesn't answer. One of her pawns is threatened.

Go away, whispers Muhlbach, go away, go away, you silly animal! and he nudges the hamster, which pays no attention. He discovers that it has eaten a series of little holes in his cuff.

Queen, says Rouge thoughfully. *En garde,* Pops.

Muhlbach surveys the board. The attack is obvious, has been so for the past six moves. Check, he replies, a bit reluctantly because he doesn't want the game to end; but she has obliged him to close the trap. He leans down again and pulls the hamster off his foot, worried that he may receive a nasty bite, but the hamster patiently returns to its task. Muhlbach hisses at it, thinking that perhaps it is frightened of cats. But the hamster with beady eyes fixed on his trousers cannot be alarmed.

With a sigh Muhlbach returns his attention to the game. The cuff already is ruined, another few holes won't make much difference. He tries to ignore the gentle weight on his foot and the soft, persistent tugs. If only I had a piece of lettuce, he thinks; and says aloud to Rouge as he moves a pawn, Check. And, I'm afraid, Mate.

She doesn't give up. She has one move left, that's true. It's inconsequential, a bit embarrassing. She should have the grace not to insist on making it, but she does, she retreats grimly. He realizes for the first time that this game has meant something to her; it must have been important that she defeat him. Well, it's too late. He can't possibly lose, there's just no way to lose, none at all. He searches the board. Perhaps he could pretend that he was working on a more intricate and aesthetically satisfying Mate and thus justify the forfeit of a piece.

He looks up, aware of two spectators. They have come out of nowhere and now stand one on either side of the table, ragged and solemn, the natural companions of Rouge. One is the boy who owns the motor scooter, still wearing his cape and plumed hat, and smoking a stogie. The other, who appears to be about Muhlbach's age or a little older, is a bearded Negro with a beret and a snaggly grin. Why are they here?

Muhlbach cautiously picks up the enemy bishop, replacing it with his own. There's no need to speak. Rouge looks at him for just an instant, she is cold with rage. He attempts to smile; he feels guilty.

Cha-boom! murmurs the Negro.

The boy in the plumed hat removes his stogie and puffs a row of tiny smoke rings.

Thank you for the game, Rouge, says Muhlbach.

Oh, rookie, Dad, rookie. Cool the crap.

Cha-cha-cha! exclaims the Negro. Ba-zoom-ba!

Rouge, still peeved, introduces the visitors. They are named Quinet and Meatbowl. It seems they would like to sit down; in fact, without being asked, they do, and Muhlbach finds three pairs of eyes trained on him. Something is now expected of him. What can it be? He looks from one to the other. Quinet clears his throat and inspects that magnificent cigar. The Negro, who is humming and tapping his fingers on the table, does not once remove his gaze from Muhlbach. Nor does Rouge. They're waiting. But for what?

Muhlbach begins to feel uncomfortable. After a few moments he takes off his glasses, wipes them with his handkerchief, holds them up to the light, carefully hooks them on again. It is almost as though he were being initiated.

Perhaps — could it be? Has he been accepted? The defeat of Rouge might be significant. Yes, now that he thinks it over, no one in the Queen's Bishop paid the slightest attention until the end of the game was near, until it was plain that Rouge couldn't win. It was only then, he recalls, that a few heads began turning their direction. Everyone in this place must be acquainted, they come here every night and have learned to communicate with each other as mysteriously as bees or ants; they've known what was going on. Rouge isn't a good chess player yet she must hold some position of authority here and I've made a spot for myself by defeating her! For a moment he imagines himself coming to the Queen's Bishop night after night, growing bolder, being less concerned with appearances, imagines himself in a beret and a suède jacket, with a mustache and goatee, saluting Quinet and Meatbowl and Pierre with casual familiarity.

Muhlbach realizes that he is smiling, first at Rouge, then at her two rococo companions, for no reason except that they have welcomed him to the sanctuary of the Queen's Bishop. It is flattering, really. Do these people care about his business, his habits, his background, whether or not he has money? No. No, they are interested in him for himself alone.

He sees that Meatbowl is grinning; Quinet grins, too, if not as pleasantly. Just then Pierre arrives, his head on a level with the table. Pierre is carrying a dented aluminum tray on which there are four large bowls of minestrone and some crackers. Obviously this is the rite, the moment when he becomes a catechumen. Now they are to break bread. Muhlbach feels powerfully moved; he feels within himself something that he has virtually forgotten—a flow of love toward his fellow man. And that he should have rediscovered this community at such a humble crossroads! His eyes are moist with tears; he is tempted to reach over the table to take Meatbowl and Quinet by the hand. It is all so unexpected.

He blinks, looks down at the steaming minestrone. He is not hungry, and as a matter of fact the minestrone does have a doughy appearance, but he will eat it and love it because this soup is symbolic.

When he lifts his head he finds the dwarf standing at his side, gazing at him attentively with one hand outstretched, palm up, ready to be crossed with silver.

The silence is profound. Every chess game has stopped.

At this instant many things become clear to Muhlbach, just as chemicals in a beaker of liquid turn instantaneously to one great glittering shard of crystal. Life is as it is, not as man wishes it to be. He has entered this house, which is not his own, which he had no prerogative to enter, and has been promptly recognized. I've been false, he thinks, and they have known it from the first. They knew me before I knew myself.

Now he is docked for this audacity, for having intruded. Now he must pay.

The dwarf is waiting.

No one speaks. Muhlbach wonders how he could have been so stripped of sensitivity. He, alone, is out of place. Even that old man in the corner who has not said a word to anyone, but has sat motionless with a tattered overcoat buttoned up to his chin and speckled arthritic hands folded over a cane — that old man belongs to the Queen's Bishop. The gangling boy in denim work clothes and flowered cowboy boots who is sipping coffee at the bar, with a guitar case at his feet — he is part of it. The fat girl in a mumu who is absently reading a newspaper and scratching herself — she is welcome here. Even the two lesbians with crisp silvered hair and masculine suits, withdrawn, hostile, frightened — yes, they are made to feel at home here, they are given refuge from the terror and confusion of the outer world. Why am I different? he wonders. Why am I not welcome? Why is it that I represent the enemy? What do these disparate people communally own that I do not share? Is it poverty? No. That must be subsidiary, it's not the principal. These people are like odd patches on a quilt, how curious they won't accept another. Well, what do I stand for? A nation's hypocrisy? The tribes of Philistia? Can they despise me as an individual because I am dressed like a bureaucrat? Am I the corporation executive gorged on stolen figs who never serves a sentence? Is it not hurtful to be accused by outcasts?

So his thoughts chase each other over and under with the alacrity of tigers in a circus.

And she has signaled these two — Quinet and Meatbowl, he thinks angrily. That leaves the sourest taste. The question now is whether to accept the imposition and pay for everybody's minestrone, or not. To do so is to avoid embarrassment, but at the same time to acknowledge a personal ignominy. Either way, I lose. If I object and complain that I've been taken for granted, if I point out that no one consulted me, say to the dwarf what he knows perfectly well — that he and they are in league to pluck me cleaner than a squab, just as they've plucked other innocents, no doubt — if I do raise my voice, what's gained? What's to be saved? Well, two dollars, but what else? Self-respect? Is this a thing that strangers are qualified to evaluate?

He looks at the dwarf's untrembling hand, the right hand of iniquity. In the Tenth Book of Augustine it is written that our fellow citizens must be also our fellow pilgrims — those who have walked before equally with those that are on the road beside us, and with those that shall come after us. We are meant to serve them, if we elect to live in the sight of God; to them we are meant to demonstrate not what we have been, but what we are and continue to be. But neither are we to judge ourselves.

Muhlbach reaches for his wallet.

Oh, Daddy, says Rouge, this gruel's the greatest. Quinet nods approvingly. The Judas kiss. Ba-boom-boom! says the feeble-minded Negro.

All of them are sure. They never doubt.

And when they have finished spooning up the soup, when the last noodle has disappeared, the final bean devoured, without one further word they get to their feet and go. He is left to reign over the table, over four bowls — three of them as empty as the day they were lifted from the potter's wheel—four bowls and the mock ivory pieces of a lengthy intellectual triumph. The flesh—the flesh he coveted—is gone. Everything considered, it's been not unlike a vision in the desert.

Tell me, what's your name? he hears himself inquire again. Not Rouge, what's your Christian name?

That's it, she seems to say. Like what else is there, you know? A chick's got a short time and then it's night, you dig? So, like, express it uptown, Pop, because you and me, we beat a different skin.

But are not the senses of our bodies mutual, he wonders, recalling Saint Augustine, or is the sense of my flesh mine, and the sense of your flesh yours? If we are not the same, how could I perceive all that I do, even though we have our separate organs?

Muhlbach disconsolately picks at the flaking table. His strength is gone. If he were at home he would fall into bed exhausted. How long he sits at the table he does not know. When he walks out of the Queen's Bishop no one looks up.

A warm wind is blowing through the trees. An ice cream vendor waits at the corner. An artist who paints bucolic scenes on colored velvet stands hopefully beside his merchandise in the light of a theater marquee and the reflections from a thousand automobiles.

Muhlbach sits down on a bench in Washington Square. Through the arch he sees the flow of traffic. He hears, as though from a considerable distance, the noise of the city. He feels slightly chilled, as though he had been without food all day. It is a weakness of privation, abstinence that chills to the bone. The sickness is deep. It will pass, of course, and it's not fatal. Yet the cure is absurdly simple. The body of a woman, that is all. That is all.

I'm both parts of a man, he reflects, body and soul. I think that the interior of me is the better, but it is also the weaker. How does any man resolve the conflict that continually rages between the exigencies of his body and the burning pod of the soul? I am famished for love and I despise myself, although it is much too easy to call myself dust and ashes. I know that there are things about myself that I do not know. Certainly now we see through a glass darkly, not yet face to face.

After a while he gets to his feet and walks to the curb where he waits for a taxi. He feels as though he has been mildly poisoned, or has had a quart of blood withdrawn; he sees his wife again, as though in a mirror, her taut body stretched across his own, her mouth yawning with excitement; but he cannot summon her warmth, and the weight of her thighs is no heavier than dust.

A taxi veers aside and stops. Muhlbach climbs into the back seat and orders the driver to take him to some night club — any one that's close by — so long as there are women in the show.

The taxi swerves and lurches through the Village, the driver cursing, and turns north.

Very soon he finds that he is being delivered to the Club Sahara. Apprehensively he considers the fluorescent sign, the doorman costumed as a sheik, and wishes that he were not alone. The club looks ridiculous but also a trifle dangerous. He has not been in any such place as this for several years.

Effendi, says the doorman, bowing and making a vaguely religious gesture with one hand. Don't miss the harem dancers. Exotic entertainment once seen only by caliphs in the privacy of the seraglio!

Muhlbach gives him a quarter and marches up the staircase to be met by another sheik. There's an admission charge, after which the curtains are drawn aside and he steps into darkness. The show has begun. On stage sit four musicians, each wearing a tasseled red fez.

This way, *effendi,* says a voice. Muhlbach discovers that he is standing next to a figure in a white burnoose.

He is led to a table in a corner. The stage is partly hidden by a post. He shifts his chair, is nudged by some invisible party whose view he has blocked, and so resigns himself to what he has. The table interests him; he has never been seated at a table so small. It is round and is about the size of a pancake griddle. A slave girl arrives by flashlight to take his order.

Meanwhile to the wicked clink of finger cymbals, Nila, direct from Beirut, Lebanon, has undulated into the spotlight. Muhlbach polishes his glasses, settles them on his nose, and after crossing his arms he prepares to watch the dance; just then the slave girl reappears with his drink. One dollar and fifty cents. He is a bit shocked. Considering the admission fee, this is too much. However, there's nothing to do but pay. She goes away to get change for the bill he has given her and returns almost immediately.

I'm afraid you've made a mistake, says Muhlbach when he has counted the change she holds out on a platter. It was a ten I gave you, not a five.

The slave answers that it was a five.

It was a ten, he knows, because he is meticulous about such things. He does not make mistakes of this sort, he never has. He remembers having looked at the denomination of the bill when he handed it to her. For a moment he wonders if he should simply give up and go home. The night to this point has been nothing if not a disaster. At best it has been a disappointment and at worst he has suffered humiliation enough to last the year. He looks helplessly at the ruins of his ten-dollar bill.

Will there be anything else, sire?

Not at the moment, thank you. For the time being this is quite enough.

Very good, sire. The slave girl switches off her flashlight and steals away.

On the stage Nila is swaying like a viper to the music of oud and darabukka. Flutes are wailing, cymbals clink. Her costume, which may or may not be authentic, consists of loose transparent pantaloons tied at the ankle, a gilded halter with loops of coins that dangle to her navel, and a Cleopatra bracelet squeezing the tawny meat of her upper arm. She dances as sinuously as though she were remembering the pasha who came to visit last night, and Muhlbach finds that he enters into the soul of her dance: America becomes distasteful—an insensate, vulgar, flatulent, bloodless subway nation of merchants, thugs, Protestants, and barbers. He considers giving up his position at Metro Mutual and moving to Lebanon.

Nila melts to the floor, heavy strings of brass coins flowing. Her pale orotund belly possesses a life of its own. The jewel in her navel winks at him. Truly it is a wondrous belly—throbbing, heaving, pulsing, quivering. It trembles, it palpitates, it almost weeps, and then mysteriously vanishes but soon returns larger than ever, rolling languorously from side to side. Muhlbach is quite fascinated; he leans forward.

However, the slave girl is at his table. Would he like another drink?

No, he replies, but changes his mind. Yes, do bring me another. Mindful that money disappears in the Club Sahara as if it were dropped on a shifting sand dune, he searches his pockets to collect the exact amount, nothing extra. Not a surplus peso, not a drachma, no gulden, no dinar, no yen, no reis—in brief, not a pfennig.

When she comes back he is prepared for an ugly scene; but having collected for the drink, the slave girl slips away into the night without saying a word, so there would seem to be an arid truce between them.

Will she serve me again? he wonders. I suppose I'll be ignored from now on, or possibly bounced. We'll find out soon enough.

A new harem dancer is on the stage. Lisa from Port Said, direct from a triumphal tour of the capitals of the Middle East, the personal favorite of Sheik Ali Bey. She is slender and charming, with a sensitive face. Muhlbach feels himself half in love with her. She's as delicate as a fawn. Her eyes are edged with kohl. A jeweled pendant glitters on her forehead. He is positive that she is looking toward him while she dances; it seems to him that she is entreating him to go with her. They will go together, hand in hand, back to the days of King Solomon; they will live in a whitewashed hut, or a tent, and mind a herd of goats. Anything becomes possible when Lisa dances. Anything. The ringing of her tiny cymbals destroys him, he does not know if he can stand this passion. She is calling him to Paradise.

Lisa, ladies and gentlemen! Lisa! A nice round of applause for the little lady.

Lisa bows, smiles like the carnival courtesan she is. As she walks into the wings she peels off the diadem.

And still, thinks Muhlbach, she's what I need. Maybe she was born in the Bronx and has no more danced in triumph through the capitals of the Middle East than I have been shot out of a cannon or gone parachute jumping, but I need her. If there's a God, a God with compassion, He knows. I cannot help it if I lust after the favorite of Sheik Ali Bey — who's probably better known as Mick, Abe, or Louie, who at this moment is lounging at her dressing table paring his nails with a switchblade knife. Yes, each inordinate affection becomes its own torment.

The question no longer is one of aesthetics or of sensibilities. The question is: how do you acquire a belly dancer for a mistress? Do you send a note concealed in a dozen roses? How should it be addressed? Do you ask the slave girl for the dancer's true name? Then what do you write? Dear Lisa Goldberg, et cetera, et cetera, signed Your Faithful Admirer. This must be ancient fiction; furthermore it would necessitate coming back again to occupy the same table, becoming a spectacle yourself, the butt of obscene jokes. Suppose that is the procedure. Consider the implications.

I can't do it, he thinks. I cannot do it. Suppose she replied, and told me to wait for her outside the stage door, in the alley, among the trash cans and mewing cats. The truth is, I simply don't understand how these things are accomplished. I just don't know how. I'm pricked and urged along by this degrading appetite and I drag after me a great load of doubt. I know that what I'm following is not happiness, or even satisfaction, but a state in which I am free of my mortal goad. This is the simulacrum of content. I think that I would settle for it. At least, thank God, I am not altogether ignorant of my ignorance.

Another dancer's on the stage — Riva, she is called, the toast of three continents, direct from Istanbul for an exclusive engagement at the Club Sahara. She, too, has a tender belly possessed of demons which she sets about to exorcize, but the slave girl has come around again and Muhlbach is distracted; not knowing whether to say yes or no, he orders a third drink. Or is this the fourth? What difference does it make? He does not feel well. He inspects the rim of the glass and wonders if he has swallowed a little something that he did not pay for. Riva fails to interest him — excepting the magic belly, which he observes with remote concupiscence. Otherwise he is not moved, she lacks the grace of Lisa, she is not half so Byzantine, has not the deep conviction or felicity. Riva does not promise much.

Just then like an evil flower blooms the thought that perhaps he could attack some unknown woman. Incredible! Muhlbach adjusts his glasses, as though he might be able to see the origin of this insane conceit. He tries to remember if some previous thought has brought up such a criminal idea from the depths of himself, or if he has overheard or seen anything that nourished it. Nothing. Nothing. The woman swaying on the stage has summoned it, but why? Already the idea has become unreal, impossible. Of course I never would, he reflects, but at the same time how interesting that I should think of it! Yes, very interesting indeed. So in spite of my intelligence I'm not much different. There, spattered across the front pages of the tabloids, but for the grace of some inherent power go I—good God! Good God, are we so near the precipice, each one of us?

He squints against the smoke, realizing for the first time just how crowded, uncomfortable, and perfidious the Sahara is. And to say that it is expensive is to put it courteously. He looks at the leader of the four musicians, at the great beaked avaricious nose and snapping black eyes, the trimmed mustache, the tassel on his fez. Abdul Somebody. Abdul, nodding and smiling rather like a crocodile, leads the authentic Arabian band while Riva slithers around the stage to a flute obbligato of sorts. She is barefoot, with fingernails like the talons of the phoenix and the profile of a hawk. She is fierce and she is mean, there's little doubt; also, she looks dirty, as though she had spent her life in the back rooms of the club. He thinks again of Lisa: no matter if she's a fraud, her lithe body was altogether genuine, and because he will never enjoy that body—and he knows he will not—he wishes he had never seen it.

The lights go on, the musicians put away their exotic instruments. The next show will begin presently, but Muhlbach decides he will not be there. He joins the crowd struggling through the curtained exit and while he is being jostled and elbowed and struck in the back, and perhaps fondled, he asks himself what he has gained by coming here. Nothing, of course, except a clearer knowledge that his temptation has not ended.

Once outside the club he asks himself what to do next. He is standing on the corner with his hands clasped tightly behind his back when someone speaks to him — a naval officer, a stoop-shouldered lieutenant commander with a Southern accent, and Muhlbach recognizes the adult face of the boy who used to be his closest friend, who had been his college roommate twenty years ago.

Puig, for that is his name, promptly insists that they have a drink together.

He'll ask what I'm doing, thinks Muhlbach, if I'm married, if I have a family, and so forth. I know every question he's going to ask.

What is it that's disappointing about Puig? Is it that he's changed so little? He does look older, yes, and his face is still disfigured by those hairy brown warts. He looks somehow depraved, the cold agate eyes blurred by a hundred barrels of sour mash bourbon, the ribbed stomach of youth collapsed and grossly distended. Puig's khaki uniform is wrinkled, the little black shoulder boards are perched askew. His cap is set too far back on his head and he is perspiring. And he's so delighted, Muhlbach reflects, that we've run into each other after all these years.

The longer he looks at Puig, the more it does appear that Puig has changed; but still, the first thing he'd noticed was not any outward modification but that, apart from having physically aged, he might still be mingling with college boys. There's been no inner growth, merely this deterioration of the surface. Muhlbach remembers that Puig had been very fond of music, particularly of Victor Herbert and

Sigmund Romberg; now he guesses that although twenty years have elapsed Puig's not yet graduated. He loved the jingles and the macabre stories of Poe; probably he still does. Puig reached his highest point of sensitivity with Rodin. That's real carving, he used to say.

Any old port in a storm, Puig is saying.

Muhlbach follows him across the street into a dank saloon, and there they sit on high leather stools. Puig insists on paying for the drinks, then he swivels back and forth and talks and appraises every woman that walks by. He's married and has four boys. He's executive officer of the U.S.S. *Huxtable* which dropped anchor only last night. After the war ended he stayed in the Navy, it seemed the simplest thing to do; now the pay is good, there are benefits, and when he's not at sea he gets in quite a few rounds of golf. Life's all right in the peacetime Navy, not really bad, claims Puig.

Well, probably it's neither more nor less satisfying than the insurance business; and certainly to be based in Casablanca one year and on the other side of the world the next is far more stimulating than year after year in the dust-free, odorless, subdued and regulated neutrality of Metro Mutual.

Just then with a lecherous little squeak Puig slides off his stool and whispers that he will be back in a moment.

Muhlbach nods and remains at the bar, contemplating his drink. He is envious of Puig, who has no scruples, who has never been concerned with dignity. Puig is at home in the gutter because he does not recognize it as such; if asked, he might very well admit to being in the gutter, but of course to identify a place or a condition of the soul doesn't mean that it's been recognized.

Minutes go by. Muhlbach has finished his drink. What's become of Puig? Foul play? Is he stretched out unconscious in a back room? Not likely. His uniform implies that the total weight of the United States Navy would fall on any malefactor unwise enough to despoil its wearer. Whether this is true or not, Puig never was the type to be victimized. Wherever he is, and whatever he's doing, he's all right. It's almost certain that during these past twenty years nothing unfortunate has happened to him, nor will anything damage him more than temporarily until the day of his death; even that he may turn to some account — triple indemnity taken out the day before, something similar.

It is this blithe ease and fortune of Puig that annoys Muhlbach, that causes him to turn restlessly on the leather stool; because Puig is so average, so direct and ponderous, and because tonight his snuffling chase is similar to Muhlbach's own, equally discreditable. This is not comforting.

Both of us suffer the muddy cravings of the flesh, he thinks, the bubblings and foggy exhalations that demean the spirit. Only he is not aware of how he has fallen; he sees nothing despicable or ridiculous in his acts. The truth is that I must be considered inferior to him because whatever it is possible to corrupt is inferior to what cannot be corrupted. Whatever cannot be damaged or lessened is undoubtedly preferable to what can be, just as whatever suffers no evident change is better than what is subject to change.

Restless in his weariness, Muhlbach can do nothing but wait.

Puig returns, but not alone. He brings Gertie, with the inevitable shiny black handbag. She is as drunk as the grape can make her.

You're all alike! shrills Gertie. No good sons-of-bitches, every blessed one of you. Always after the same thing, by Christ! Only one thing ever on your mind! I should've listened to my first husband. He's got the number of guys like you! Who needs you? Answer me that! Triumphant in her rhetoric, she leans soggily against Puig, who has trouble holding her upright.

Stand by, Gert, we're casting off. See you, buddy, mur-

murs Puig, somewhat apologetically. Together they go leaning out the door.

What about me? thinks Muhlbach, once more abandoned.
I was hoping he would invite me to go with them. I'd share
her, God help me. I would have, if I had been invited. Then
he looks around—for the first time seeing the bar in which
he has been seated—and realizes with amazement that he's
been descending: it resembles the entrance to a sewer.

He does not know how he got here, but what alarms him
is not that he has reached this low step but where the next
might take him, since he has not descended deliberately;
some inner force has been diligently at work, a despotism
too deeply buried and silted over to be uncovered. Realizing
this, he believes he should be able to control it, but is not
sure.

Immediately he gets off the stool and walks out.

The city air is not clean, and it seems to have become
much warmer during the past hour; it is almost uncomfortable, as though summer would begin again. A polluted
river breeze hangs in the soot-blown street. His suit feels
thick, the collar tight.

There's a taxi parked at the curb. The driver, like a messenger from above or below, is looking directly at him.

Times Square, says Muhlbach without enthusiasm and
climbs into the back seat. I've got to get off these dark
avenues, he thinks. I've been too long at the periphery.
Other people are finding happiness, they evidently know
where it is; strange that I don't. And stranger still, I've the
feeling that I too could have found it, if I'd been able to
recognize the form it takes. Doubtless the saint was right in
telling us that those things are not only many but diverse
which men witness and select to enjoy by the rays of our sun,
even as that light itself is one, in which the sight of each one
beholding sees and holds what pleases; so, too, there may be

many things that are good, and also differing aims of life, out of which each chooses as he will. Now, in matters of the flesh, it's said that whatever you perceive through the flesh you perceive only in part, and remain ignorant of the whole, of which these are parts; yet still these parts do delight you.

Times Square, says the cabbie, taking off his yellow hat to scratch his skull.

So soon? Muhlbach is surprised. He sits forward, blinks in the artificial light, and reaches for his wallet. However, his pocket is empty. Never, in fact, has a pocket felt so absolutely empty. The wallet has been stolen. He is positive of the moment when it was stolen — as he was jostled by the crowd leaving the Club Sahara. He remembers that in the bar with Puig he started to reach for it but Puig caught his wrist; the last time, therefore, that he touched it was in the Sahara. But this is merely the deduction of the conscious mind, which is a useful tool but a blunt one; the wallet was lifted by somebody in the crowd, and now that he has been informed by the emptiness of his pocket that it is gone he realizes that the perpetually vigilant self within himself has been trying to notify him ever since it happened.

To placate his incredulous brain he methodically feels through all of his pockets, then, with the cabbie's assistance, searches the back seat. The wallet's not found, of course.

The cabbie is prepared for a struggle, since nothing's half so important as being paid. You want to go back?

No, says Muhlbach, take me to the Tyler Plaza. I'll cash a check.

You know somebody there?

I do. The manager's a friend of mine.

You better hope so, pal.

There's more insolence than sympathy in this remark. Why did I attempt to justify myself? Muhlbach asks while the taxi works its way through the crowd. What business is it of the driver who I know at the hotel, or if I know anybody at all? That's not his concern. He'll be paid. I'm stripped of my money and all at once I'm as insecure as a schoolboy. As for going back to the club, I'd rather lose a dozen wallets. I'll telephone and ask, I can do that. But I couldn't walk up those steps again. This has been a wretched night. Good God, I've been robbed. Robbed!

The cab driver follows him into the Tyler Plaza.

May I please speak to Mr. Sproule, says Muhlbach to the clerk.

Mr. Sproule, according to the clerk, is not there; he's at home sick in bed with the flu. Could Mr. Ascagua be of any assistance?

I need to cash a check, says Muhlbach. Sproule is a close friend of mine. I'm sure it will be all right.

Just let me speak to Mr. Ascagua, suggests the clerk, who is unctuous enough to run a mortuary. He then disappears for ten minutes. Finally it develops that, most unfortunately, Mr. Ascagua has stepped out for a little while.

What time do you have? asks Muhlbach.

Almost two in the morning.

Call up Sproule and I'll talk to him.

The desk clerk is afraid he couldn't do that.

Then you give me the number because I cannot remember it, and I'll damn well call him.

Reluctantly, peevishly, and with a look of insane discomfort, the clerk agrees. So the call is made.

David, says Muhlbach, I'm sorry about this. It's a long story and I feel like an imbecile. Somebody took my wallet and here I am. I need help. He listens, nods to the cabbie, and hands over the telephone to the clerk.

Yes, sir, of course, begins the clerk, I'll be glad to. Yes, sir! Right away, sir!

Muhlbach has no difficulty visualizing Sproule propped

up in bed, eyes bulging, mustache and jowls aquiver with indignation.

No trouble at all, sir. Certainly, sir. Not a bit, sir! I certainly will do my best. And a different breed of clerk comes off the telephone.

By the way, says Muhlbach, are there any rooms left? Because I think I'll stay overnight, provided you can locate something away from the street.

The clerk is positive that he will be able to find a very nice room, meanwhile the cashier will be delighted to take care of Mr. Muhlbach's check.

In a few minutes the cabbie is paid and tipped and goes on about his nocturnal business; and Muhlbach with a modest roll of bills lodged carefully in his trousers pocket feels somewhat better. He calls home to tell Mrs. Grunthe that he has decided to spend the night in town.

Mrs. Grunthe is not asleep as he had supposed she might be; she is wide awake. He is oddly touched by this, but also slightly irritated. She has been sitting in her favorite chair, watching television and knitting and every once in a while no doubt lifting her eyes to the clock on the mantel.

How are the children? he inquires. They're asleep, naturally. Everything is under control; as usual, nothing is ever much out of control while Mrs. Grunthe is present.

I'm tired, he explains. I don't feel like riding the train back at this hour. I've decided to stay overnight, that's all.

Mrs. Grunthe does not take to this idea; she suspects something. Muhlbach remembers that she now and then preaches against the wickedness of gambling; probably she thinks he has become involved with a bunch of card-playing Italians. She always has been suspicious of Italians. Puerto Ricans, Greeks, Negroes, Chinese, they're very much the same, they are not devils, however foreign; but Mrs. Grunthe knows that sinfulness dwells in the Italian breast.

So be it. Good night, Mrs. Grunthe. Dream of Salvador.

Now there is only one call to make, and it will be futile. He calls the Club Sahara, explains that he was there earlier and that his wallet is missing. Just by chance has it been found? No answer. He hears the clink of glasses, laughter, remote voices, and once more the music of oud and dara-bukka inscrutably beckoning him across the wire. Time goes by while he holds the receiver and blinks his eyes to keep awake. Finally, without explanation, somebody at the other end of the line hangs up.

This insult is one too many. He had planned to go to bed but now, after this, there is only one possible resolution to the night—he will get drunk. He has not been filled to the brim since his wedding day and that was fourteen years ago. Now seems like a good time. No doubt the time was long past. Probably a man's anguish and his troubles are best washed away once in a while, since they are bound to return. In any case, where's the nearest cocktail lounge and how fast can it be achieved? He calculates that half a dozen ought to finish him, after which he'll get a good night's sleep. It may be joyless, that's not the point. I'm half out of my senses, he thinks, with grief and shame and mummified passion. I'm a coward and a celibate. I don't have guts enough to approach a kootch dancer, I don't have either the brains or the sex to interest a Bohemian girl. I'm a fake, a pompous ass, a stuffy bourgeois pedant and a—well, what's the use? I could go on and on. And a blessed son-of-a-bitch not the least of these. Oh, but I am miserable! How miserable I am.

This causes him to feel a little improved. He heads grimly for the cocktail lounge. To his surprise it's nearly deserted. There are a few lonesome men at the bar, who look around as he comes in, a waitress, and two bartenders. The thought of joining his fellows on a stool is disagreeable; he selects a table in the darkest corner.

The waitress begins walking toward him. She does not

wear a dress but red mesh stockings to the hip, a black Merry Widow, and a marvelous blond wig.

Muhlbach knows that he is staring at her like a provincial, but he does not care. Frustration, disgust, anger, disappointment, the badly stained and spattered image of himself, mauled dignity—whatever the night and this impossible city have proffered is wrapped up and tied in one vulgar bundle which he might throw away if he can bring a light to the eye of this steamy wench. Pride and confidence may then be restored, may grow and flourish. He knows in the midst of his dejection that such a thought, such hope, is madness, that he will fail again. Yet he is a man, no matter what else; lecherous and unrepentant in the depths of exhaustion; desirous of much more than can be reckoned; muddied by concupiscence; made wild with shadowy loves; halted by the short links of his mortality and deafened by conceit; seldom at peace; adulterous and bitter; stuck and bled by thorns on every side; rank with imagined sin; exiled forever and yet ever returning, such he is. Brambles of lust spring up on all sides while he plots the course. He learns that Carmen is her name.

As she walks away her fat thighs torment him and he is heavily swollen by lascivious plans. With a dull, furious gaze he follows the gathered pink chiffon decorating her extravagant rump like a rabbit's flag and wonders if he will explode from passion before she comes back. Jesus, oh Lord! I've been taken prisoner by this disease of my flesh, he says to himself, and of its deadly sweetness, and I drag my chain about with me, and I dread the idea of its being loosed.

Carmen doesn't wear a ring, he notes when she returns. He introduces himself, but she replies with a shrug.

He mentions that she could be the sister of someone he used to know years ago in Washington. She doesn't say a word.

Well then, says Muhlbach, tell me, what time is it?

She doesn't know.

I'll be wanting another drink as soon as you can get it, he says, leaning back against the cushions, and is grateful that she goes away without so much as a glance at him. He swallows most of the drink and looks around. The lounge is not uncomfortable, in a rather calculated way, as though it had been designed to solace defeated men. Muhlbach shuts his eyes. It's true that Carmen does remind him of somebody in Washington; he tries to remember, but cannot. He remembers that he had been attracted to whoever it was, but then, just as now, nothing came of it. The reason was the same, as it is invariably the same. It never will be different.

I'm trapped like a bird in a loft, he thinks.

Carmen is returning and it occurs to him that she, too, is a bird—a glorious bird of the jungle with plumage as indescribable as a tropic dawn. When she bends over to serve him he seizes her wrist. She utters a little cry and draws back; there is a momentary struggle before he lets go, more shocked than she.

Porfirio! she calls.

That one word brings out of some gloomy recess in the lounge a dapper, swift, and unmistakably dangerous Latin with a diamond stickpin on a white silk necktie. He stares at Muhlbach through tinted glasses and inquires if he may be of service, although this is not why he has come to visit. He conveys a very different message.

Muhlbach, shaken doubly by his own conduct and by the implied threat of violence, has difficulty answering. Exposed to Porfirio's pitiless gaze, he takes out his handkerchief and weakly pats his face. He is glad that Carmen has gone. If anyone must witness his shame, it should be another man.

I'm afraid I feel a little sick, he says.

You had enough for tonight, says Porfirio, not unkindly.

Muhlbach nods, perspiring.

You make it to the door by yourself?

In a few minutes I will. Let me sit here until I recover.

Take your time, says Porfirio, and sidles away.

Oh my God, asks Muhlbach during his moments of grace, what has become of me?

Before getting up he reminds himself that he is seriously drunk, at least that is what the evidence suggests, and if he has not acted nobly anywhere else tonight, he will manage somehow to leave this place unassisted. I'll do that, he says, if I drop dead one step beyond the arch.

Cautiously he gets up. He walks with unspeakable dignity past the piano and the bar and so into the lobby to the desk where he asks for his key, while the meditations of Saint Augustine sing loosely through his head. There is no place that I can rest, he thinks; backward or forward, there is no place. I have dared to grow wild and touch a multiplicity of things in order to please myself, but each consumed itself in front of me because I exceeded the limits set for my nature. But is there not attraction in the face and body of a woman that is very great and equal to the face and body of gold? For the flesh has like every other sense its own intelligence.

Holding the key in both hands so that he will not drop it, he heads for the elevator. He does not know what time it has become, except that it must be quite late; and he is amazed by the determination of his body, which does not care whether it is three or five or twelve but would as soon walk out again into the street.

In the elevator he is relatively certain that he is going to vomit; he concentrates on other matters in the hope of deceiving his stomach, and once inside the room he does not feel quite so sick. In fact, after a very few minutes, there seems to be no reason he should not refresh himself with a shower and go out. Really, a man's luck changes. Yes, of course, things should improve.

But this is the voice of the Devil—that wheedling tone is familiar. Muhlbach refuses to listen. He sits down on the edge of the bed to examine the cuff of his trousers. The hamster has eaten more of it than he thought. Tomorrow he must buy a new pair of pants. But tomorrow is Sunday. All is wretchedness and cross-purpose.

The softness of the bed soon affects his body. He lies down but immediately gets up and walks back and forth wrestling with the devilish proposal. He mutters, squeezes his hands, turns around, explains to himself that it is all a fabulous absurdity. Some time later, fully dressed, not able to sleep naked if there is no other body for companionship, he stretches himself on the floor. Hours pass. He sleeps nervously, aware that he is alone; it is as though the troubled evening continues.

By morning the night phantoms have not been vanquished; at breakfast he scarcely tastes his food but sits gazing through the window of the coffee shop at the sensual movements of women on the street. Even their shadows on the pavement suggest and hint at Babylon. The morning is brilliant, and morning is reflected everywhere, but he cannot enjoy its splendor. This is Sunday, he reflects, a time for Christian worship, but I am obsessed. This is the seventh day, yet I am unable to rest.

Then, whether it is a hallucination or not, he believes that he sees Rouge across the street, accompanied by Meatbowl and Quinet. If he is not mistaken, and he wonders, they are standing outside a bookstore. Quinet and Meatbowl are gesticulating—stock characters in an old folk comedy—while Rouge, like Columbine, perhaps invisible to mortal eyes, stands just apart as though waiting for Harlequin. Now imploringly she looks toward him; she has discovered him at his table. He cannot remain where he is. He quickly pays for his breakfast and hurries out.

Yes, they are there. They do exist, all three of them, outlandish spirits. And has Rouge truly seen him? Is she beckoning? Is there something that she wants? A book, a meal, a game of chess, a diamond to exchange for a night of love? No matter, he will give it to her. How different from the pains of youth. Here is no thought of pressed flowers, moonlit walks along the beach. Here is the meaning of the body's work, its need; the rest is wasted time.

Impatiently he waits for the light to change, worried that Meatbowl and Quinet will wander off and she will follow and be lost forever.

But Columbine is there, looks up with great grave eyes at his vigorous approach. Bright indeed is this morning, fortunate are those who have found each other. Is not the very air filled with clapping wings?

So the deus ex machina, a pigeon, one gray pigeon otherwise quite nondescript and indistinguishable from the millions, unaware or indifferent to the magnitude of its act and to the finality with which it will score a human life, possibly two lives, briskly cocks its head, winks once, and without a ruffled feather sends down from Heaven the fateful message.

Muhlbach, in mid-stride, hears the liquescent thunder against his hat. He takes it for a distant earthquake because the sky is blue. But no! Informed by Rouge's insane shriek of laughter, by the looks of horror, sympathy, and stupefied amusement from passers-by, as well as by his own desperate inner certainty, Muhlbach takes off his hat. One glance certifies the pigeon's mighty blow. After this, what can befall a man?

With the hat held upside down in one hand as though he were collecting coins he stalks up Broadway. Perhaps, he thinks, this is for the best. I've hoped for what was never meant to happen. I have spent one whole night attempting to distort the truth which was born in me; now I have learned. Whatever I touch henceforth—whether it is the body of the earth or the air itself—I must be sure that it is within my province and does not belong to any other. But still, knowing this was not meant to be, does not, nor ever shall diminish the yearning. I know this, as I know that seven and three are forever ten.

The Short Happy Life
of Henrietta

Henrietta had a marvelous time in Paris. She came from a very small town in Nebraska and did not understand a word of French, but this did not bother her in the least. No matter what was said to her she would eagerly nod her head and begin laughing.

Henrietta enjoyed everybody, and she explained to whomever she met that when she had seen and done everything there was to do in Paris she was going completely around the world by herself. She could be seen at almost any time of the day or night scurrying through the Latin Quarter or sitting in a café on Montparnasse, laughing, nodding excitedly, sharing her table or her umbrella with all kinds of people — Arabs, streetwalkers, students, tourists — it did not matter.

Somewhere near the Seine, probably in an alley, she met two jolly little men from Algiers. She was seen wandering about the streets with them, all three laughing heartily. These Arabs spoke no English.

Some weeks later, when one of the Algerians was located, the story of their hilarious evening came to be known. The three had gone from one café to another, from Latin Quarter to Pigalle, drinking vermouth — Henrietta buying — and laughing till the tears rolled down their cheeks. None of them had ever had such a good time. Late in the evening one of the Arabs proposed they get a wicker basket, a great big wicker basket, and go out to the Bois de Boulogne and there they should cut off Henrietta's head and stuff her in the basket. Henrietta did not understand a word they said, but thought whatever they were suggesting must be enormously funny, and when pressed for an answer she agreed.

The Arabs slapped each other and screamed.

They asked her again if she would like to be murdered and stuffed into a big wicker basket. Henrietta said yes indeed.

The two Arabs could scarcely believe she meant it, so they described with their fingers what they meant to do to her, whereupon Henrietta was overcome with laughter. So, after a time, they got into a taxicab and they went in search of a wicker basket.

The three of them entered various shops that were still open, and in one of these they found exactly what they were looking for. It was a fine, stout basket. They put it down in the middle of the floor and one of them helped Henrietta climb into it. She sat in the basket with her knees drawn up to her chin and she laughed until her eyes brimmed with tears while the shopkeeper shrugged.

If one wishes to buy a wicker basket — so the shopkeeper later explained to the police — one is entitled to buy a basket.

The Arabs put on the cover and found that it contained Henrietta quite nicely. So Henrietta climbed out of the basket and bought it, and her friends carried it to the taxicab and put it in the trunk. They had the driver take them to the Bois de Boulogne.

If one wishes to go to the Bois de Boulogne with a girl and a wicker basket — so the taxicab driver later explained to the police — there is no law against it.

After the taxi went away they stretched out on the grass,

Henrietta and her friends, and they rolled around helpless with mirth, for it was a truly wonderful evening they were having. Then the question was once more put to Henrietta, and once more she was certain their idea must be a fine one, whereupon they picked up their basket and went staggering into the woods and it was there the police found her body in the basket.

The Corset

I think that you are, she had said, enunciating each word, unutterably disgusting. I think, to tell the honest truth, that never in my entire life have I heard such an inexpressibly vulgar suggestion. Just in case you care for my opinion, there it is. To think that any man would even propose such an idea, especially to his wife, which, just on the chance that you've forgotten, I happen to be, is, to put it in the simplest possible terms, unutterably disgusting.

Mosher shrugs. Okay, never mind. It was a thought, Alice.

What you did while you were in the Army, and the type of women who prey upon lonesome soldiers in foreign countries, or for that matter, how foreign women in other countries behave with their husbands, are things I'd just as soon not care to hear about. I don't know if I'm making myself clear. It simply does not concern me, first of all, and then too, I don't see why you keep harping on these things, as though I were merely some sort of concubine. I guess that's the word. To be perfectly frank, because certainly I've always wanted you to be frank with me whenever anything was bothering you about our relationship, and I'm sure you've always wanted me to express my feelings just as frankly, I appreciate the fact that you thought enough of me to mention it, but it's just so revolting, I mean, I honestly do not know quite what to say.

I thought it might be fun, says Mosher. Overseas the women would —

Fun! Did you say *fun*? When we've always had such a marvelous relationship? I can't understand you any more. You've changed. We used to agree that we had the most beautiful relationship in the world, at least you said so every time I asked, but now I don't know whether to believe you or not. I should think you'd want to keep it the way it was. When two people sincerely respect each other they surely oughtn't to jeopardize their affiliation, do you think? A moment ago I could scarcely believe my ears. I never dreamed that you could be so — so —

Vulgar?

Exactly! Not by any stretch of the imagination.

Then you think it's an unreasonable request? asks Mosher after a pause. Listen, Alice —

What you did in Europe is one thing, and I try not to dwell on it, which is more than most wives would do, but now you're home and we ought to go on the way we did before.

Alice, it's a damned strange thing, says Mosher, that my own wife should know less about me than a whore on the Rue de la Paix.

For a moment she gazes at him. Then all at once she remarks: Tell me what you want. I love you, you must know that. I'll do anything on earth for you. Tell me specifically what would please you and I'll agree to do it, on the condition that it means preserving our relationship.

I don't want it that way! Mosher shouts, and bangs his

fists together. Can't you understand? Oh my god, don't look
so miserable, he adds. You look like I was getting ready to
flog you.

That wouldn't surprise me. Nothing you do any more
could possibly surprise me. I don't know what's come over
you. Honestly, I don't. You're a perfect stranger.

Mosher, enraged and baffled, lights a cigarette.

Smoking isn't good for you.

I know it isn't, I know, he says, puffing away.

You never listen to me.

Alice, he replies with a gloomy expression, I don't miss a
word, not a word. Oh hell, I love you as you are. Don't
change. You're probably right, we'll go on like we used to.
I don't want you to change. Forget I said anything.

But you *do*! You do want me to change, and I've got to be
everything to you, otherwise our —

Don't! Mosher groans, falling back on the bed. Don't
keep calling the two of us a relationship, as though we were
a paragraph in some social worker's report.

For better or worse, she says as though she had not heard
him, I've made up my mind to behave exactly like one of
those European women. I'm quite serious. I mean that.

Mosher, rising on one elbow, gazes at his wife curiously.

I do mean it. I'm going to be every bit as depraved and evil
as they are, you just watch!

What the hell's got into you? he demands. You're out of
your mind. You're as American as Susan B. Anthony. Then
he continues: But if you want to, fine. Go ahead.

What do I do first?

I don't know. Don't you?

No, this was your idea. Give me a suggestion.

Well, says Mosher uneasily, I'm a spectator, so to speak.
I don't really know. He realizes that she has started to
unbutton her blouse. What do you think you're doing? he

asks. I mean, good God, it's three o'clock in the afternoon and the Haffenbecks are coming over.

I don't care, she says. I simply don't care about a thing anymore.

But wait a minute, Alice. We invited them for drinks and a barbecue, remember?

I don't care! I don't care about the Haffenbecks. And she takes off her blouse, asking: Shall I take off everything?

Oh, yes, yes, everything, everything, says Mosher absently, gazing at her shoulders. With his chin propped in his hands he watches her get undressed.

I really should have paid a visit to the beauty parlor this morning, she says. My hair is a fright.

The beauty parlor! he shouts. What the hell has a beauty parlor got to do with this? Life's too short for beauty parlors!

However, she's doing her best, he thinks, all for me, because she does love me and wants to please me, isn't that odd? She's not a bit excited, she's just ashamed and embarrassed, so I am too. He feels deeply touched that his wife is willing to debase herself for him, but at the same time he is annoyed. Her attitude fills him with a sense of vast and unspeakable dismay. In Europe, now, romping in a bedroom, there would be no stilted questions, no apologies or explanations, no pussyfooting about, no textbook psychology, nothing but a wild and fruitful and altogether satisfying game. Alice, though, after the first embrace, customarily looks to see if her clothing is torn or her hair has been mussed.

Why, he asks with a lump like a chestnut in his throat, do you wear that corset?

It isn't a corset, it's a foundation.

Mosher waves impatiently. Alice, I hate these Puritan bones. Those Boston snoods. You haven't the slightest idea how sick and tired I've become of Aunt Martha's prune-whip morals. Whenever I touch you while you're wearing that thing it's like I've got hold of a bag of cement. Didn't I ever tell you how much I hate that corset? Didn't you ever realize? I mean to say, I think of you as flesh and blood, but that freaking thing makes you look like a python that swallowed a pig. Why do you wear it? You have such a marvelous shape all by yourself. It would look wonderful to see you out in public without that damned corset.

I should think a man wouldn't want his wife to be seen on the street bulging at every seam.

Well, I would, says Mosher with great bitterness. I'd love it. Anyway, right now I want you to take that bloody thing off.

She does, with no change of expression; her eyes remain fixed on him rather like the eyes of a frightened tigress, bright and watchful and unblinking.

Do you love me because of this? she asks.

Because of what?

My figure.

Yes, he says earnestly, I certainly do. A moment later, to his amazement, a tear comes wandering down her cheek.

I hoped it was me you loved, she says, weeping a little more but holding her head high.

I should have been a monk, he thinks. I'd have a nice quiet cell with bread and porridge and books to read — it would all be so simple. On the other hand I wouldn't make a very successful monk. I know what I'd spend every day praying for.

You can leave those beads on, Alice, he says, I like the effect.

He gazes at her body with immense interest; it is as pale as a melon. In the undergloom of her belly, he thinks, a little bird has landed — a fierce little falcon with tawny wings. He lifts his eyes once more to her face and sees a lock of hair almost, but not quite touching the lobe of her ear. She is as divine and inimitable and perfect as a snow crystal or an April leaf unfolding.

You mentioned some girl over there who was a dancer, who used to dance for the soldiers.

Oh yes, yes, and she was magnificent, Mosher answers. Her name was Zizi. She used to go leaping around like the nymphs on those Greek vases, and when she wriggled across the floor you'd swear she was made out of rubber. I never saw anything like it.

Well, look at me, says Alice. And to Mosher's astonishment she lifts both hands high above her head and turns a perfectly splendid cartwheel.

What do you think of *that*? she demands, on her feet once again, tossing her hair over her shoulders.

I didn't know you could turn a cartwheel, says Mosher. He sits up briskly, spilling cigarette ashes on the bed.

You haven't seen anything yet, she calls from the other side of the room, and bending backward until her palms are flat on the floor she gives a nimble kick and is upside down.

I didn't know you could stand on your hands, says Mosher, looking at her in stupefaction. Even with your clothes on you never did that.

Does it please you?

I should say it does! Mosher replies.

Men are so peculiar. Why should you want me to do these things?

I don't know, Alice. Somehow it makes me love you all the more.

I simply cannot understand you, she remarks, and begins walking around the bedroom on her hands. Could your old Zizi do this?

I don't know, he mutters. I can't remember. You've got

me confused. I don't think I ever saw anything in my life like this.

Not even in Paris?

Not even in Heidelberg. You look strange upside down, Alice. What else can you do?

Just then the doorbell rings.

Oh my word, she exclaims, that must be the Haffenbecks!

No doubt, says Mosher. Either it's the Haffenbecks or the police.

What on earth are we going to do?

I don't know, he replies, unable to stop staring at her. Who cares? Do you?

I suppose not, she answers, still upside down.

The corset is lying on the edge of the bed. Mosher picks it up, flings it out the window and, reclining comfortably, takes a puff at his cigarette.

Now, he commands, turn a somersault.

The Promotion

"The trouble with you, Lester, is," she had said almost as soon as he got in the door; and she did not stop talking while he took off his coat and his shoes, loosened his necktie, fixed himself a double martini, and scanned the headlines of the evening paper. He knew what she was saying so there was no reason to listen. Sylvia didn't expect him to answer, she assumed he was listening and she would be annoyed if he tried to interrupt. It worked out very nicely.

"— and take your feet off the sofa!" she concluded. "How many times must I tell you! Suppose somebody should walk in and find you lounging around like a factory worker."

Lester put his feet on the floor.

"If you must take off your shoes the moment you get in you might at least wear your slippers. Is that asking too much?"

Lester set his drink on the table and walked into the bedroom to get his slippers.

"You don't like them, do you?" she called after him. "You've never liked those slippers. The fact that I spent half of one entire morning shopping for them doesn't mean a thing."

"I like them," he said, coming out of the bedroom. "But why is it that I always have to go and get them? Can't you put them beside my chair?"

"If you think for one instant I have nothing better to do than trot back and forth waiting on you, Lester, you'd better think again. I'm not a servant, after all. And I do wish you wouldn't walk around with a cigarette in your mouth. Honestly, there are occasions when you show remarkably little consideration."

"It's one of my worst faults," said Lester.

"I'm in no mood to endure your sarcasm. I've had a frightful day."

"Me, too. My God, it was hot. Air conditioning broke down at the office."

"It looked simply impossible outside. I cancelled my appointment with the hairdresser."

"Hundred-and-three at two o'clock. Fourth day in a row it's topped a hundred. That office felt like the inside of a casserole. I thought I was going to have a coronary."

"You spoke to Mr. Gumbiner?"

Lester glanced down into his martini.

"You didn't ask, did you? You promised me, Lester — you gave me your solemn promise."

"It was too hot, Sweetie. It was just too hot. He'd have thrown me out. This was no day to nudge the boss. Maybe tomorrow, if it cools off."

"There are times, Lester, when you make it impossible for me to respect you. I suppose I really shouldn't blame you for being what you are. I suppose it isn't entirely your fault, but really, you're such a weakling."

"You've told me before."

"If it weren't true I wouldn't say it."

"Plenty of people in that organization would be delighted to change jobs with me. Plenty of them!" Lester added, nodding significantly.

"How self-satisfied you look! It would never occur to you to try to improve yourself."

"I earn enough to pay the bills, don't I? You aren't going hungry, are you? I don't see why you have any complaint."

"Are you accusing me of trying to ruin you?"

"I am not."

"Then why did you bring up the subject of bills? I get sick and tired of hearing about bills! If you had your way I'd be wearing last season's clothing one year after the next. Do you expect me to do my shopping in the ten-cent store? And as long as you've brought up the subject, suppose you tell me just exactly what you do expect of me!"

"Come on now," Lester said mildly.

"You make me wish I'd never divorced Roger. Whatever his faults, Roger wasn't stingy. And he wasn't a weakling. Roger had his faults but in many ways he was three times the man you are."

"So you've told me more than once."

"You're not a man at all."

"I'm a chicken."

"You disgust me."

"I'm a capon."

"I won't say what you are."

"Sylvie, all in the world I'm trying to do is hang on to a pretty good job, that's all. I work like a bloody slave but at least I'm working, and jobs aren't so easy to find."

"Roger wasn't afraid to ask for what he wanted."

"I'm a bit sick of hearing about precious Roger."

"Then let me tell you something, Lester. I'm sick of your whining and I'm sick of your dilly-dallying. I don't know why I put up with it. There are times I could scream. And for goodness sake stop toying with that olive, either eat it or leave it alone!"

"It's too bloody hot to argue," Lester said as he began chewing up the olive.

"I'm going to cry."

"You've never cried in your life. You're hard as a rock. Hard as nails. If you were a man you'd march into old Gumbiner's gilded palace and let him know who the boss really is. Tell him there's going to be a promotion and a big raise in salary right now, otherwise he can take his job and shove it."

"Do you have the slightest inkling how utterly I despise your vulgarity, Lester? No, I don't suppose you do. I don't suppose you could. Furthermore, I believe you're proud of it. Actually proud of it! I believe you are."

"That's right," said Lester.

"Stop it! Stop it this instant!"

"Okay," Lester said, "but as you keep pointing out to me, I can't be anything except what I am."

"I was trying to be helpful. I don't enjoy being humiliated, nor do I intend to put up with it, do you understand? Do you understand? Are you listening to me?"

Lester nodded.

"Then open your eyes."

"Sylvie, I'm tired. This heat. I feel like a leg of mutton, I just want a chance to relax."

"Sit up and pay attention to me. I'm not going to speak into a vacuum. I won't be ignored. You're not the only person who had a wretched day. Do you think for one single instant that it gives me pleasure to sit here hour after hour waiting for your arrival? Frankly, Lester, I'd far far rather be a number of other places. And for the last time—I'll not have you scattering ashes on the carpet! Roger, do you hear me?"

"My name isn't Roger."

"It was a slip of the tongue, Lester. I'm sorry. But you do infuriate me. Now, where was I?"

"On the subject of my faults."

"I will not listen to any more of your sarcasm. I will not. If I criticize you it isn't because I enjoy it."

"No?"

"One more such word will be one too many."

"Sylvia, it's too bloody hot for this. Four days in a row, one right after the other."

"According to the weatherman on television we'll have more of the same tomorrow. I wish you'd stop saying 'bloody'."

"Tomorrow morning I'll grab old man Gumbiner by the throat and strangle him. Beat his bald head on his big walnut desk, smear his brains all over the walls. Would that satisfy you?"

"I've been trying to point out that if Roger had been working at the same job for as many years—"

"Please!" Lester said with a look of anguish. "Please please. Not after a day like this."

"Are you the only one who feels the heat? How do you think I feel? Do you suppose I've enjoyed myself?"

"I imagine so. You haven't accomplished a bloody thing. You lie around half the day watching the idiot box and spend the other half giving orders to the maid. Who are you to be complaining?"

"Thank you."

"Sweetheart, I'm sorry," Lester said. He reached over and took her hand. "I didn't mean to say it, really I didn't. Forgive me."

"I forgive you, Lester."

"Sylvia, truly I am sorry. Believe me."

"I'm a parasite. Is that what you're saying?"

"I called you no such thing."

"Now I'm a liar as well. How very nice. At last I've discovered what you honestly think of me."

"I didn't say you were a parasite. I didn't call you a liar."

"Don't repeat it. I'm not deaf. Now if you have finished cataloguing my faults for the moment, let me tell you a thing or two."

Lester sighed and leaned his head against her shoulder.

"Well," she said, "if you imagine I take any pleasure in these arguments you couldn't be more mistaken."

"Then let's have no more."

"Promise me one thing."

"What's that?"

"Ask Mr. Gumbiner. I want you to promise me faithfully that you'll ask."

"Done. I swear."

"Are you making fun of me again?"

"Absolutely not. I'll ask the old crook. I'll walk in there, sit right down, lean back and put my feet on his desk."

"Tomorrow."

"Well, it depends," said Lester, letting go of her hand.

"That's what I thought. That's exactly what I thought. I wish I'd been a man."

"You'd have been something, you would."

"I wouldn't be the sort of man you are. I'd make a success of myself."

"Thank you, thank you, Sweetheart."

"Lester, at certain moments I wish I'd never laid eyes on you."

"As they say, the feeling is you-know-what."

"Damn you, Lester. God damn you!"

"Well, who started this?"

"You're the most despicable man I've ever met."

"And you've met plenty."

"Every word you speak reminds me of something I prefer not to think about."

"But you do think about it, don't you? Don't you?"

"Thanks to you."

"The pleasure is mine. Every ounce! Every gram!"

"You've never cared for me. You've never cared. You treat me as though I was a creature you'd picked off the street."

"That's a lie and you know it!"

"It's how you make me feel."

"Sylvia, I love you."

"I want to believe that," she replied after a moment. "I do want so very much to believe it."

"It's a fact," said Lester, reaching for his drink.

"Then why don't you prove it?"

"I do my best."

"When was the last time you told me you loved me?"

Lester glanced at her in astonishment. "What are you talking about? I just now told you. Just this minute."

"No, I mean really, Lester. You weren't sincere just now."

"Certainly I was sincere, why else would I say it? Don't be stupid."

"Lester? Lester, tell me something. Do you have somebody else?"

"Somebody else?"

"Are you cheating on me?"

"My God," said Lester, "what kind of a joke is this?"

"I wouldn't put it past you."

"My God," said Lester, "you're kidding!"

"Don't lie to me."

"After a full day in that office? What do you think I am, some sort of nineteen-year-old international galloping stud? Look at me! All I want when I get away from that office is a chance to sit down and have a few drinks. My feet hurt. My back hurts. Everything hurts. My God, Sylvia, you're out of your mind!"

"I can remember when you used to say you could hardly

wait to get away from the office so we could be together."

"Yes, well," said Lester uneasily, "you've got quite a memory."

"You never say things like that anymore. You don't care for me."

"Yes I do," Lester said, "yes I do."

"Other men find me attractive."

"I'm sure they do. You're a very attractive woman, Sylvia."

"Only yesterday a man followed me in the street. I was ready to call a policeman. I didn't want to tell you because I was afraid it might upset you."

"Why didn't you call the cop?"

"Just exactly what is that supposed to mean?"

"Nothing."

"Lester, I want to know where we are. I don't like this situation. When are we going to get married?"

"I've told you before, as soon as I'm free. Nine in the morning as soon as I'm a free man."

"You keep saying that, but I don't really believe you want to marry me."

"I do, you know I do. You know I've spoken to Louise about a divorce, what else can I do? You know the situation as well as I do. My hands are tied. It's up to her. She's promised to think it over, but until she makes up her mind we're helpless. I don't like this situation either."

"We could be so happy."

"I know, Sweetheart. Already you've made me very happy. Happier than I've ever been in my life."

"Think what it will be like when we're together constantly."

"I often do," said Lester.

"We'll be married as soon as she lets you go?"

"I wish it could be sooner."

"Are you eager to marry me, Lester?"

"I just said so, didn't I? Why do you keep asking?"

"I need to be sure. You do care for me, don't you?"

"I do. You know I do."

"How can a woman be so self-centered?"

"Louise? I don't know, nobody knows. That's how she is. I suppose she was always that way but when I met her I didn't recognize her true nature. I was blind. I must have been blind."

"Did you love her?"

"In a way, perhaps, although we were both kids. I've almost forgotten."

"Only a man would forget."

"That was a long time ago," Lester said. "These last few years with her have been hell on earth. Absolutely hell on earth."

"Will you forget how you feel toward me?"

"Of course not, Sylvie. You're everything Louise isn't. I've wished a thousand times that we'd met before I happened to run into Louise."

"That's how I feel, too, Lester. I mean, concerning me and Roger."

"It's not much fun when you get married and then afterwards you meet the right person."

"I wonder if it happens to very many people."

"Probably. Probably it does."

"How tragic."

Lester nodded and finished his drink.

"Darling, I'm sorry if we argued. It must not be easy for you — living with that woman."

"Every night when I get home she starts right in. Nag nag nag. If it isn't one thing it's another. Lester, you drink too much. Lester, you said you were going to have the car washed. Lester-this and Lester-that! You wouldn't believe it, Sylvie. Nobody could believe it."

"I can imagine."

"The way she pecks at me! Peckety-peck-peck! I wish I didn't have to go home."

"I wish you could stay."

"Ah, that would be marvelous!" Lester said. He bent over to reach for his shoes but winced and straightened up cautiously. "It's nothing," he said. "Just my spine."

"You work too hard."

"Well, it wouldn't be any easier if I was promoted."

"You're going to ask, though. You told me you would."

"All right," Lester sighed, rubbing his back. "I'll ask."

"Tomorrow?"

"Tomorrow."

"I don't want you to think I'm nagging. It's simply that as soon as Louise lets you go and we're married we ought to move to a nicer place. We'll need new things. These drapes won't do," she began, gazing around the room while Lester fumbled for his shoes.

The
Caribbean Provedor

At four o'clock the sun was burning like a green lemon above the coconut palms. The ship's rail was too hot to touch. Koerner stood in the shadow of a lifeboat with a cigarette between his teeth and looked around. In the water alongside the stern some garbage was floating. On shore a few Negroes in straw hats sat on boxes in the shade of the customs house. Nobody else was in sight. There was no breeze, and not a sound except the hissing ball of the sun. Aboard ship nothing moved and there was a smell of hot canvas.

Koerner felt suddenly that his skull was as empty as a gourd. He looked at the deck to be sure that if he fainted he would not hit his head on a piece of iron. Then the feeling passed, but he thought it would be a good idea to go inside. A cold drink would be a very good idea. For almost eight hours he had been playing chess with the surgeon from Ohio. Neither of them had eaten since breakfast. They had played without stopping and were planning to continue until dinner time as usual, but the surgeon's wife got angry. After five days at sea the score stood 23 to 17 in the surgeon's favor, but he was going as far as Vigo and if his wife did not cause too much trouble there would be time enough to overtake him.

Koerner squinted at the shore to see if there was anything he might have missed but the town looked worse during the day than it had the previous night, and there had been nothing worth seeing even then. It was a port of call and they would leave in a few hours. The loading had been completed.

He dropped his cigarette into the water, stepped back inside the ship and descended to the lounge where he took a stool at the bar next to a fat man who was wearing a short-sleeved shirt. The fat man was stroking a little bottle of champagne as tenderly as though it were a cat and talking to the bartender in Portuguese. He stopped talking but continued playing with the bottle, wiping away the moisture with his fingers.

"Um Magos," Koerner said to the bartender.

The champagne was good and very cheap and it was cold and he thought he would be drinking a number of these little bottles while crossing the Atlantic.

"Are you on this boat?" the fat man asked in Portuguese.

Koerner nodded. The man was probably a merchant seaman, both of his thick hairy red arms were heavily tattooed. On his left wrist was a bright new watch which looked as though he had just that afternoon put it on.

"Are you a passenger?"

The heat, no lunch, and so much chess had been exhausting and Koerner did not want to get into a conversation. Besides, the man was anxious to talk and therefore probably did not have much to say. He began to roll the bottle between his palms and tried to remember when the ship was scheduled to arrive in Vigo.

"It's nice to be rich," the fat man said in a voice that was almost threatening. "I'm poor. I work for a living. I can't afford to go on a voyage."

Reluctantly Koerner looked at the man directly for the first time. He was about fifty years old, with a flattened nose and protruding lips and skin that burned but would never tan. Underneath the fat he was solid. He could have been a wrestler. Koerner noticed that the top of one of his ears was missing, sliced off quite cleanly.

"What do you do on this ship?" the fat man said.

"Not a thing."

"You don't do nothing at all. Is that what you tell me?"

"I play chess."

"Ah! You play chess, do you?"

"Every day. I've been playing this entire day since breakfast and I'm very tired."

"Every day. So you been on board a few days. You didn't come on board this ship last night?"

Koerner shook his head.

"I can't waste time playing around. I got a lot of work to do."

"All right," Koerner said.

"When you are not playing games what do you do?"

"I travel."

"That's all you do. You don't do nothing else?"

Koerner took a drink of champagne and then said, "Nothing else."

"You don't work on this ship?"

"No," Koerner said.

On a shelf behind the bar there were trinkets for sale. Portuguese galleons with billowing sails of filigreed gold, carved wood boxes inlaid with ivory squares, black lace Spanish fans, postage stamps from different countries in cellophane packages, flags, and miniature cork life preservers with the name of the ship. Some of the postage stamps were quite beautiful, especially the Japanese which looked like tiny woodcuts. There was snow on Mount Fuji, and waterfalls, and animals. He thought he might buy a package of them.

"I have business here. I'm the provedor," the man said. "I

finished loading eight tons of food and drink on this ship. It's all done. I was working while you were asleep in your very pleasant cabin."

Koerner continued to look at the stamps.

"Now everything is on board so I'm having a drink. I'll buy you a drink, too."

"Thank you," Koerner said, "but I've already got one."

"I have been supplying this ship, all the ships of this line, and a lot of other ships for sixteen years. You don't know what it means to work hard like that. I have never done anything wrong. I have made friends all those years. Tomorrow I give the company my bill, then in a few days they pay me everything. Just sign the papers. I asked to buy you a drink. If you don't want to drink with me it's your business. I don't give a damn."

"Dois Magos," Koerner said to the bartender and took out his wallet, but the fat man pushed it aside.

"I can do this much," he said. "You don't get yourself in trouble drinking with me. You got nothing to worry about. Anyway, nothing worries you."

Koerner didn't answer.

"What's your name?" the fat man asked.

Koerner told him.

"That's what you call yourself. All right, if that's what you tell me it is. You say you're a passenger on this ship."

"I am."

"If you're a passenger on this ship where are you going?"

"Lisboa."

"Then you come back again?"

"Maybe."

"Traveling. That's what you said."

Koerner nodded.

"You work in Martinique?"

"I don't work in Martinique."

"You don't work for the French?"

"No."

"You look French, whatever your name is. Are you a tourist?"

The word was a little degrading but Koerner decided to accept it. "All right, call me a tourist."

"Where do you live? You live in Lisboa?"

"No."

"You don't live on this island. I'm sure about that."

"You're right, I don't live on this island."

"In Curaçao?"

"No."

"I seen you once in Curaçao. A long time ago. Maybe three years ago."

"I was there once," Koerner said while he tried to remember when he had been in Curaçao. Then he remembered it had been about three years ago.

"In a cafe holding a newspaper, pretending to read. But you was watching somebody. I don't forget."

Koerner had not thought of it for three years but now he remembered sitting in a cafe with a newspaper, although he could not remember that he had been watching anybody.

"It was some English newspaper."

"Sure," Koerner said in English.

"Sure. Me too. Hell, yes," the fat man said in English but then continued in Portuguese. "I speak eight or nine languages. I don't know how many, maybe more than that. Spanish. German. French. Just about anything. In my work I got to. You didn't see me in Curaçao?"

"No."

"I can see you like a photograph. In Curaçao I could show you what table you was sitting at. I could tell who you was watching."

"You notice a lot."

The fat man stopped talking. Koerner drank some more champagne, then without turning his head he glanced at the wristwatch.

The man said immediately, "You want it?"

"No."

"You want this watch I'll give it to you. It don't mean nothing to me." He was starting to unbuckle the strap.

"I don't want your watch," Koerner said. "I've got no use for it."

"Listen, whoever you call yourself, you know what my little girl said to me this morning? She said 'Papa, I know you have to go to work today because loading the ship means plenty of money for you, I know that.' Do you know what I said to her? I said 'No, Sweetheart, the ship means you can go to school and it means nice things for you. It don't mean the money is for me.' That's what I told my little girl this morning. But you don't know what I'm talking about because you don't have no little girl. You don't have no idea at all what it means to bring a present to a little girl. A little ten dollar watch from Switzerland. You don't know how much that means to a child. Something she can show her friends and tell them her Papa got this for her and it comes from Switzerland. A little ten dollar watch. A ten dollar watch! But you don't care about these things. They don't mean nothing to you."

Well now, Koerner thought, I believe he's going to smuggle that watch past customs.

"You want it? You want this watch I'll take it off and give it to you if that's all you want," the provedor said. He was breathing heavily.

"Keep it. I don't need it."

"A man like me works from the day he's born but he don't get very rich. What do you want?"

What is he saying? Koerner wondered.

"I don't forget you, not for one minute. A long time ago in Curaçao I told myself 'There he is. That's him.' I feel sorry for you, William Koerner, if that's what you tell me your name is. I feel sorry for anybody like you that goes around like you do, doing what you do. Not having any wife to come home to, not having a little girl throw her arms around your neck when you get off work. Eating by yourself every night. It don't make no difference to you, I know that, but I feel sorry for you. I'd rather be in my place."

Koerner waited to hear what the man would say next.

The provedor shrugged his shoulders. "A cheap watch. What difference does it make? Who cares? It don't hurt nobody. You want another Magos?" he asked in a voice that tried to be friendly.

Koerner shook his head.

"A man like me. What am I? All my life I work hard, but I don't amount to nothing. Maybe you're important. Probably that's what you think you are. You're proud of yourself, but I don't envy you. I don't want to trade places with you."

He realizes I know about that watch, Koerner thought, and he's afraid I'm going to tell the customs officer. But why should I? It's no business of mine. He can smuggle half the watches in Switzerland for all I care. I don't work for customs. He knows that.

Or does he?

And then everything the man had said gradually began making sense.

He believes I'm an inspector. This man thinks I work for the shipping company or for some government. He doesn't believe a word I've told him.

"Maybe you like what you do," the provedor was saying. "Maybe you don't. You do it just for the money? If that's what you do it for nobody's going to care if you live or die. A man like you could get killed and nobody cares. What good does money do? Sure, plenty of things. A lot of things. I know. I know that. But what kind of a life have you got?"

Suppose I were an inspector, Koerner said to himself, and suppose I had just now caught him with this watch. At the moment he's not guilty of anything because he hasn't taken it ashore. So why is he worried? I don't understand. Suppose that in a few minutes he does try to take it through without paying duty and he's caught, what would happen? Nothing. They wouldn't let him keep the watch, that's all. I can't understand why he's worried. Of course if he'd made a habit of this, if he'd been smuggling things ashore for sixteen years that might be a different kind of horse.

So that's it! Not just a wristwatch this afternoon, my fat friend, you've got a business going on the side. Coming aboard and going ashore day after day, one ship after another, for all these years. No wonder you're worried. I would be, too. And you don't know who I am, do you? If I were in your britches I'd be scared to death.

It mounts up, doesn't it? Sixteen years multiplied by how many ships? How many people do you deal with? And what do you bring ashore? What were you and the bartender talking about when I walked into the lounge, and why did you stop talking? Will there be a few cases of cognac hoisted ashore late tonight? That ten dollar watch is nothing. That's a peanut, isn't it, my friend? You've finished work and you feel so good you decided to wear it ashore right past the customs officer, right past his nose because you feel so good. Ordinarily you'd slip it into your pocket and nobody would search you because you're the provedor. Everybody knows you. After all, you've been here sixteen years.

Yes, indeed, it does mount up, doesn't it? But something else mounts up too, my friend, my ambitious businessman. Every day you've got to worry, like every other ambitious businessman. And you wait, and you wait, because you've juggled the accounts, and each day the waiting is a little harder. But you've got to keep on because you're not quite strong enough to let it go. Just one more time. One more time. Then suddenly I'm here.

Koerner put his elbows on the bar and smiled.

"William Koerner," the provedor said, "if that's what you call yourself, I feel sorry in my heart for anybody like you. Nothing makes any difference to you. I got to pity you."

"Ah," Koerner said, and shrugged.

"Sure," the fat man said, "you can be like that. How many people you hurt don't mean a thing in the world. You don't care for nobody. You got no family. No little girl waiting at home asking her Mama when you're coming in."

He loves his daughter, Koerner thought. She's the only person or thing on earth this man loves.

"Why don't you get married?" the provedor asked. He was trying to pull his face into an expression of intimacy but he could not get rid of the fear. "When a man gets married he knows what's worthwhile. He don't run around hurting people."

Whenever I please, Koerner told himself, following the idea slowly, as though it was a speared fish pulling him through the water, I can destroy this man. I can ruin his life. I can destroy his business, his reputation, and probably his marriage. Whenever I want to, from now on. I can do it because he thinks I can. He himself gave me the power, which means he can't possibly doubt it. I'm powerful because he thinks so. And whatever I want to do with him, I can do. If I order him to go ashore and wait for me, he will. If I stand up and beckon to him he'll follow me like a toy on a string.

"Give me a cigarette," he said.

The provedor picked up the package and offered it; Koerner took one and waited and the provedor lighted it for him.

So this is how it feels, Koerner thought, this is the way it feels. I'd never have guessed. I can actually destroy a man and I can hardly keep from laughing. I can put an end to a man's life and I feel a kind of elation. I feel as though I'd like to do something nice for this man. I don't know why, but I rather like him.

"What do you call yourself?" Koerner demanded, and smiled.

The provedor gave him a curious look, almost of surprise, or of some deep and sudden confusion.

"Oh, come on now," said Koerner, trying to control his excitement.

The provedor continued to look at him with a speculative expression, but finally said, "I am Hans Julio García."

It had been a stupid question Koerner realized too late.

"Ah," he said, turning his face aside, "for some reason that sounds familiar. Did we meet in Curaçao?"

The provedor didn't answer.

Koerner looked into the mirror behind the bar. He could see the fat man's ear. The top of it appeared to have been taken off with a razor swipe, and he remembered his first impression of the provedor, of how solid he was under the creases of fat. It occurred to him that Hans Julio García probably was a very dangerous man, and that he had been threatening this man.

I wonder what might happen, he asked himself, when this man decides I'm not who he thinks I am. I don't know. What happens probably will depend on how he feels about me. If he thinks I never suspected the truth he won't have any feelings about me and he'll forget me. No, not that. He won't forget this afternoon, or me, for a long time. I'll be the tourist he talked to in the bar.

But if he thinks I did suspect the truth? If, let's say, he thinks I've guessed. What then?

I don't know that either. I don't want to think about it. I don't know how I got into this but I don't like it. I feel like I've put my hand inside a jar full of spiders. I didn't realize what I was doing. This could get ugly. I don't know how it got started. It was that watch. I noticed the watch because it was new and it didn't belong on his wrist, his wrist is too big for it. Then I looked at it again because I was hungry and wanted to know how soon I could eat but he didn't know that. I should have asked the time instead of trying to see the dial, but I didn't want to talk to him. How was I to know this would happen?

But if I go on pretending to be an inspector how could he find out I'm not? He's afraid of me, he's quit asking questions. He's pretending more than I am. Sorry for me, he says. I pity you, he says. He doesn't pity me, he hates me. He's terrified of me, his hand was shaking when he tried to light my cigarette. He thinks I know everything about him. By God, why couldn't I turn him in? Why not? I didn't ask for this, it's his fault. I came here to get a drink, that's all, and now he's involved me with his guilt.

Damn this man's soul, Koerner thought, and felt himself becoming angry. I could see this man in Hell! Why should I care what happens to him? He means nothing to me. Nothing! All right, by God, let him suffer! He deserves it — the lousy thief!

But could I do it? Say I have the power, can I use it? If I ruin him who else is ruined? His daughter, for one. His wife. I don't have any idea who else. What difference does it make to me? For all I know they're both as rotten as he is. Yes. The little girl, too. And how do I know she exists? Because he talked sentimentally about 'my little girl' and what she'd said to him this morning. How do I know it's true? How many lies have I heard since he started talking?

Koerner had been leaning on his elbows, rocking the

stool slowly backward. He glanced at García. The fat man was gazing at him very seriously.

He's waiting. I've got to make up my mind. Suppose on the other hand I let him off. But how? He's never admitted anything. Just the same he's guilty and he knows I know it. He's waiting to see what I do. Suppose I've decided to let him go. What do I say? "I feel sorry for you, Hans Julio. I pity you. I don't want to hurt your daughter. I'm not going to do to you what I thought I would." Oh yes. He'd believe that on the day he'd believe my name is William Koerner. He'll believe me only when I act the way he expects me to act, whether it's false or not. And if I've come here to get him I'd never let him go, not unless I was corrupt.

Suppose I hinted about a bribe. And say he agreed to pay me. What's to stop me from being twice as corrupt? Turn him in as soon as I get the money. Or come back later. Bleed him again and again.

I must be out of my mind, Koerner thought and shook his head. I'm trying to figure out whether I can untangle this mess by accepting a bribe. I must be going mad. This is a dangerous man beside me who assumes I'm somebody that I'm not. If he ever finds out how much I've guessed he might kill me. Right now he's wondering. He knows I've learned something and he realizes that I'm playing with it. He's about to lose control. He thinks he's already lost, he has no more to lose. This man is brutal, he could put a knife into me. He's almost ready. I can feel it. I've got to do something, there's not much time. I can't take a bribe. As stupid as I've been so far, that would be worse. The ship leaves tonight. He has people on board who will know about me.

What's left? If I try to turn him in, exactly what do I do? Go ashore with him following me like a sick bulldog and present him to the customs officer? "Look here, officer, just have a look at what I found!" Oh yes. Sure. Oh hell yes.

We're at the bottom of the world and I've cornered a man who thinks I'm Death. He's waited for me. He's been waiting all these years. Once he saw me in Curaçao and he believed I was Death. Oh yes, we understand each other. There's no need to speak. But at this moment what's he thinking? I don't know. All I know is that he believes in me and therefore he must hate me. It was he who gave me this authority, yet he hates me because I have it.

Koerner went over the situation carefully with himself.

I have an authority that I don't want and I'm not able to give it away. I'd throw it in the water if I could, there's nothing I want less. What do I do?

Say I can't accept a bribe, and say I don't dare to let him go. I've made one false move already; one more and he'll sense the truth. I'm no actor. Why hasn't he found me out already? Because he wants so much to believe, that must be it. And because I made no effort to persuade him, which makes it hard to doubt.

All right, say that's the case, yes, and I couldn't possibly turn him in. Supposing I did act well enough to lead him off the ship, where's the proof? There's none. Only what I've guessed. He'd get rid of that watch in a minute. And maybe the customs officer is his partner, I don't know. It doesn't matter. I can't finish him. I should never have started this. But I didn't; he was the one. He built this into what it is. The fault's not mine; he can't blame me. When I learned what was going on I helped a little, but not much, and I didn't think it would come to anything like this. I didn't realize. He can't blame me. But he will. He will.

Why argue with myself? There's not time, and that's all I've got. He's got the rest. No, there's one more thing, the knowledge that I have. If I could use that. If I understood how to use that.

I'm trying to be logical, but I can't think. My head's full of mice scrambling in every direction. How much longer will he believe? I can't even guess. My strength exists in his imagination and when he no longer believes in its existence it no longer exists. Then how much longer do I have it? He must have told himself I wouldn't be here unless I was confident. He imagines I have every exit blocked. He imagines he can't escape unless I allow him to, which is the reason for the servility and fright and the lies dripping and sliding from his lips, yes, and the threats I heard. Only through me can he escape. And I have this power over him precisely as long as he believes.

Koerner had been gazing almost stupefied at the Japanese stamps, at the waterfalls and the tiny white cone of Fuji-yama. He blinked and looked at himself in the mirror and was relieved to see that he appeared unconcerned. He picked up the bottle, poured out the rest of the champagne and drank it quickly. The champage was warm and he knew he was beginning to get drunk.

Either I make use of what I know or I don't, he said to himself, and I think I'd rather not. I'd rather back out of this without getting my skull crushed or a knife in the ribs. I'm not a hero with celluloid teeth. When we get to Lisbon I could talk to somebody who might be interested. I don't know who, but somebody ought to be interested. I could do that much, although I doubt if anybody will listen. But I can't break this up by myself.

Then if I'm not going to use what I know, and if I don't dare let him know what I know, I've got to get out of this by seeming ignorant. How easy is that? I don't know, I've never tried. But if I can give no hint of understanding what both of us have sensed, he'll never ask directly. I'll be the simple tourist that I am. I travel and I play chess and I see no evil and time itself takes care of me. This man can't believe forever. He's got to know. He's got to ask. Already he's suspicious. Soon he's going to ask more questions. If ever in my life I've been careful, I'll be twice as careful now. All right, William Koerner, clever enough to move into the mind of another man, are you clever enough to be a fool?

"You're just traveling," the fat man said. "That's what you told me."

Koerner nodded.

"You said you were on vacation."

Koerner shook his head.

"That's right," García said, "you didn't tell me that. I forgot. If you're not on vacation what kind of work do you do?"

"I work at a desk."

"In Lisboa?"

"New York."

"I don't know what kind of work you do," the provedor said finally. "I never got a chance to have a job like you, so I could go traveling around playing games. I work hard."

Koerner listened carefully.

"You got friends on this island?"

Koerner knew instantly that he must not hesitate about answering, or show the slightest caution.

"No," he said, "in fact I couldn't give you the name of anybody within a thousand miles of this place."

"No? Who do you play games with?"

Koerner laughed. "Right you are! I do know somebody's name."

Hans Julio García smiled.

"You told me your name, too, a while ago," he said, "but I forgot."

Koerner told him again.

"Sure. I got a bad memory."

Then suddenly García said, "You're not Poigt."

Koerner appeared puzzled. The provedor began to laugh. He pounded Koerner on the back.

"Listen, William Koerner, I want to buy you another drink. I'm going ashore pretty soon but I'll buy you another drink."

"It's almost time to eat. I didn't have any lunch."

"That's right. You're a chess player," said Hans Julio García laughing.

Koerner grinned.

"Well, you go eat dinner," said the fat man, and he was laughing to himself. "Goodby, whatever your name is."

"Goodby," Koerner said.

He walked out of the lounge and went up on deck instead of into the dining salon. The deck still smelled of hot canvas but the late afternoon air seemed not so deadly. Beyond the breakwater the Caribbean lay dark blue-green and slightly broken like a stained-glass window.

So somebody exists, he thought, whose name is Poigt, or who calls himself Poigt, who causes the fat provedor to wake up in the middle of the night. It's for him that Hans Julio García waits. And one afternoon Poigt will step into the lounge as quietly as I did. Yes, the day will come. Or maybe it won't. It might never. What a shame, I'd like to know. Not that it concerns me very much, but still I would like to know.

He wandered to the other side of the deck. The sun looked larger and was wedged between two palm trees like an orange or a pomegranate. A few gulls were soaring above the ships in the harbor. On the quay some people were getting out of a taxi. He put his elbows on the rail and waited. Presently he saw the fat man go ashore. The watch was not on his wrist.

It must be in his pocket, Koerner decided. Isn't that

curious. He's not so sure of himself anymore. I took the edge off his confidence. In fact I believe what I may have done was make things more difficult for Poigt. My fat smuggler is going to be much more cautious from now on. I hadn't expected that.

The provedor waved to somebody in the customs office, then walked through the gate and into a warehouse.

The Scriptwriter

Koerner leaned against the glass wall of the booth and stared at the moonlight on Malibu beach while he listened to the telephone ringing.

Somebody picked up the receiver and a woman's voice said, "Yes?"

"Dana?"

"Who is this?"

"I'm calling Morris Reisling," he said because the woman did not sound like Dana. "Do I have the right number?"

"Who are you?"

"My name is William Koerner."

"It's you," she said. "Where are you?"

"On the highway near the ocean. Not far from the house."

He expected her to turn away from the telephone saying, "Morrie, Bill Koerner's here!" or "Morrie, guess who's calling!" And then Morris would be on the telephone asking if he remembered how to get there, saying the extra bedroom was waiting and there was a pot of chili on the stove.

"I suppose you remember how to get here," she said.

"I'll find it."

"Are you staying in Malibu, or just passing through?"

"I'm on the way to Mexico," Koerner said. It was not

what he should be saying and not what Dana should have asked, though more than a year had gone by without a word from them. He wondered if they had been divorced.

"I look forward to seeing you," Dana said as though he was nothing but an acquaintance.

"How's Morrie?"

"Morris died."

Koerner blinked. Then he said: "What?"

"I told you," she answered in a flat voice. "He's dead."

"Morrie?"

"Yes, Morrie. How does that grab you?"

After a few moments Koerner said, "I didn't know."

"I realize you didn't. I'll look forward to seeing you. Goodby." Then she had hung up.

Koerner walked across the highway to his car and started driving slowly toward the house where he had spent so many nights. The house with those two people in it had meant as much as almost anything he knew, but now he did not want to see it again. Morris was dead and she had remarked 'How does that grab you?'

Several minutes later he coasted to a stop in front of another telephone booth and sat for a while without moving, but then continued on the highway and presently turned into a canyon. The night was warm and a deer sprang over the road, bursting through the headlights like an image on a movie screen. Going up the hill the lights followed a furry shape lumbering along, probably a small brown bear, which soon disappeared among the trees. Koerner put his head out the window to smell the pines. All of this he could remember and he had wanted to experience it again, but now none of it was pleasant.

Morris is dead, Morris is dead, he thought. Yet it might be a joke. They both were there when I called and Morris decided to give me a scare. Or he's working on a script and needs to know how people react to shocking news. He could do that because he uses people. He's experimented on me before, but it never hurt like this.

Dana was alone, wearing the ragged sweatshirt, dungarees and sandals. She shook hands calmly and asked what he wanted to drink. After that she sat down on the hassock where she always used to sit and listen while they talked; and she asked how he was, and Koerner wondered how soon he could leave.

"You were suspicious on the telephone," he said.

"I've become afraid of the telephone. There were so many bad calls after it happened. Anonymous obscene calls at night. I began to hate people. I can't pick up the receiver anymore without being frightened. But that doesn't concern you. I suppose you want to hear about Morris. He died a year ago September. It was in quite a few papers. Not as many as I expected, but quite a few."

Koerner remembered that Morris was overweight and at times his breathing sounded like a locomotive.

"Did he have a heart attack?"

"No."

"An accident?"

"Not an accident."

Koerner wondered if she expected him to guess again.

"Morris was murdered."

He realized that instead of being shocked he was annoyed. She had deliberately tried to shock him. Morris, who had been his friend and her husband, was dead and she had played a scene. He tried to excuse her because she had been an actress.

"Nor do I mean it figuratively," Dana said, looking at him with one eyebrow lifted.

Then he understood that she was playing not a scene but a role, and had been playing it ever since Morris died. Her questions on the telephone, the remoteness and the artifice, shaking hands instead of throwing her arms around him, forcing him to ask about what had happened.

"Morris was shot."

Koerner knew she would go on with it. He had done his part, now it was her turn. How many times had she behaved like this? Since Morris died how many friends had driven up the canyon road to the light burning above the door like a backstage entrance? Dana there to greet them with both hands outstretched, the palms turned down, perhaps, if the visitors were movie people, or if she happened to feel that way. Now she was sitting on the leather hassock as indifferently as a cat.

Suddenly she glanced up and said, "I know who did it."

Koerner hoped the exasperation he felt did not show on his face. She had resorted to acting because she had been hurt, and knowing this he knew he would not get angry, but still he wished she would stop.

"Actually there's no mystery. The man was tried for what he did and acquitted. He's walking around free today. He's a film cutter named Huggins. Poor little man. Morris was shot to death by a little film cutter. What do you think of that?"

Koerner said, "This isn't what I asked for. Please, Dana."

"It happened in a cheap motel on the beach. Morris was in bed with the film cutter's wife. It seems that Huggins suspected his wife was having an affair so he hired a private detective. The detective found them together one afternoon when Morris had told me he was going to the studio. The detective did something that is not ethical. He told Huggins exactly where they were, with the result that the man left the studio and took a taxi to the motel. He was not supposed to be in possession of a gun because he was an ex-convict, nevertheless he had one. He proceeded to kick open the door of the cottage and begin shooting. He shot Morris only once, but he shot his wife seven times. Both of them were naked. She was very fat. Isn't it amusing?"

"Not to me," Koerner said.

"I realize that."

"Dana," Koerner said, and waited until she would look at him. "Dana, for God's sake."

"You wanted to hear about it. I'm simply telling you. The man's wife died immediately. Morris lingered for nearly three weeks and for most of those three weeks I was at the hospital. He died in agony. His stomach was bloated like a sausage. I knew he was going to die. I knew before the doctors knew. I knew it even when they told me he was going to recover. Morris didn't believe them either, although he would nod his head when they told him. Do you know what he said to me one morning? He said 'It was a roll in the hay.' That's all the affair meant to him. Don't you find it amusing? People we know aren't murdered, are they? Gangsters are murdered and South American generals are murdered and occasionally a Brooklyn grocer is murdered by a boy who was trying to rob the cash register, but people you and I know aren't murdered, are they? Are they, Bill?"

Without any expression or any tears she was crying.

Koerner looked at the row of framed certificates on the brick wall above the fireplace and said, "Did he get another one?"

"Two since you were here. The one at the end is from a Brussels festival. He was killed before the awards were announced. Everything seems like such a waste."

Then she talked about it some more, and played a record of songs from a new musical comedy which was very popular, and before midnight Koerner was driving out of the canyon. He had hoped when he telephoned to find them both at home and if that had been so they would have insisted that he stay with them. He had hoped this is how it would be. Next, after learning that Morris was dead, he expected Dana would invite him to stay overnight in the guest room; but she had not offered and after a little while he would have refused. He thought then that he would stay at some place near the beach and perhaps go for a swim during the middle of the night as he and Morris used to do. But when he turned out of the canyon onto the Malibu road he did not slow down. From that house something was seeping like a poison and he felt it staining everything for miles in all directions. Whatever he looked at became disagreeable—the trees, the beach, the moonlight on the water—and the ocean wind had a foul odor.

Morris died without speaking, she had said, but he knew what was happening because he put on his glasses. Those horn-rimmed glasses, Koerner thought, mounted like a machine gun on that enormous nose. How could he meet Death without being able to see its visage? And he had died because of a lapse of taste, as well as poor judgment; died in a hospital, a setting he had used more than once in his scenarios, with a white plastic tube curling from his intestines into a pail beneath the bed, wagging his head slowly from side to side because he believed none of it.

She was sitting beside the bed when Death finally got around to his room. She had been reading a magazine when she knew Death was in, and quit reading and turned the magazine over on her lap and looked at her husband. Everything had been done for him that could be done, so with no particular surprise, and not much sorrow, she observed the meeting. She had loved him but her esteem for him disappeared when he was shot. He had been caught so stupidly. She had respected his intelligence, it had been the foundation of her love for him. They had lived together eighteen years and she had admired him even when she felt critical of things he did or said, but then one afternoon he was caught in bed with an overweight tramp in a roadside motel. He was caught like a foolish sailor. The stupidity of it disturbed her; three weeks she spent reading magazines and watching him suffer, and she began to feel insulted. She had selected as her husband a man who turned out to be a fool. She could not forgive him this. She might have forgiven his poor taste, because that was a thing men were often guilty of, but she could not forget or forgive his stupidity. She would have taken him back if he had believed he was in love with the woman, because men are easily confused; often they think they are in love when a woman knows it is only the body that absorbs them. If Morris had believed he was in love there would have been some dignity to the affair, at least there would have been that if nothing more. But he knew he was not. Or she might have overlooked it if the woman had been beautiful, but she was not. She was fat and ordinary, while he was a superior man. So she had quit reading that afternoon and dispassionately watched while Death strangled him, sorry that he was in such pain but otherwise not caring.

I never dreamed he would plot against me, she had said. I knew he plotted against other people, but not against me. Not in my wildest dreams. Not against me. As long as we were married I never once considered another man.

Then she attempted to explain something, which Koerner understood easily enough, although she was not sure she had made it clear. It was how she had observed herself, Dana, observing her husband's death. Did that make sense? Morris used to observe himself, many times she had noticed him doing it, and from him she had gotten the habit. He used it professionally. He would step out of himself and stand distinctly to one side observing Morris. In fact he made notes of his own behavior, she said, and later in one of the scenarios she would read what he had discovered about himself. Was this clear?

Yes, Koerner said, because he too had seen it.

As he was dying, Dana said, I did what he had taught me. I stood far away. I could see him suffering from where I was, and I was curious to learn what would happen next. As though my husband was the subject of a script. How could I be like that? Do you know?

She did not expect an answer. Koerner was looking at her and noticed how neatly her brown hair was parted and how carefully she had plaited it and closed the long braid hanging down her back with a rubber band.

Really, she said, it's a shame he never knew. He had such a sense of humor. He would have loved that touch of irony, and probably would have found a way to use it. He was so clever. But he was occupied with himself during those last few minutes. He didn't pay any attention to me. And there were other touches which were terribly reminiscent of his scenarios. He always employed at least one scene of violence — shots, screams, a door slammed, the sound of running feet. Imagine him doing the motel. The woman shrieking and collapsing on the bed while her husband was firing shot after shot into that enormous body. She was quite dead when the police arrived. She must have been as bloody as a Spanish crucifix. Morris would have enjoyed writing it, if he had lived. People used to say he was a genius. He wasn't, as we both know, but he was awfully smart. Isn't it amusing that he was shot to death by a nobody?

That doesn't amuse me either, Koerner had said.

Then he stood up and she walked with him to the door where they said goodby. She seemed to know he would not come back again. She was not blaming him for this. She had discovered within herself certain thoughts and feelings that she had never known existed, and no doubt the same was true of everyone.

The light still burned above the door when Koerner turned the car around and started through the canyon.

Halfway to Mexico he took one hand off the wheel, pointed a finger at the moon and said while wiggling his thumb: "Pok pok pok pok!" the way Morris used to do when reading one of his scripts aloud, as though by such a gesture he might get rid of the disgust and the oppression, but the moon would not fall into the sea.

Mademoiselle
from Kansas City

GRAND ENTRANCE

"First trip to New York?"

Ruth turned to look at him—the stranger and opportunist—without surprise. He was furtive; he was cheap. "I've always lived here," she said. "Now hop on your scooter and roll. Make it fast."

He hurried along the street. She picked up her suitcase and climbed the brownstone steps. Already she felt at home in New York. Kansas City?—it was as though she had lived there once upon a time. The midwest belonged to another life, it had not meant very much. One day she would go back to visit. Yes, and what bitter pleasures there would be! Someday, yes, she would go back, just long enough to be seen, to be talked about. She pressed the bell and waited.

"The room looks fine. I'll take it," she said, and paid for the first week.

And then for half an hour she sat on the edge of the bed and gazed down into the street thinking only that here in New York, at last, she belonged. The room was not fine, it was not half so fine as it sounded in the newspaper, or by telephone; it would not do for long, but it would do until she could find a job and learn the city. As for the Wenzells—
"I've written them to expect you," her mother had said at

271

the station, "but of course they won't know where to find you." No, the Wenzells didn't know where to find her, thank Heavens. "Be sure to look them up!" her mother had called—anxious, waving. "They're awfully nice! Have a good trip! Don't forget to write!" Yes, Mother, yes, yes. Ruth kicked off her shoes and fell backward across the bed. The ceiling, she noticed, was stained. A scrap of paper hung down. But it would do; yes, anything at all would do for a little while. The heat, now, in mid-June; the sleazy, filthy men like spiders on the street; garbage and papers in the gutter—even this was preferable to life in Kansas City. Now, she thought, shutting her eyes, it would be four o'clock in the afternoon and her brother would be swimming at the country club, diving from the high board to impress whoever cared enough to watch. And sister Carolyn?—playing golf, beyond doubt. And her father?—still at the office, perspiring, or perhaps at court again. Nobody thought about him between breakfast and supper. Yet that was not so; her mother must think of him. And what would Mother be doing now?—lying on the sofa with a damp cloth over her eyes, the shades of the house pulled down, the house cool and dank, insufferable as a closed museum!

In New York it was growing dark. Ruth lay on a strange bed. What was past was soon to be obscured. She had not lived until now. And was it not strange, she wondered, that the first words she should speak in this new home had been a lie?

THE VICTIM

Early one Sunday morning, before dawn, Ruth was wakened by someone tapping at the door. Then there was silence. Whoever it was, she thought, had gone away. But the tapping resumed and she heard her name whispered, and knew that Lenny was outside. She lay motionless, with clenched teeth, and waited for him to leave; but he tapped louder, and called her by name. "I've got to see you!" he said. "Ruth, I'm going to shoot myself!" She turned over in bed, the springs creaked. "I know you're in there," he said, and rapped sharply on the panel. "Let me in, please! Ruth! Ruth!" His voice was becoming hysterical. "I need you! Christ! Christ! It's Lenny, Ruth, it's me!" She did not answer; and the man who lay next to her, whom she had met a few hours before, was wakened by the noise. Ruth could not think of his name; when she tried to remember it but could not she felt a rush of hatred against him, against all men for their lack of discretion, their indelicacy, because they could not control their passions — they seemed to her despicable and contemptible for eternally running after women. Then she thought of his name, Howard, but remembered nothing else about him. His body was rigid with fright; in the darkness she smiled, knowing that he was wondering now, as he had not bothered to wonder earlier, who she was, if the man knocking at the door was her husband. Ruth lifted one hand to his face to comfort him because he had started to tremble. From the corridor came the sound of Lenny weeping, then a furious hammering at the door; she turned her head to look at the man beside her but could not make out his features. He was shaking with fear and she decided that whoever he was she would never see him again. She reached across him to the night table for a cigarette, then sat up in bed with her chin resting on her knees, smoking and waiting. She imagined herself in another bed, in another woman's place, and wondered how she would feel if that woman returned in the middle of the night. It was difficult to imagine. It would not happen, but if it did happen what would she feel? Not fear, certainly. No, I would be angry, she thought. I'd be infuriated.

After a while there was silence in the hall. She sensed that Lenny had gone away.

Monday morning, at coffee, she saw the story on the second page, and a photograph of Lenny. He had gone into Washington Square and sat on a bench until almost noon, then suddenly stood up, pulled the gun from his pocket and killed himself. There was no explanation, except that offered by his landlord—he had seemed despondent for several weeks.

Ruth looked with distaste at his picture, the familiar supplicating smile, the enormous soulful Jewish eyes that once had seemed to her so beautiful. Now the face looked merely weak, vaguely hopeful. There weren't enough bones in him, she thought. Why should he have gotten so upset about me? We didn't mean anything to each other, I told him that.

Later, when she happened to think about him, less and less frequently, as days and weeks went by, she would think that she ought to feel some sense of regret. She might have spoken to him through the door, she might have done that much at least, for she had known that he did mean to kill himself if she rejected him. At that hour there had been only one person on earth who could have saved him—that had been herself, but she had preferred to sit in bed smoking a cigarette and waiting for him to go away. She asked herself if she would have opened the door to him if she had been alone, and it seemed to her that probably she would have allowed him in and would have talked to him, tried to console him without becoming involved. But this was an idle thought; she had not been alone, she had been with someone, therefore she could not let him in. Lenny had been a victim of circumstances, that was all.

MESSALINA

This one was no different. She listened, feigned a smile, accepted the drink he poured, which was, as she had known it would be, as it always was, too strong—not a drink so much as a poison, an attempt to relax her, to drug her, so that he might do more as he wished, might half-live the absurd masculine fantasies. She swallowed the drink and looked about the room; like the man himself, the room was no different. She looked for the closet and got up and walked across the room to open it, as she always did, feeling his eyes greedily upon her. I despise you, she thought. If only you realized how I despise you! Before she touched the handle of the closet door she knew that nobody was hiding inside; so, at the last instant, she turned toward the window as if that had been where she intended to go, and stood, holding the curtain aside, staring down into the mid-city night. She knew he was watching her from his chair and that he was quietly starting to remove his clothes. A shoe bumped on the carpet but she did not turn from the window. This is the scene, she thought. This is the hour, the place, the tragedy. This is where the unhappy girl opens the window and the music rises to a crescendo as she plunges to her death. How does it always end? The final scene? Focus on the salesman, briefly, see his shocked expression. But only briefly because he's not important. Do we close with a crowd gathering on the street? Fade out. Ruth unlatched the window and pushed it open. Would he be alarmed? She turned; he promptly smiled. She did not think he had been worried, he had been staring, staring at the flesh he had bought for a little while, but then, seeing her smile, he must pretend that she was human.

"Gettin' late!" he grinned.

"Well now, do tell," she said, and saw the effort he made to conceal his displeasure—his southwestern accent, her mimicry. "Where are you from?" she asked. Then he said he was from Kansas City. For a moment of horror she glared into him, into the gelid green eyes, but saw no malice, nothing.

"I guessed you were from Texas," she said.

"Folks do," he remarked, and for a moment she almost understood everything about him. He meant no harm. There would be a family back home, he was away from his wife—perhaps he loved her, or perhaps she had bored him for twenty years—what did it matter? Ruth looked at him more softly.

"Truth is," he said, and he was ready to talk, and she saw that he might talk for an hour, "truth is, now, I come from Louisiana. Saint Charles, Louisiana. Know where it's at?" Ruth shook her head. "Sleepiest place ever was, full of moss and bugs. I lef' some time back, though. Lived lots of places. Thinkin' I might move to Noo Yawk!" He laughed; it was a joke; and yet he wished to know if she would encourage him to move here. Now, *that* would be something to talk about back home. Pretty little whore wanted me to move there. His voice echoed from the sleepy towns of the past; she remembered Harrisonville and Joplin, darkened lobbies of old hotels, yellowing magazines untouched in the stained oak racks.

"Tell me about Kansas City," she said.

"Been livin' there these past two years," he answered, chuckling. "Man's got to go where the company sends him. Don't give a man no choice in the matter." He poured himself another drink and wagged his head. "Nice enough. Lord, I suppose. Lakes and trees. Hot in summah, though. Hell, on the other hand I don't mind that so much. It's them cold wintahs that freeze up a man like a drum."

"Two years you've been there," Ruth said. "You must have friends. You must know a great many people by now."

"I meet easy," he said, nodding. "That's how come I'm in this good position. That whole territory belongs to me. I know how to put people at ease. That's always been m'strong sellin' point. People meet me and think to themself right off, why, I think I met that man somewhere before. You'd be surprised," he added and suddenly, seriously, looked up at her where she stood leaning against the wall.

"I feel the same—as though we'd met before," she told him. Immediately she regretted saying this, even before he answered. She had meant this as an insult too subtle for him to perceive. He had not perceived it, but it reminded him of his purpose. He would not forget again. He winked at her and patted the bed.

"If we ain't met befo', I'm sure that's my errah. Come along now, little lady, you sweet thing."

"I'll take the money first," she said, and snapped her fingers for emphasis. Always she had asked for it before she undressed, but never like this, never directly. She glanced at herself reflected in the half-opened window and for a moment thought she was seeing someone else.

"It's a powerful lot of money, what they told me it would be," he said, and waited. He was hopeful. She knew she should not have talked to him; it was a mistake to ask about Kansas City.

Don't argue, she thought, gazing down into the street. For God's sake, don't be one of those!

"Well, sho," he said at last and cautiously took his wallet from an inside pocket of his coat. She walked across the room and stood silently in front of him while he counted the bills into her hand, wetting his thumb before releasing each one, wrinkling each one to be sure that another had not clung to it; and she wondered if when he had finished she would crumple them and throw them at his face. Then he was through counting; she folded the money, tucked it into her purse, and without hesitation reached back, unzipping her dress and pulling it over her head before he could try to help. She did not want his hands to touch her clothing.

When, soon, she lay beside him, both naked, and he set to

fondling her, kissing her body and whispering suggestions, she pretended that he was arousing her. She listened to the noise of the midnight street and imagined herself walking to the theater. Some night it would happen, and crowds would follow. The unimportant people of the world would point to her. She turned her face aside from his kiss, caught her breath when he lunged. Underneath the heaving obese body, insulted by the odor of cheap talcum, disgusted by his clumsiness, she heard with indifference his groans of ecstasy. Now she did not need to pretend; his face was pressed into the pillow while he labored. She opened one eye and gazed at the ceiling, waiting for him to be satisfied. She wondered if she really did despise him, and decided that she did not. She felt nothing in relation to him, nothing at all. Now for a little while she was free; there was no need to talk to him, and she began to think of her mother, of a different time, and values that were lost.

Heavily, flabbily, like a sea lion he moved across her, clutched at her shoulders, at her breasts, choking and trembling, crying softly in his agony that he loved her, and begged her to love him. Then Ruth sighed, brought back regretfully through the years from her dream of childhood, which was the dream she always dreamt, of a summer evening, her brother yodeling from the darkening heart of an elm in the green yard, her sister meticulously skipping rope, seventeen, eighteen, nineteen, twenty! and the enormous moths batting patiently against the screendoor while her parents waited on the porch swing for a cool breeze — evening that would never end. Beneath the spasms of the corpulent, aging body which she could neither hate nor love she wondered what had driven him to this. What futile need possessed him? Why was he here? Is this, she wondered as he grunted and tried once more to kiss her lips — is this the image of my father? Never before had she needed so deeply to understand, yet this man had not the wisdom to explain. Had anyone? If the nature of man was always to be a mystification, what had she to hope for? And it seemed to her that it would be unnatural, in the face of their mystery, to do other than acquiesce.

A Brief Essay on the Subject of Celebrity

With Numerous Digressions and Particular
Attention to the Actress, Rita Hayworth

West of Albuquerque a hundred miles or so there is a
national monument that nobody visits. It is maintained by
the Department of the Interior, but except for a picnic area
there are no accommodations, and it is considerably off the
highway. The road is passable, the monument is not difficult
to reach, but when you arrive you find only a small government station with an American flag snapping in the windy
silence, juniper and prickly pear, and a gigantic sandstone
bluff standing like a memorial tablet on the valley floor. Few
birds are visible, no people, no animals, only an occasional
glossy black beetle struggling with mindless determination
through the crumbled rock at the base of the enormous cliff.
Tourists do not come here: Paradise lies at the end of Route
66; immortality waits in Beverly Hills. A monument such as
this can be overlooked; it is academic — one brief paragraph
in a guidebook, a red star on a road map — surely nothing
speaks from this dead land of Zuñi Indians, from the shadows of the Seven Cities of Cíbola. There would be only
broken walls, pictographs, shards of coarse white pottery a
thousand years old, and inscriptions left by early travelers
who paused for a little while. So it is.

Paso por aquí adelanto
Don Juan de Oñate
del descubrimiento de la mar del sur
a 16 de Abril de 1605.

Oñate, who rode through this valley before the Pilgrims arrived at Plymouth Rock, took thirty men along with two priests to the Gulf of California and stopped on his return to set down the fact that he had discovered the sea of the south. Nearby another inscription, partly hidden by a yucca plant, is carved in Spanish on the cliff:

By here passed the Ensign Don Joséph
de Payba Basconzelos
the year he bought the cabildo of the realm
at his own expense
the 18th of February, of the year 1726.

Just what Basconzelos meant is not clear, but what is unmistakable is that here was another who set down his deed, his name, and the date, in order that he should not be forgotten.

The 28th day of September 1737,
arrived here the illustrious Señor
Don Martin de Elizacochea, Bishop of Durango,
and the day following, went on to Zuñi.

By here passed Pedro Romero
on the 22nd of August, year of 1751.

I am of the hand of Felipe de Arellano
on the 16th of September, soldier.

Then the Spaniards were gone, leaving records only a little more complex than those of the primitive Zuñi; and the first Americans arrived, rested, watered their horses, wrote, and went away. Lt. J. H. Simpson. E. Pen Long of Baltimore. Mr. P. Gilmer Breckenridge. Mr. Engle. Mr. Bryn.

Today around this cliff the wind boils through ponderosa

pines and acorns drop from scrub oaks on the mesa. Beetles clamber insistently toward an incomprehensible goal while the wispy trail of an Air Force jet miles above fades into cirrus clouds. Inscription Rock no longer is a crossroads; it is now meaningless, except as evidence of the human wish to be remembered, for indeed there are not more than two things that we want: the first being our fair share of corporeal bliss, generally consisting of food, warmth, and sex; the second being that after we have been tucked away we shall be remembered. Little else concerns us. Symbols of affluence, say, are merely to remind the neighbors that we are of some consequence and will not easily be forgotten. Exploration and conquest, works of art, singing, dancing, humors of every sort — modesty, lust, wrath — all may exist to perpetuate our name just as children do, notifying the future that we are worth at least a minor celebration.

Now, if you keep traveling west from Inscription Rock you come ultimately to California on whose golden shore all promises must be honored. Let this be noted. Without knowing why, we do believe that in California we will discover what we started toward so long ago. Yes, we say in our hearts, when we have reached California our value cannot go unrecognized. There, without question, we will be happy. We will be fulfilled. Our needs will be ministered. Afternoon may find us loitering beside a private pool in the shade of imported palms, while a vulgar public clusters outside the gate. This is the promise that somewhere, once upon a time, was made to us, and we do not doubt it.

Mirabile visu! The promise is kept, usually. Just once in a while, to one or two or three of us, does it seem that the salty smell of fraud has mingled with the orange blossoms.

Take this example. A few weeks ago about five o'clock one pleasant evening in Los Angeles when Wilshire Boulevard was populated with the homeward-bound after another day when the contract had not quite been honored, there came one woman steadily marching up the boulevard with a businesslike expression, a woman so average in each detail that she became formidable. She neither spoke to nor looked at anyone. Perhaps she was reflecting on the inequities of life. Who can be sure? She wore a pair of ballet slippers but nothing else, because forty years had come and gone and as yet nobody cared. The magic words had not been spoken. So much time had elapsed and nobody had told her how valuable she was, how significant, how inestimable and precious. Not one man, woman, or child thus far had stepped aside or bowed when she went by, because she was as unremarkable as Felipe de Arellano, who could put after his name only the one word: Soldier. So she had grown tired of waiting and thought that she would cause the world to take some notice. It did, of course. To be sensational is not particularly difficult. For five full minutes there was no one more famous. The crowd opened, quietly subservient, as though she were the wife of Caesar.

However, to carve one's name on a cliff and to take a spectacular stroll along Wilshire Boulevard are more or less identical, being surrogates of fame. If there is some genuine talent or resource, a strangeness of proportion to the body or to the mind that elevates a person so that he or she exists in the sight of millions, there is no more need to walk blindly naked through a crowd than to carve private data on a rock. Such secretarial work may then be left to others, the amanuenses: they shall note that a distinguished individual passed by this place, giving the style and nature of the accomplishment.

To these few, the authentically famous, we are attracted. We follow them and we speculate. We wonder in what respect they are different from ourselves. Is it circumstance? Or has a genie chosen them?

Let us consider. Let us say that there is a ballplayer seven feet tall, which there is, whose name is known to a certain part of the population. In his way he is talented, he is muscular, and energetic; but suppose that he were six feet tall, who would ever have heard of him? Is this not, therefore, the purest kind of circumstantial celebrity? A game exists for which a uniquely suitable body was born. Whistles blow, drums beat. Had such a man been twelve inches shorter than he is, his name would be recorded only with a crayon on the bricks of a tenement, scratched with the tip of a switchblade knife on a lavatory partition, and the date he was there.

Or is this true? Possibly we still would know of him. He might have become the warehouseman who one afternoon for no evident reason opens fire with a rifle from a window of his apartment, the epilogue as follows:

Tell us, Bud, why did you shoot those people?
I dunno, man, I dunno. I felt like it, that's all.

If such is the case, circumstance becomes peripheral and we must conclude that within certain individuals a genie resides, directing them to eminence of one sort or another, however commendable or bizarre. Then we wish to descry this genie, to find where he or it lives, and fathom its nature; knowing that if we too possessed the daimon we would not go unrecorded. Then Earth's bright doors should swing open for us as well.

So we look after the celebrities of the world, whether they are statesmen, actors, athletes or murderers, wondering at their essence. Hopefully, wistfully, we send them gifts and write to them; we seek to make friends with them in order that we may divine their secret and appropriate this to our own purpose.

But the secret is hidden, ordinarily. We look and wait and listen, but divine nothing. The genie is not visible, not audible. Only once in a while can we perceive him.

For example, in San Francisco are thousands of middle-aged Italian gentlemen playing boccie on the public greens, solemnly sitting in hotel lobbies, shuffling along the narrow streets of North Beach, and they are very nearly as indistinguishable from each other, unless you happen to be acquainted with them, as twenty thousand herring. They mind small shops, they work around Fisherman's Wharf, and each one is attached to a baggy suit and a stout wife and a clutch of children and grandchildren and more relatives than there are mushrooms in Tuscany. Because their differences are negligible you cannot tell them apart, just as you cannot identify particular fish, bowling balls, or women at market. However, some evening, perhaps browsing through a bookstore, you may encounter one of these greying little Italian men and pay him no attention unless you meet his gaze. Then, after he is gone, you inquire:

Who was that?

The sculptor, Bufano. Gandhi was a friend of his, and Roosevelt. . . .

A year goes by but you do not forget that cold electric-blue gaze. You pass him on the street, watch him on a scaffold — apparently a laborer cleaning St. Francis — and there is nothing to tell you that he is who he is, nothing unless you look into his eyes. Then you know, instantly, beyond doubt. Sometimes, as it is with Bufano, the mystery is visible to those who look closely, even to those who don't; but more often the spirit is bottled, the radiance concealed, the mask set, a curtain drawn, so that you spend hours, days, or weeks in the presence of some exceptional person without detecting much. That is how it is with the supreme Aphrodite of a splintered age, Rita Hayworth, singularly American, who offers acquaintances a mild and friendly brown eye, nothing more.

There is the Hollywood mansion, yes, and the blue-painted swimming pool, the palm trees tilting against the

Pacific sky like totem poles, or, more properly, like symbols of national insanity. Nor can there be the least doubt that the United States of America is mad. Symptoms are too numerous to catalog. Let us take one, possibly two: Respectable citizens seated on the pavement outside their homes because there are neither public benches for loitering nor sidewalk cafés. Why are there none? Because it is believed in the United States that there is something depraved and subversive about those who are not occupied, something scurrilous, ominous. If you go for a stroll through Beverly Hills the police will stop and question you. It is quicker to get wherever you are going by automobile, therefore if you are walking you must be bent on wickedness.

Or say that you draw pictures of a man and a woman fulfilling the promise of love; you will be positively arrested, you will be imprisoned. You may represent hate in the most egregious fashion, you may picture all conceivable butcheries, that is permissible, but love is more alarming. However, that is a third instance. There are thousands. It is futile to itemize them; better to content yourself with abstract knowledge.

So there are the palms, the painted pool, and the rest. Everything you expected. Visualize the scene. Whatever you imagine is valid. The long drive winding away from the street, high guardian hedges, a maid in a black uniform to answer the bell. You are ushered in, instructed almost crisply to choose a seat.

A few minutes later, after you have had time to wait, because that is the way it is done, Rita Hayworth enters—swiftly, rather silently. The delayed entrance is the only sign of artifice. She would open the door herself, except that she was long ago taught otherwise and now thinks no more about it. That is the way things are.

Presently she is seated, not quite at ease on the sofa,

fingering her necklace, occasionally tugging at the hem of an Irish green dress. She no more displays the imperial mannerisms of a Love Goddess than does Mamie Eisenhower. There she sits, Rita Hayworth, the subject of poems, technicolor dreams, threats, grotesque fantasies, memories and speculation, the warm brown eyes telling much of what she is not — mendacious, spiteful, conniving, treacherous — but little of what she is. She inquires if you would care for sugar in your tea.

Would you care for sugar in your tea?
Thank you, no, this is fine.

That is the memorable conversation. What is significant is the omission.

Would you care for sugar in your tea?

The mundane query lodges in the mind like a bug sealed immutably in amber. Because these are the words of Aphrodite, because they are natural, inevitable, and unexpected, because she fails to say what you half-anticipate, gradually you recall other omissions: the publicity agent, Rick Ingersoll, in a booth at the Brown Derby who carefully answered all questions and brought out of his briefcase a five-page resumé.

"Few stars in the history of Hollywood have captured the public's imagination with the magnetic impact of Rita Hayworth. Internationally renowned as the 'Love Goddess,' Miss Hayworth casts an aura of glamour wherever she appears. One of movieland's all-time greats ... was born Margarita Carmen Cansino ... curvaceous, exotic star ... turned down numerous offers ... returned to dramatic parts ... created memorable characterizations ... presently lives in Beverly Hills. . . ."

It is complete, but of course it tells nothing. Ingersoll is a handsome, affable young man who zips through the pink stucco majesty of Beverly Hills in a Volks as black as a Zuñi beetle. Assiduously he is polishing the Image; perhaps he is not unlike Bufano tending St. Francis. It is not his job to promote iconoclasm, but to make certain that the idol remains on the pedestal. It is not his fault if he presents a five-page summary of nothing. He is doing his appointed job, he is paid for this, he has a family. It is easy to be critical or cynical. Most of us are obliged to work for a living, which necessitates some adjustment.

All the same, it isn't there. The truth has been circumnavigated. Not deliberately, not even consciously, perhaps, but effectually.

The actor Mark Roberts, who years ago played in one of Rita Hayworth's films, thinks back and at last observes in his leisurely voice that she was a sweet, likable girl. She could dance, says he, just a little bit better than I could. But then, he adds reflectively, her old man taught dancing so she'd been practicing.

Well, yes, but is that all? Did she make no deeper imprint? She casts an aura of glamour wherever she appears. She is internationally renowned as the Love Goddess. Surely you must have been excited?

Roberts leans back, tries to remember. He is from Kansas City where his name was Bob Scott. He is as substantial as a Missouri farmer. He is not going to be rushed. He thinks. He scratches his jaw. I haven't seen her in fifteen years, he says finally. She was always sweet and worked hard. . . .

Nor is it found in the movie magazines nor in the yellow journals, not that it could be there. But most of all it is absent in the presence of the woman herself. The difference is that she knows it is absent; the others do not. Somerset Maugham points out in *The Summing Up* that the celebrated develop a technique to deal with the persons they come across. They show the world a mask, often an impressive one, says Maugham, but take care to conceal their real selves. They play the part that is expected from them and with practice learn to play it very well, but you are stupid if you think that this public performance corresponds with the person within.

Immaculately she has prepared herself; she knows that she is not going to say anything. That is as it should be. All the chic lady journalists, all the inquisitive males, with pad and pencil, with photographic mind—they have trooped in and out of London suites, premieres, banquets, et cetera, et cetera, and they have asked and they have asked. Tell us the truth about Orson Welles! About Aly Khan! She has answered. It was not obligatory, but she has answered because she is polite, and each time has said nothing. It is splendid to have such dignity. Nor does she smile unnecessarily. That, too, is a relief and a pleasure, for there is nothing so tiresome as a decided smile. One may draw sustenance from a woman's somber face.

Half-hidden among the records beside her phonograph is an album of Haydn. Ingersoll, omnipresent if not omniscient, is quick to point out the record of *Pal Joey*. But that is his job; she was in *Pal Joey*.

Just visible in the hall stands an archaic stone figure. Near it hangs a painting by Derain. On a corner table repose *House Beautiful* and *Harper's Bazaar*, two sleek and wealthy sisters eternally congratulating one another. There also is the seventy millionth copy of a vapid little book of cartoons; Ingersoll, slightly abashed, mentions that this is not indicative of the star's taste in reading. All right, there is nothing criminal about owning a book as ephemeral as a moth.

On the coffee table in the center of the room lies an old edition of a drama by Edna Millay. Its very existence seems a reproach to the commercial pap. Like Derain, like the sculpture, or Joseph Haydn, the presence of Millay could be calculated, might be there to suggest Culture, but that is not so; the volume lies on the coffee table because it is being read. Rita Hayworth explains this almost apologetically; she is undeniably American.

Rick Ingersoll will inform you that she was born in New York, but it doesn't matter, it could as easily have been Des Moines, and even now she is not far from home. After the soirees and the safaris she speaks one language, English, like all reasonable Americans. She shoots a good game of golf, drives the ball 175 yards. She doesn't go to the movies much. One day in Ireland she saw a leprechaun. There again, as with Millay, she becomes a bit apologetic, explains that on closer inspection the leprechaun was a tree stump. It requires an American, a Puritan down to the marrow of one's bones, to say such a thing.

She has traveled four directions, married herself to baroque and talented men. She has lived the life of a celebrity for thirty years, yet has failed to acquire the sheen of a sixth-rank European countess. It is not plausible. Indeed, it is altogether impossible. You conclude that she must be somebody else. She isn't Rita Hayworth after all, she's Ike's niece in disguise.

How many weeks were you in Germany entertaining the troops, Rita? inquires Ingersoll, who already knows. Dutifully she answers, revealing nothing.

Would you care for . . . ?

So the shadows of the wild palms turn across the fabled swimming pool, whose waters are rocked by nothing. Evening comes, wan and feckless, to Beverly Hills. Tourists ride past the mansion, stare at the protective hedge, wondering. There is the gate to Paradise, is it not? It is so, according to our map, which cost a dollar. Yes, there it is, the home of Love. We have come so far to see it and we are very near. Only guess what pleasures we would find if we could enter. Tomorrow, perhaps, we will be invited.

Illusion is our price and purchase. Love and Fame, both are adulation. Various warmths encourage us to the end of each desperate centennial. If the reign of a singular goddess is too soon ended, as it soon ends for the warehouseman with his rifle, for the Spanish foot soldier plodding through the dust of savage lands toward some far blue ocean, an ocean bluer than a dream, for Mr. P. Gilmer Breckenridge and Lt. Simpson—if it is quickly ended, still each has contrived to make himself remembered. It seems necessary. Even the Zuñi pictograph says that I was here, this is from my hand. I have watched two animals by a pool of water, yes, and a strange woman. It was I who saw these things. I was here. Behold me.